BIG BOOK OF
BART SIMPSON

C. Hart

W9-BDM-509

Perennial
An Imprint of HarperCollinsPublishers

Dedicated to Burpo:

How you ended up in Kitty Heaven we'll never know.

BIG BOOK OF BART SIMPSON

HarperCollins books may be purchased for educational, business, or sales
promotional use. For information please write:
Special Markets Department
HarperCollins Publishers Inc.
10 East 53rd Street, New York, NY 10022

FIRST EDITION

ISBN 978-0-06-008469-1

07 QWM 14 13 12 11 10

Publisher: MATT GROENING
Creative Director: BILL MORRISON

Managing Editor: TERRY DELEGEANE
Director of Operations: ROBERT ZAUGH
Art Director: NATHAN KANE
Production Manager: CHRISTOPHER UNGAR
HarperCollins Editors: SUSAN WEINBERG and KATE TRAVERS
Legal Guardian: SUSAN GRODE

Contributing Artists:
IGOR BARANKO, KAREN BATES, JEANNETTE BOSE, JOHN COSTANZA, DAN DECARLO, MIKE DECARLO,
FRANCIS DINGLASAN, JASON HO, NATHAN KANE, CAROLYN KELLY, SCOTT MCRAE, BILL MORRISON,
PHIL ORTIZ, MIKE ROTE, SCOTT SHAW!, CHRIS UNGAR, ART VILLANUEVA, AND MIKE WORLEY

Contributing Writers:
JAMES BATES, GEORGE GLADIR, SCOTT SHAW!, GAIL SIMONE, AND CHRIS YAMBAR

PRINTED IN CANADA

TABLE OF CONTENTS

5 BIG FAT TROUBLE IN LITTLE SPRINGFIELD

16 GRRRL-WHIRL

23 CLOSE ENCOUNTERS OF THE NERD KIND

34 BART'S DAY AT THE ZOO

44 TALENT HUNT

49 MAXIMUM BART

54 FUTILITY BELT

63 TERROR ON TRIOCULON PART 1

69 TERROR ON TRIOCULON PART 2

74 TERROR ON TRIOCULON PART 3

80 BATTLE OF THE BOY BANDS

85 SKY-HIGH BART

92 WHO WANTS TO WIN A
   POCKETFUL OF
   QUARTERS?

107 QUANTUM COLA

113 BULLY FOR YOU

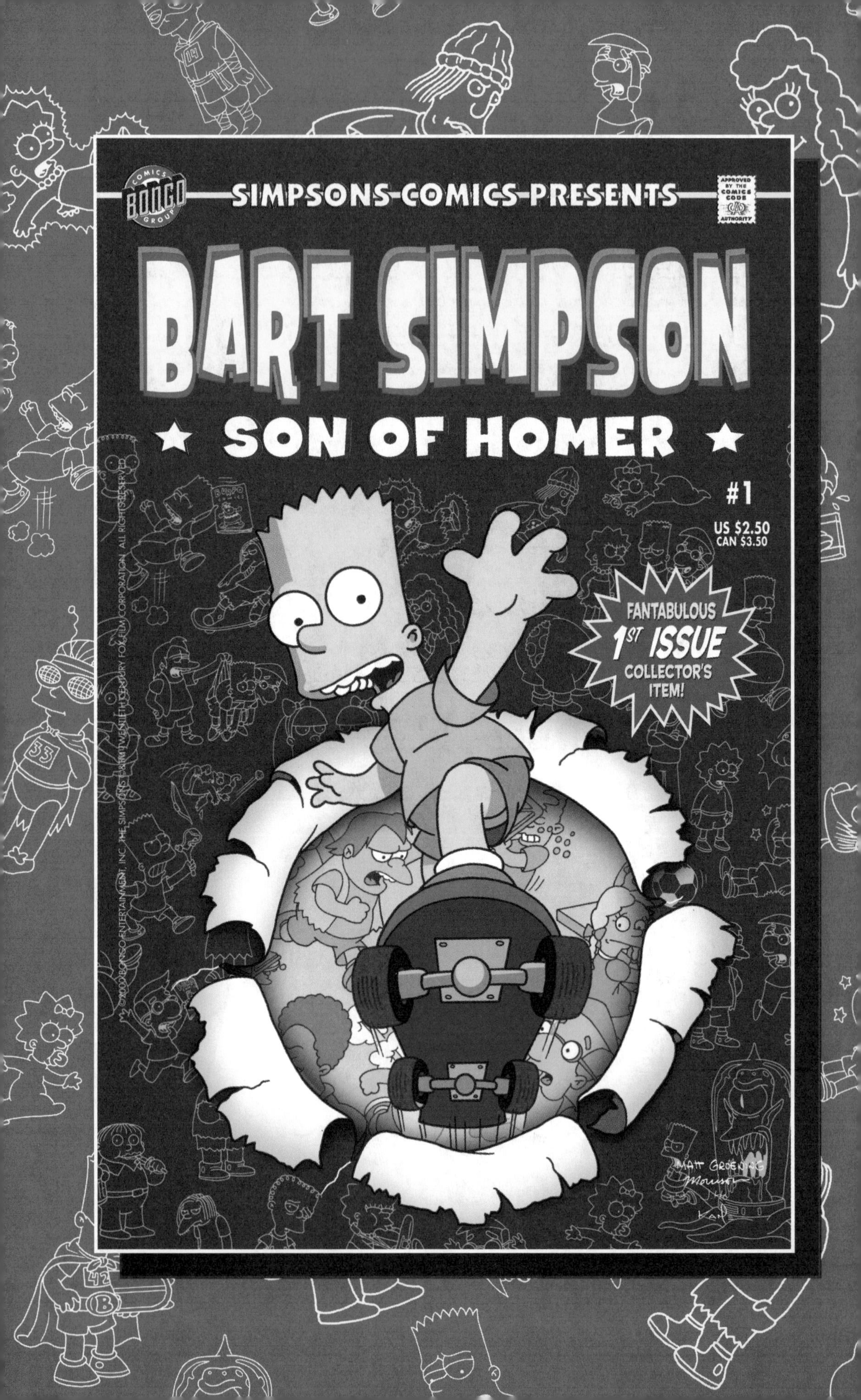
BONGO COMICS GROUP
SIMPSONS COMICS PRESENTS
APPROVED BY THE COMICS CODE AUTHORITY
BART SIMPSON
★ SON OF HOMER ★
#1
US $2.50
CAN $3.50
FANTABULOUS 1ST ISSUE COLLECTOR'S ITEM!
©2000 BONGO ENTERTAINMENT, INC. THE SIMPSONS © & ™ TWENTIETH CENTURY FOX FILM CORPORATION. ALL RIGHTS RESERVED.
MATT GROENING

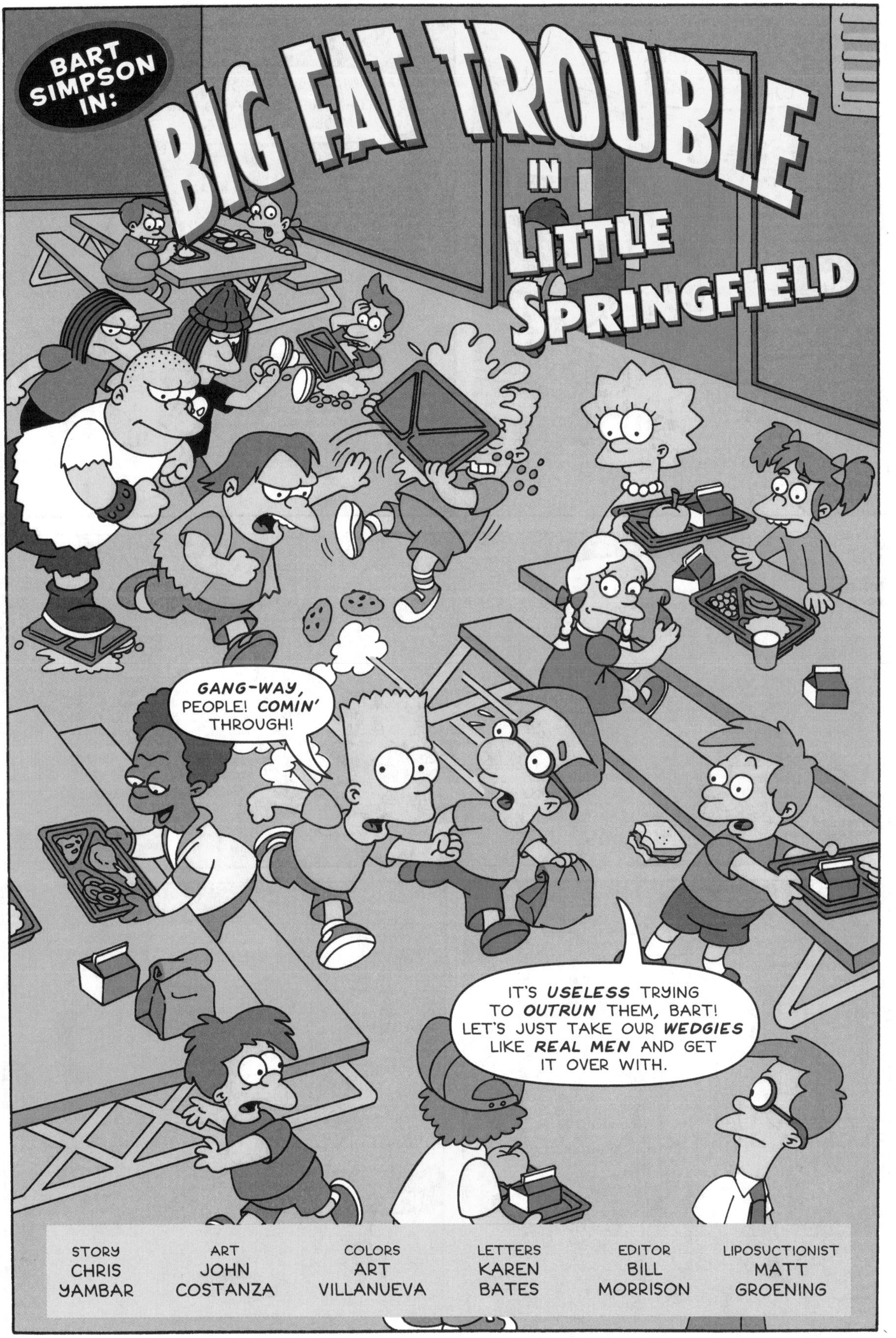

BART SIMPSON IN:
BIG FAT TROUBLE IN LITTLE SPRINGFIELD
GANG-WAY, PEOPLE! COMIN' THROUGH!
IT'S USELESS TRYING TO OUTRUN THEM, BART! LET'S JUST TAKE OUR WEDGIES LIKE REAL MEN AND GET IT OVER WITH.
STORY CHRIS YAMBAR
ART JOHN COSTANZA
COLORS ART VILLANUEVA
LETTERS KAREN BATES
EDITOR BILL MORRISON
LIPOSUCTIONIST MATT GROENING

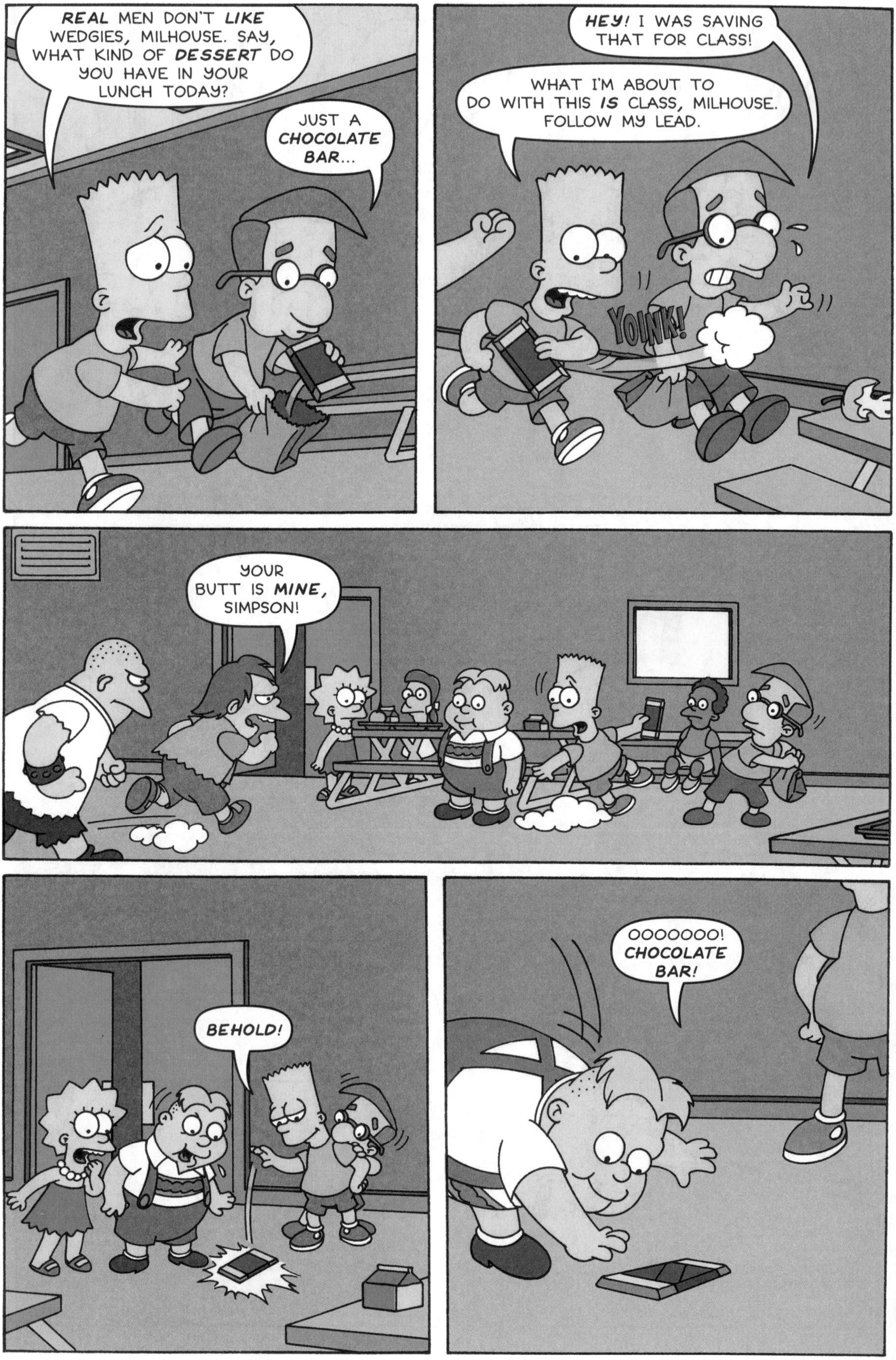
REAL MEN DON'T LIKE WEDGIES, MILHOUSE. SAY, WHAT KIND OF DESSERT DO YOU HAVE IN YOUR LUNCH TODAY?
JUST A CHOCOLATE BAR...
HEY! I WAS SAVING THAT FOR CLASS!
WHAT I'M ABOUT TO DO WITH THIS IS CLASS, MILHOUSE. FOLLOW MY LEAD.
YOUNK!
YOUR BUTT IS MINE, SIMPSON!
BEHOLD!
OOOOOOO! CHOCOLATE BAR!

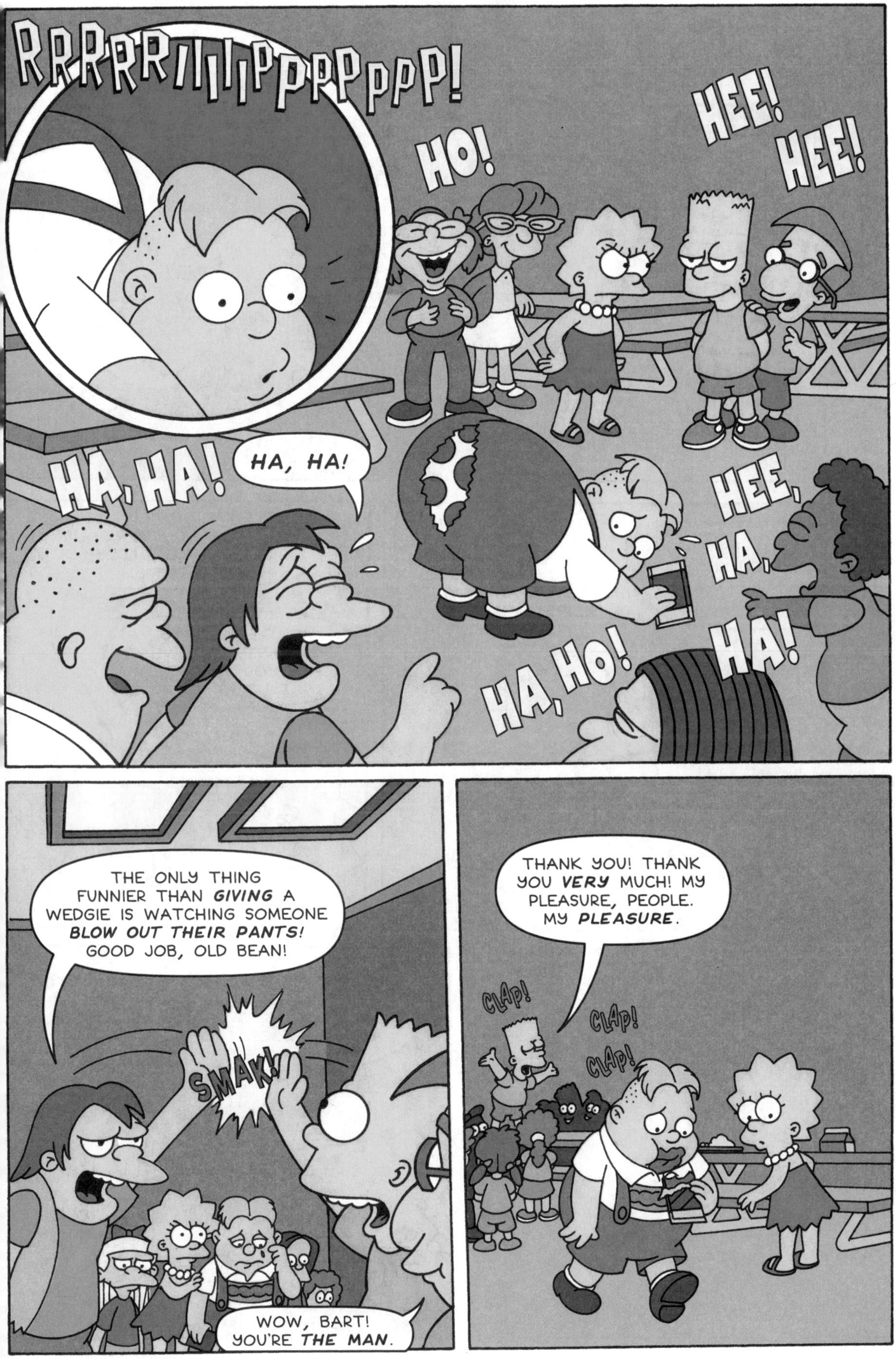
RRRRRIIIIIPPPPPPP!
HO!
HEE! HEE!
HA, HA!
HA, HA!
HEE, HA, HA!
HA, HO!
THE ONLY THING FUNNIER THAN **GIVING** A WEDGIE IS WATCHING SOMEONE **BLOW OUT THEIR PANTS!** GOOD JOB, OLD BEAN!
SMAK!
WOW, BART! YOU'RE **THE MAN**.
THANK YOU! THANK YOU **VERY** MUCH! MY PLEASURE, PEOPLE. MY **PLEASURE**.
CLAP!
CLAP!
CLAP!

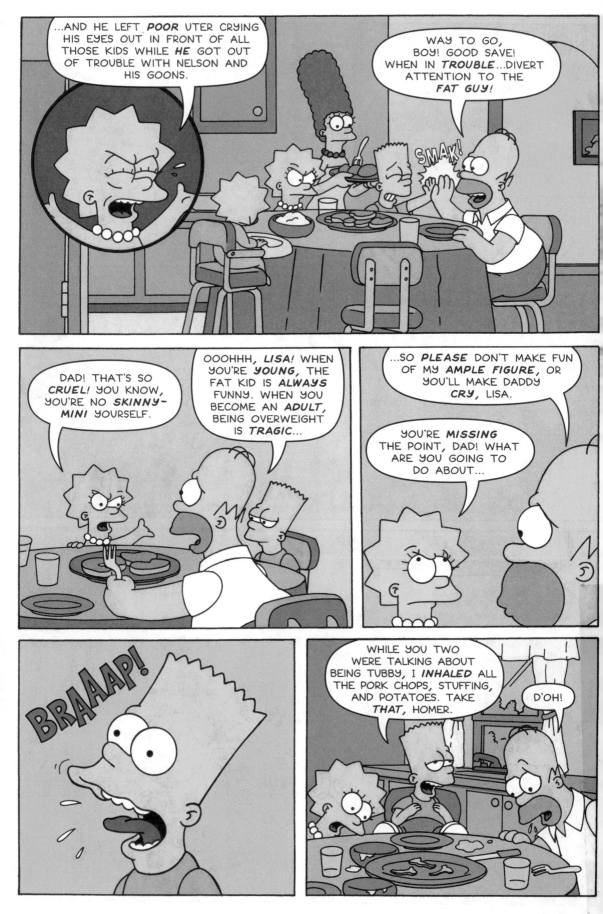

...AND HE LEFT *POOR* UTER CRYING HIS EYES OUT IN FRONT OF ALL THOSE KIDS WHILE *HE* GOT OUT OF TROUBLE WITH NELSON AND HIS GOONS.

WAY TO GO, BOY! GOOD SAVE! WHEN IN *TROUBLE*...DIVERT ATTENTION TO THE *FAT GUY!*

SMAK!

DAD! THAT'S SO *CRUEL!* YOU KNOW, YOU'RE NO *SKINNY-MINI* YOURSELF.

OOOHHH, *LISA!* WHEN YOU'RE *YOUNG*, THE FAT KID IS *ALWAYS* FUNNY. WHEN YOU BECOME AN *ADULT*, BEING OVERWEIGHT IS *TRAGIC*...

...SO *PLEASE* DON'T MAKE FUN OF MY *AMPLE FIGURE*, OR YOU'LL MAKE DADDY *CRY*, LISA.

YOU'RE *MISSING* THE POINT, DAD! WHAT ARE YOU GOING TO DO ABOUT...

BRAAAP!

WHILE YOU TWO WERE TALKING ABOUT BEING TUBBY, I *INHALED* ALL THE PORK CHOPS, STUFFING, AND POTATOES. TAKE *THAT*, HOMER.

D'OH!

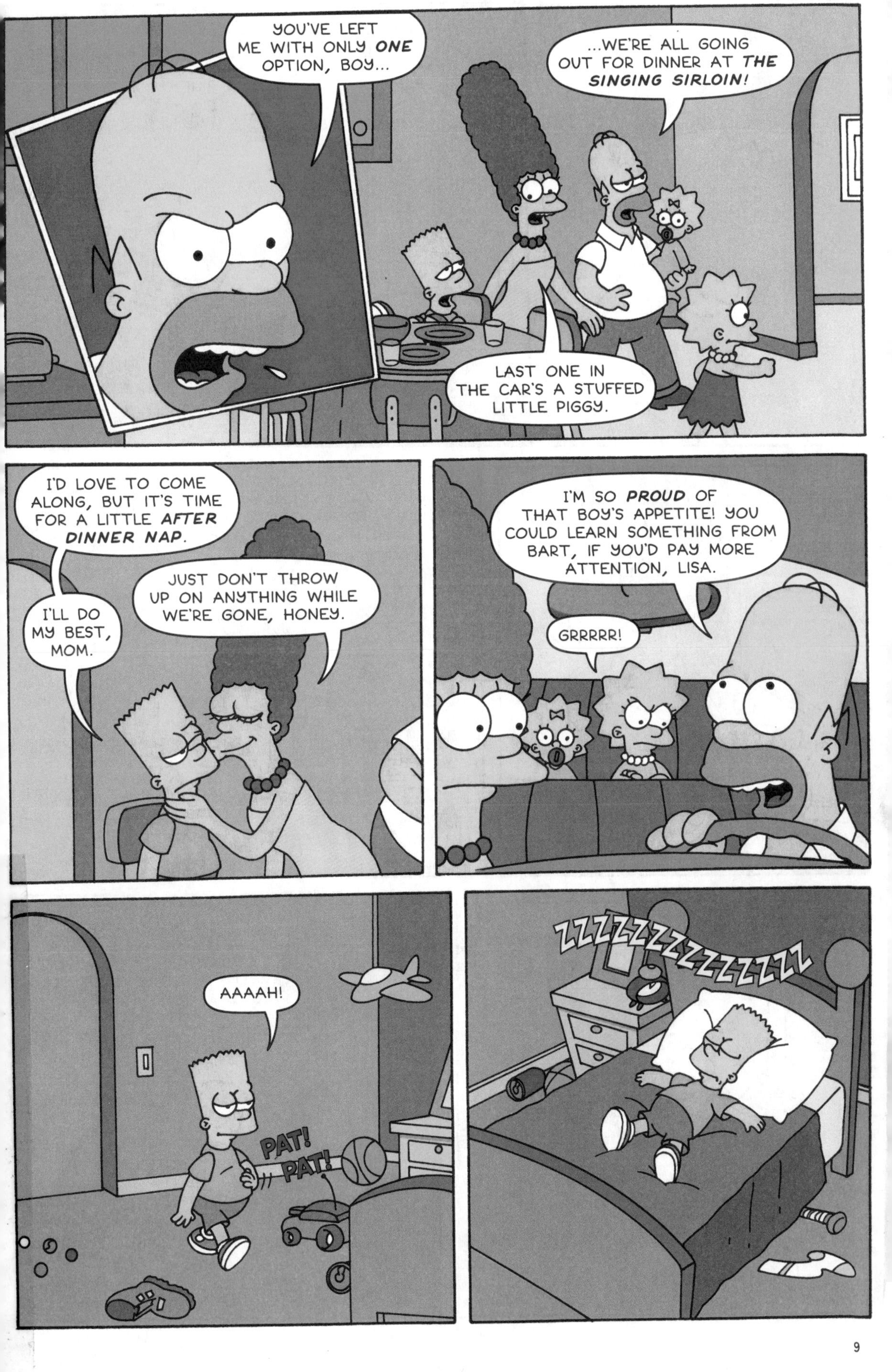
YOU'VE LEFT ME WITH ONLY ONE OPTION, BOY...
...WE'RE ALL GOING OUT FOR DINNER AT THE SINGING SIRLOIN!
LAST ONE IN THE CAR'S A STUFFED LITTLE PIGGY.
I'D LOVE TO COME ALONG, BUT IT'S TIME FOR A LITTLE AFTER DINNER NAP.
JUST DON'T THROW UP ON ANYTHING WHILE WE'RE GONE, HONEY.
I'LL DO MY BEST, MOM.
I'M SO PROUD OF THAT BOY'S APPETITE! YOU COULD LEARN SOMETHING FROM BART, IF YOU'D PAY MORE ATTENTION, LISA.
GRRRRR!
AAAAH!
PAT! PAT!
ZZZZZZZZZZZZZZZZ

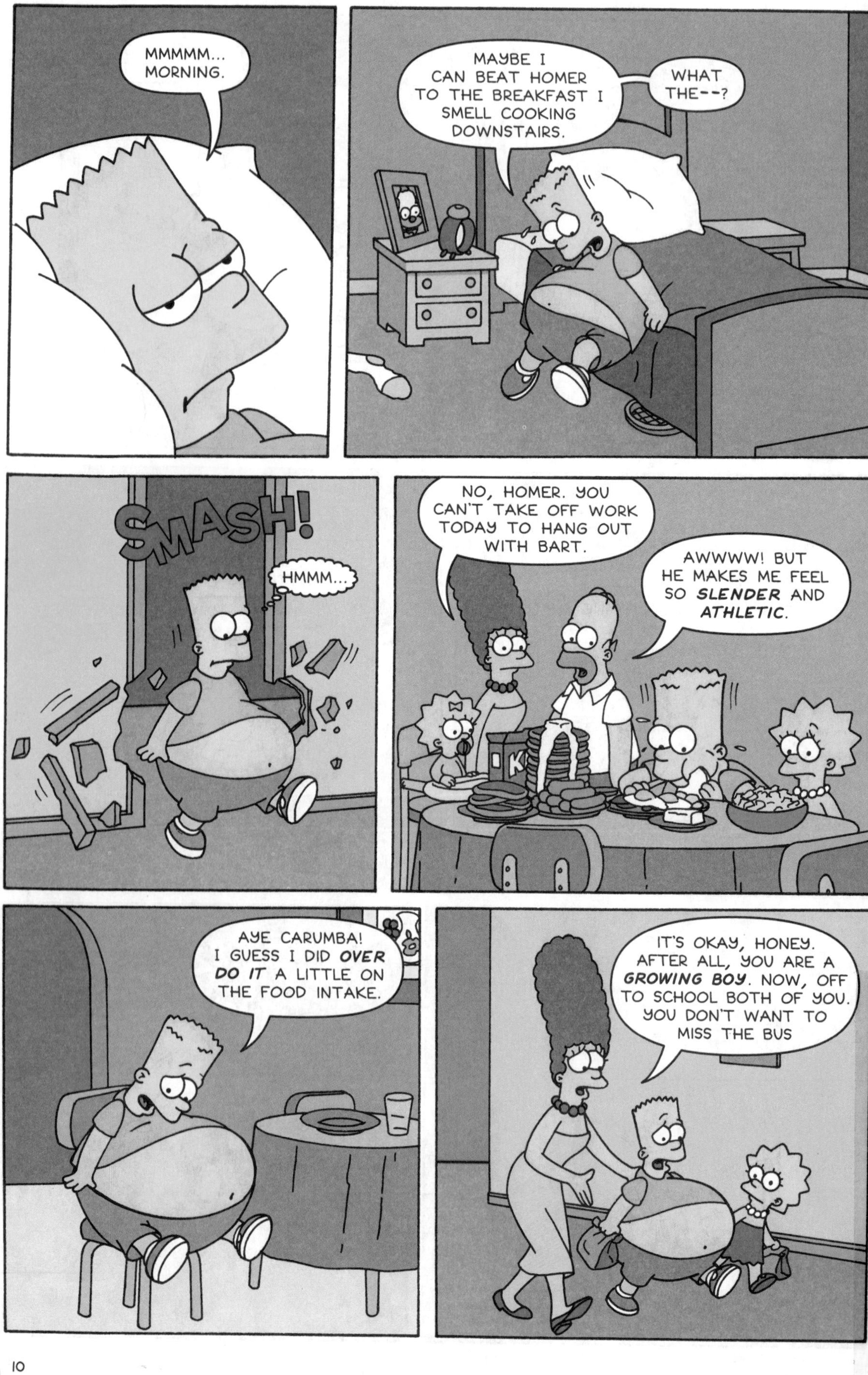
MMMMM... MORNING.
MAYBE I CAN BEAT HOMER TO THE BREAKFAST I SMELL COOKING DOWNSTAIRS.
WHAT THE--?
SMASH!
HMMM...
NO, HOMER. YOU CAN'T TAKE OFF WORK TODAY TO HANG OUT WITH BART.
AWWWW! BUT HE MAKES ME FEEL SO **SLENDER** AND **ATHLETIC**.
AYE CARUMBA! I GUESS I DID **OVER DO IT** A LITTLE ON THE FOOD INTAKE.
IT'S OKAY, HONEY. AFTER ALL, YOU ARE A **GROWING BOY**. NOW, OFF TO SCHOOL BOTH OF YOU. YOU DON'T WANT TO MISS THE BUS

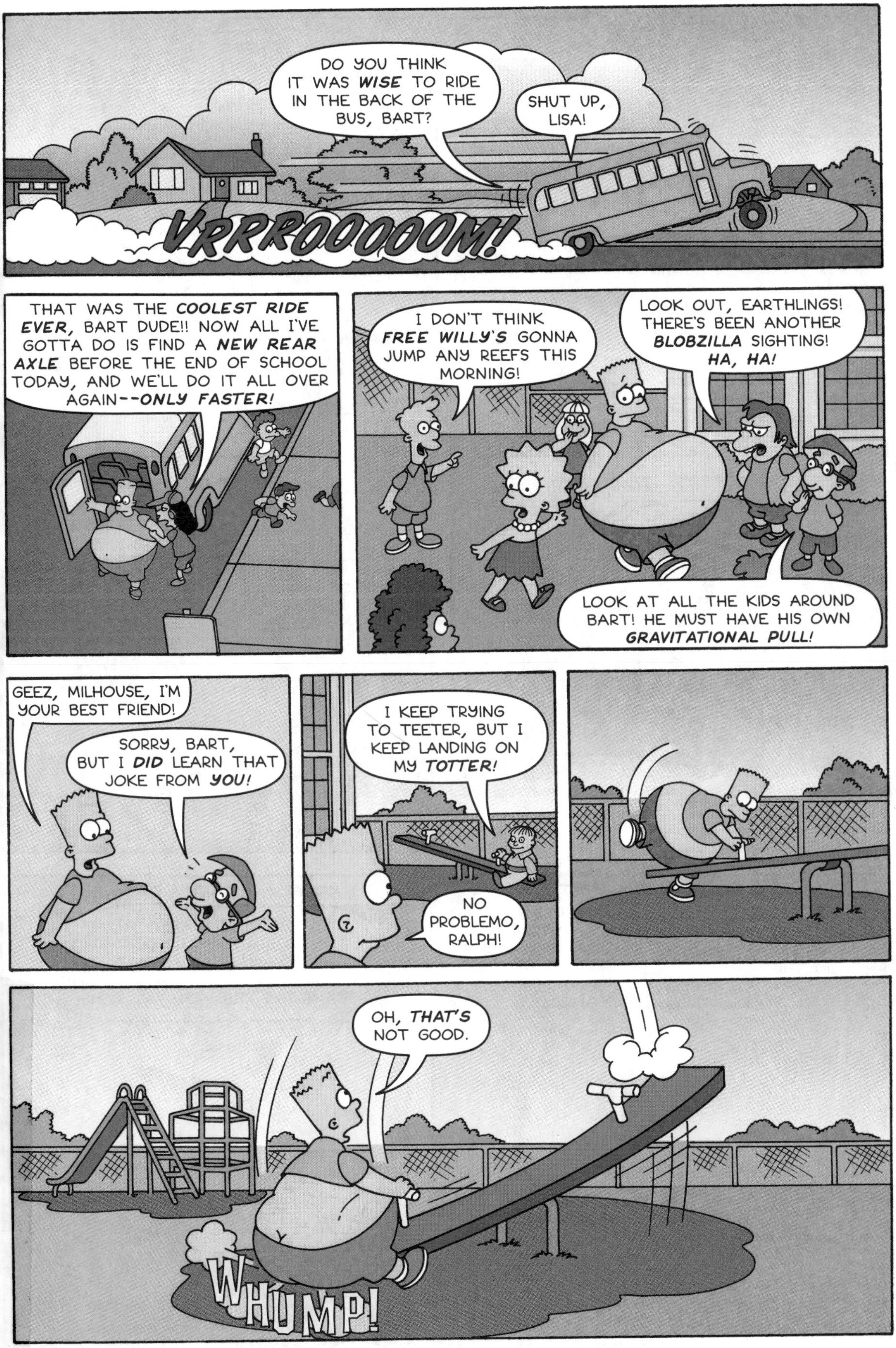
DO YOU THINK IT WAS WISE TO RIDE IN THE BACK OF THE BUS, BART?
SHUT UP, LISA!
VRRROOOOOOM!
THAT WAS THE COOLEST RIDE EVER, BART DUDE!! NOW ALL I'VE GOTTA DO IS FIND A NEW REAR AXLE BEFORE THE END OF SCHOOL TODAY, AND WE'LL DO IT ALL OVER AGAIN--ONLY FASTER!
I DON'T THINK FREE WILLY'S GONNA JUMP ANY REEFS THIS MORNING!
LOOK OUT, EARTHLINGS! THERE'S BEEN ANOTHER BLOBZILLA SIGHTING! HA, HA!
LOOK AT ALL THE KIDS AROUND BART! HE MUST HAVE HIS OWN GRAVITATIONAL PULL!
GEEZ, MILHOUSE, I'M YOUR BEST FRIEND!
SORRY, BART, BUT I DID LEARN THAT JOKE FROM YOU!
I KEEP TRYING TO TEETER, BUT I KEEP LANDING ON MY TOTTER!
NO PROBLEMO, RALPH!
OH, THAT'S NOT GOOD.
WHUMP!

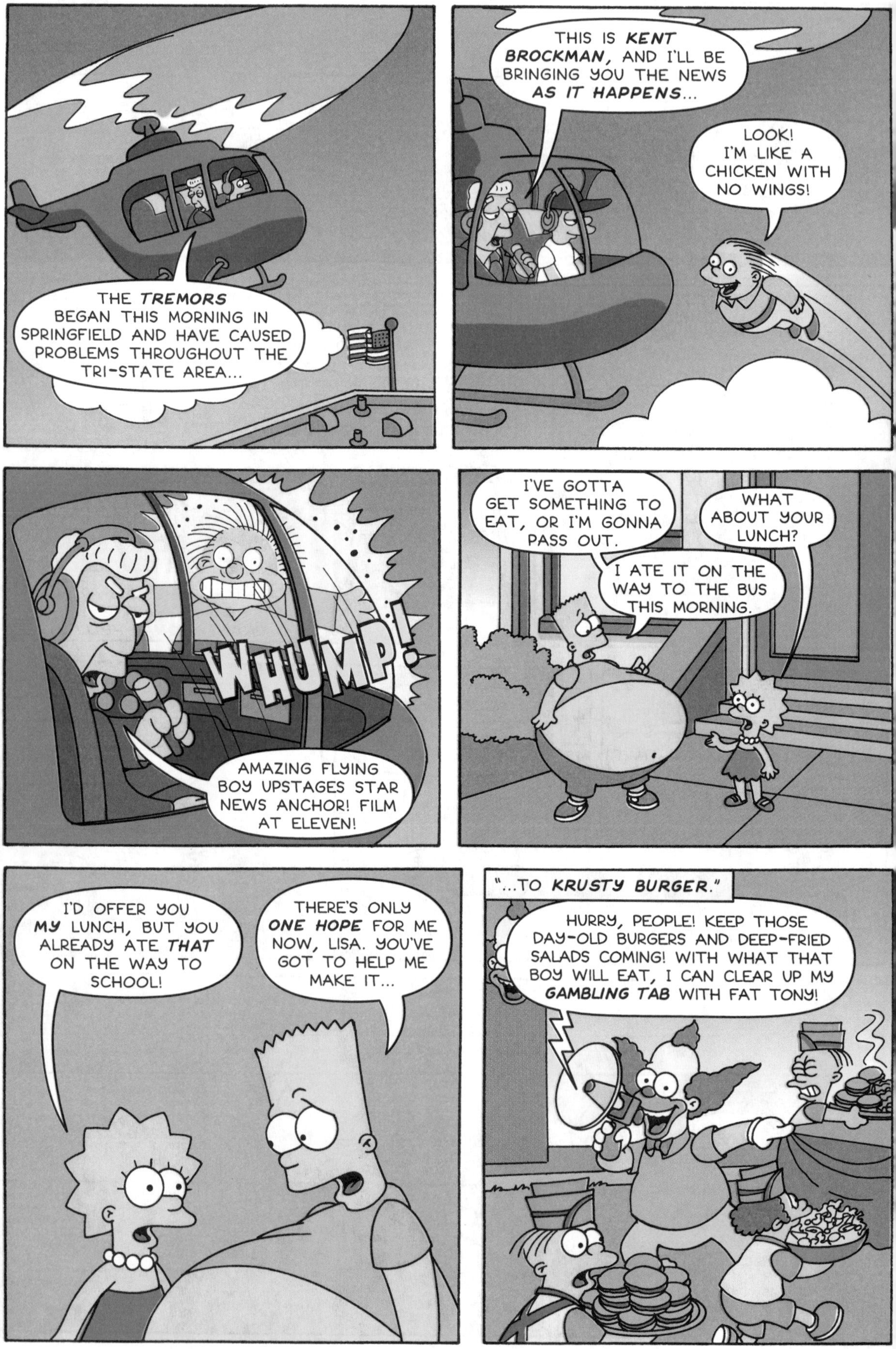
THE TREMORS BEGAN THIS MORNING IN SPRINGFIELD AND HAVE CAUSED PROBLEMS THROUGHOUT THE TRI-STATE AREA...
THIS IS KENT BROCKMAN, AND I'LL BE BRINGING YOU THE NEWS AS IT HAPPENS...
LOOK! I'M LIKE A CHICKEN WITH NO WINGS!
WHUMP!
AMAZING FLYING BOY UPSTAGES STAR NEWS ANCHOR! FILM AT ELEVEN!
I'VE GOTTA GET SOMETHING TO EAT, OR I'M GONNA PASS OUT.
WHAT ABOUT YOUR LUNCH?
I ATE IT ON THE WAY TO THE BUS THIS MORNING.
I'D OFFER YOU MY LUNCH, BUT YOU ALREADY ATE THAT ON THE WAY TO SCHOOL!
THERE'S ONLY ONE HOPE FOR ME NOW, LISA. YOU'VE GOT TO HELP ME MAKE IT...
"...TO KRUSTY BURGER."
HURRY, PEOPLE! KEEP THOSE DAY-OLD BURGERS AND DEEP-FRIED SALADS COMING! WITH WHAT THAT BOY WILL EAT, I CAN CLEAR UP MY GAMBLING TAB WITH FAT TONY!

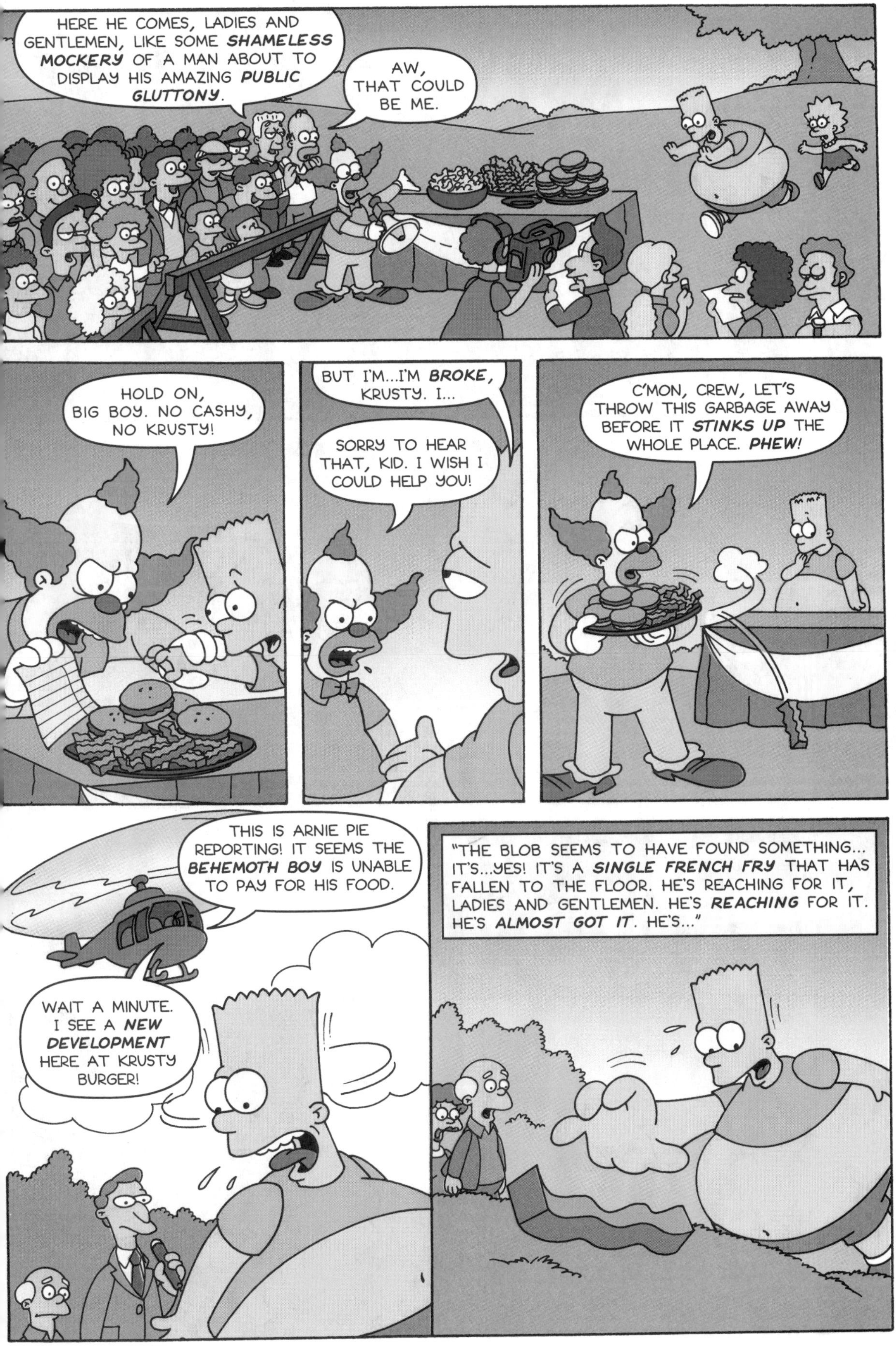
HERE HE COMES, LADIES AND GENTLEMEN, LIKE SOME SHAMELESS MOCKERY OF A MAN ABOUT TO DISPLAY HIS AMAZING PUBLIC GLUTTONY.
AW, THAT COULD BE ME.
HOLD ON, BIG BOY. NO CASHY, NO KRUSTY!
BUT I'M...I'M BROKE, KRUSTY. I...
SORRY TO HEAR THAT, KID. I WISH I COULD HELP YOU!
C'MON, CREW, LET'S THROW THIS GARBAGE AWAY BEFORE IT STINKS UP THE WHOLE PLACE. PHEW!
THIS IS ARNIE PIE REPORTING! IT SEEMS THE BEHEMOTH BOY IS UNABLE TO PAY FOR HIS FOOD.
WAIT A MINUTE. I SEE A NEW DEVELOPMENT HERE AT KRUSTY BURGER!
"THE BLOB SEEMS TO HAVE FOUND SOMETHING... IT'S...YES! IT'S A SINGLE FRENCH FRY THAT HAS FALLEN TO THE FLOOR. HE'S REACHING FOR IT, LADIES AND GENTLEMEN. HE'S REACHING FOR IT. HE'S ALMOST GOT IT. HE'S..."

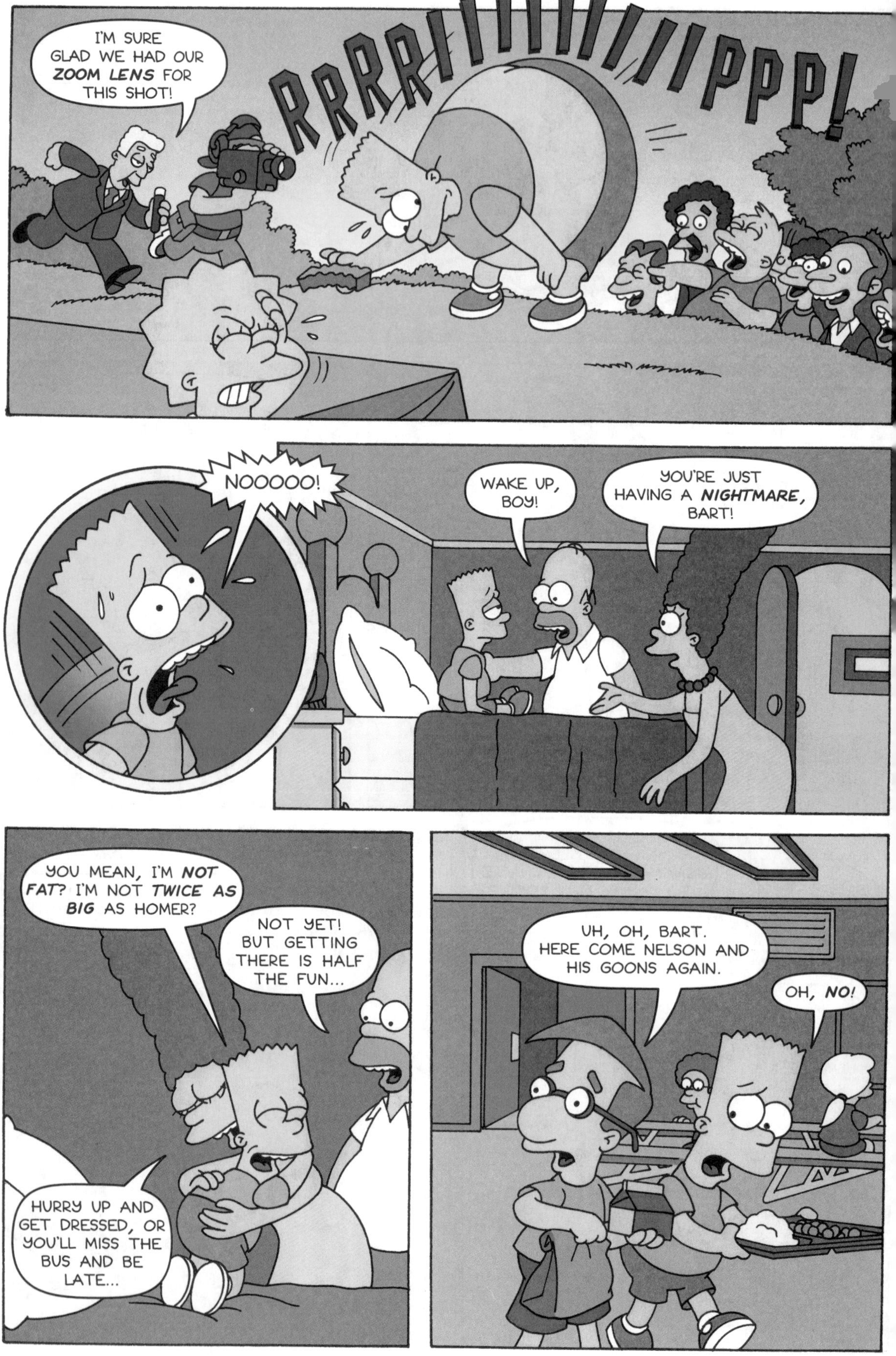
I'M SURE GLAD WE HAD OUR **ZOOM LENS** FOR THIS SHOT!
RRRRIIIIIIIIIPPP!
NOOOOO!
WAKE UP, BOY!
YOU'RE JUST HAVING A ***NIGHTMARE,*** BART!
YOU MEAN, I'M ***NOT FAT***? I'M NOT ***TWICE AS BIG*** AS HOMER?
NOT YET! BUT GETTING THERE IS HALF THE FUN...
HURRY UP AND GET DRESSED, OR YOU'LL MISS THE BUS AND BE LATE...
UH, OH, BART. HERE COME NELSON AND HIS GOONS AGAIN.
OH, ***NO!***

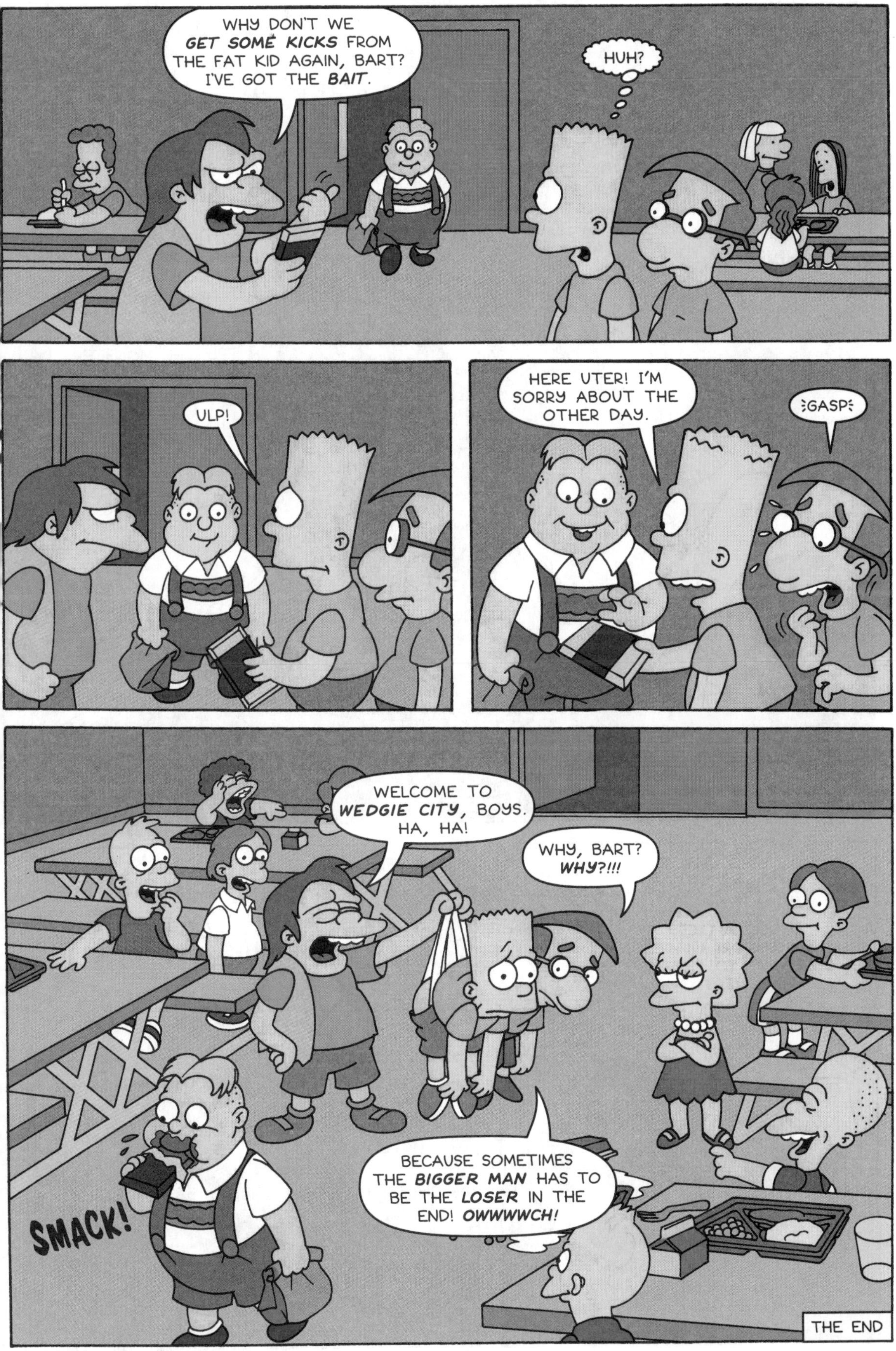
WHY DON'T WE GET SOME KICKS FROM THE FAT KID AGAIN, BART? I'VE GOT THE BAIT.
HUH?
ULP!
HERE UTER! I'M SORRY ABOUT THE OTHER DAY.
GASP
WELCOME TO WEDGIE CITY, BOYS. HA, HA!
WHY, BART? WHY?!!!
BECAUSE SOMETIMES THE BIGGER MAN HAS TO BE THE LOSER IN THE END! OWWWWCH!
SMACK!
THE END

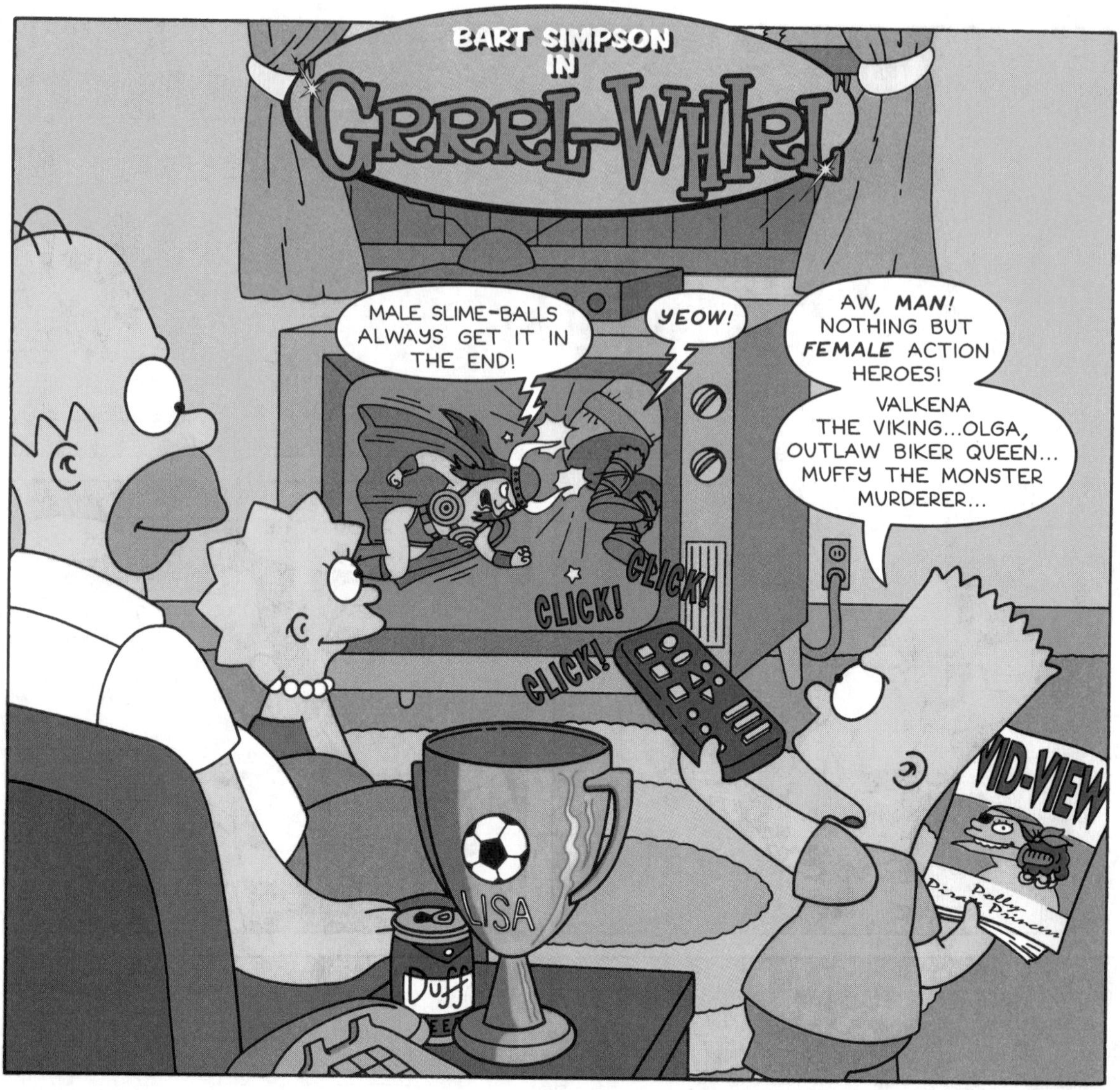
BART SIMPSON IN
GRRRL-WHIRL
MALE SLIME-BALLS ALWAYS GET IT IN THE END!
YEOW!
AW, MAN! NOTHING BUT FEMALE ACTION HEROES!
VALKENA THE VIKING...OLGA, OUTLAW BIKER QUEEN... MUFFY THE MONSTER MURDERER...
CLICK!
CLICK!
CLICK!
LISA
Duff
VID-VIEW
Polly Pirate Princess

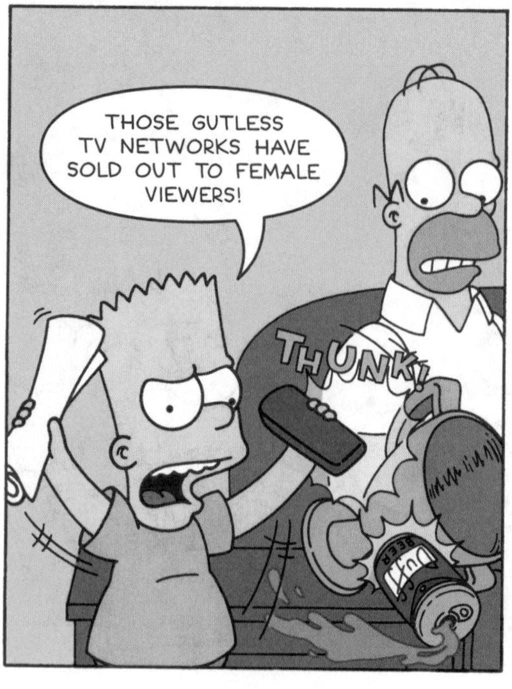
THOSE GUTLESS TV NETWORKS HAVE SOLD OUT TO FEMALE VIEWERS!
THUNK!
Duff BEER

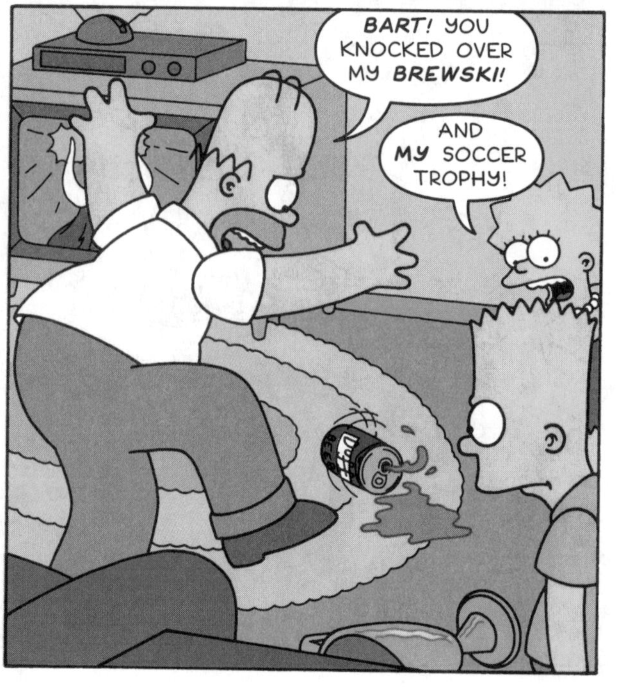
BART! YOU KNOCKED OVER MY BREWSKI!
AND MY SOCCER TROPHY!

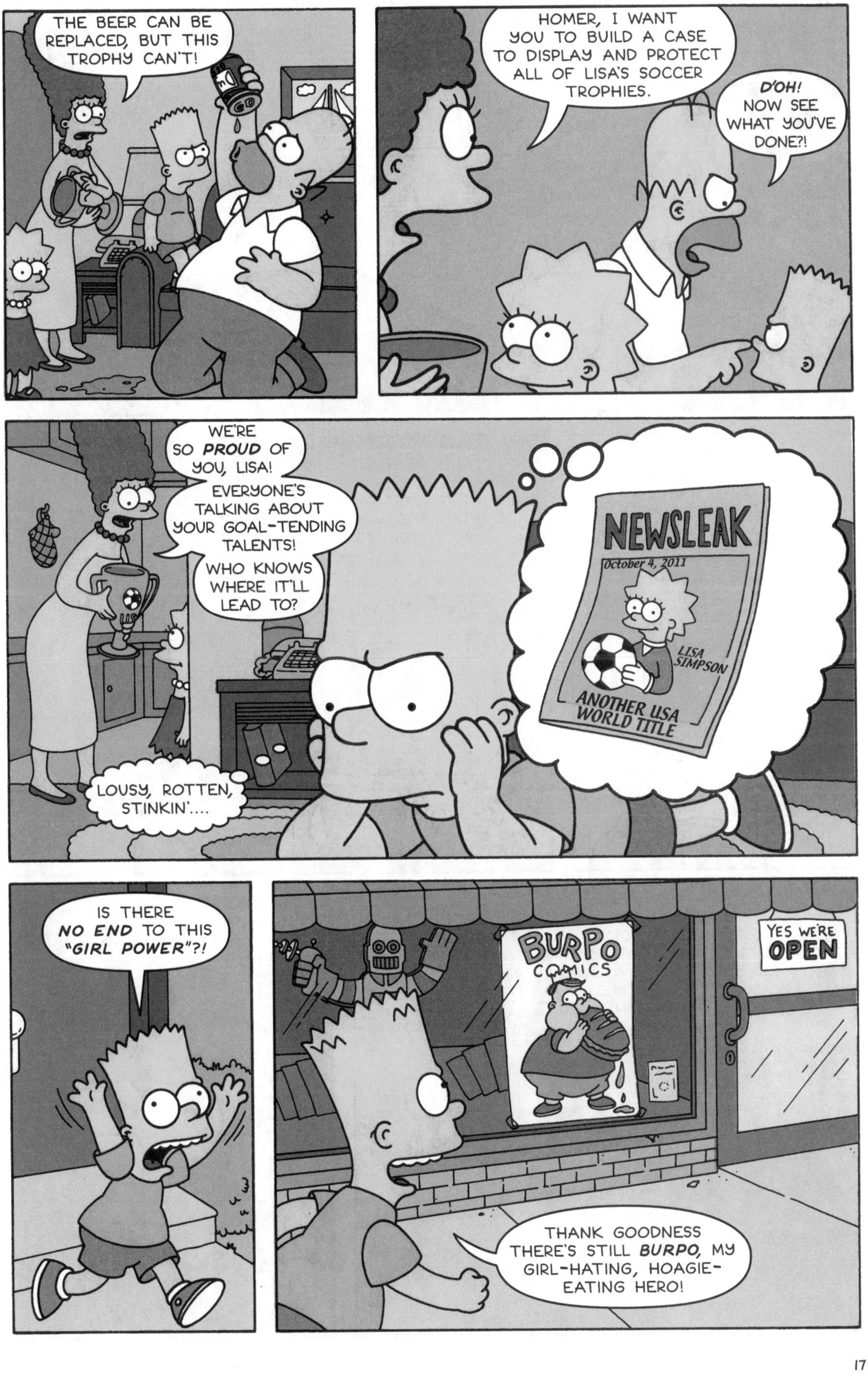
THE BEER CAN BE REPLACED, BUT THIS TROPHY CAN'T!
HOMER, I WANT YOU TO BUILD A CASE TO DISPLAY AND PROTECT ALL OF LISA'S SOCCER TROPHIES.
D'OH! NOW SEE WHAT YOU'VE DONE?!
WE'RE SO PROUD OF YOU, LISA!
EVERYONE'S TALKING ABOUT YOUR GOAL-TENDING TALENTS!
WHO KNOWS WHERE IT'LL LEAD TO?
NEWSLEAK
October 4, 2011
LISA SIMPSON
ANOTHER USA WORLD TITLE
LOUSY, ROTTEN, STINKIN'....
IS THERE NO END TO THIS "GIRL POWER"?!
BURPO COMICS
YES WE'RE OPEN
THANK GOODNESS THERE'S STILL BURPO, MY GIRL-HATING, HOAGIE-EATING HERO!

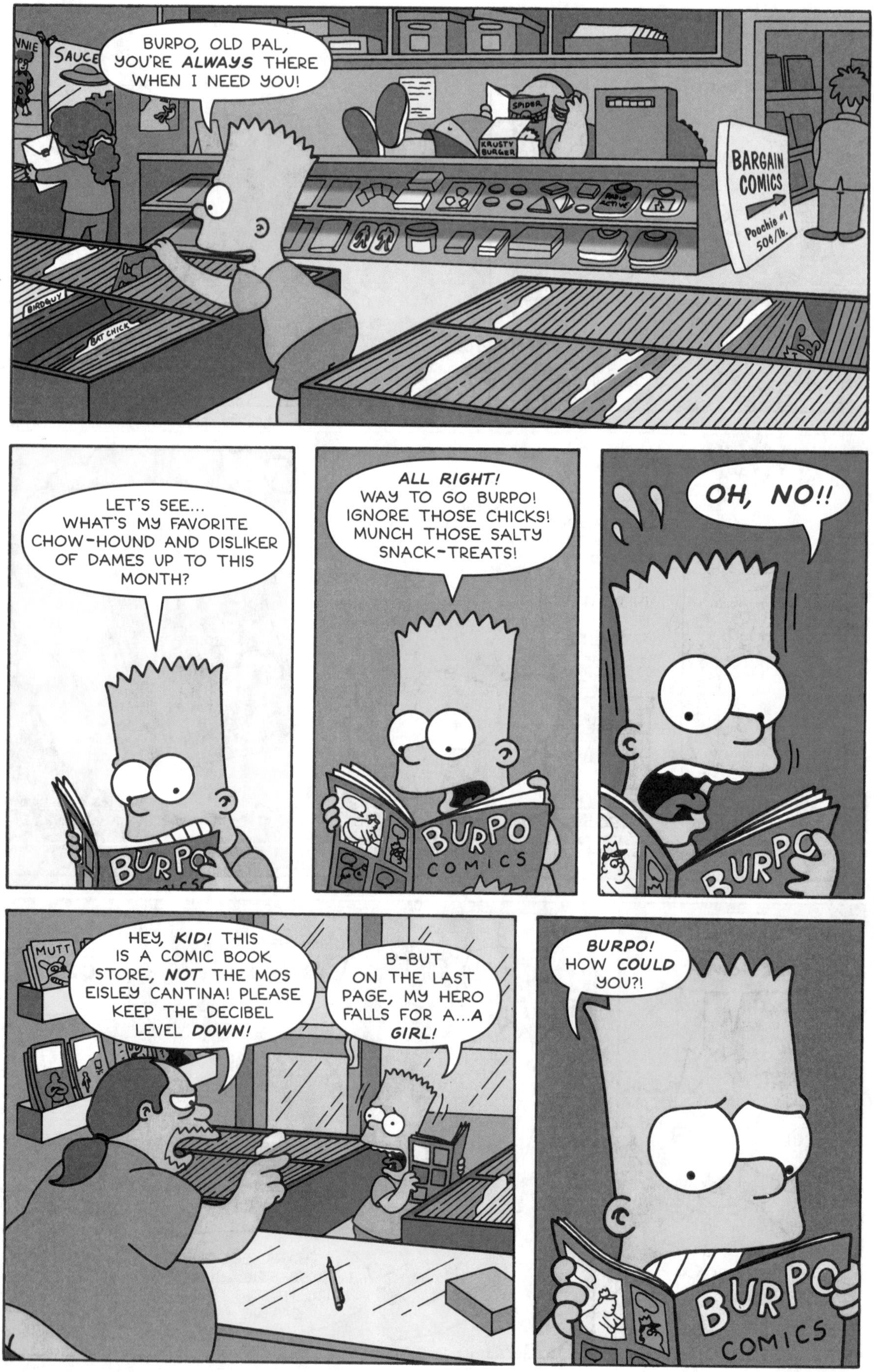
NNIE
SAUCE
BURPO, OLD PAL, YOU'RE ALWAYS THERE WHEN I NEED YOU!
SPIDER
KRUSTY BURGER
RADIO ACTIVE
BARGAIN COMICS
Poochie #1 50¢/lb.
BIRDGUY
BAT CHICK
LET'S SEE... WHAT'S MY FAVORITE CHOW-HOUND AND DISLIKER OF DAMES UP TO THIS MONTH?
BURPO
ALL RIGHT! WAY TO GO BURPO! IGNORE THOSE CHICKS! MUNCH THOSE SALTY SNACK-TREATS!
BURPO COMICS
OH, NO!!
BURPO
MUTT
HEY, KID! THIS IS A COMIC BOOK STORE, NOT THE MOS EISLEY CANTINA! PLEASE KEEP THE DECIBEL LEVEL DOWN!
B-BUT ON THE LAST PAGE, MY HERO FALLS FOR A...A GIRL!
BURPO! HOW COULD YOU?!
BURPO COMICS

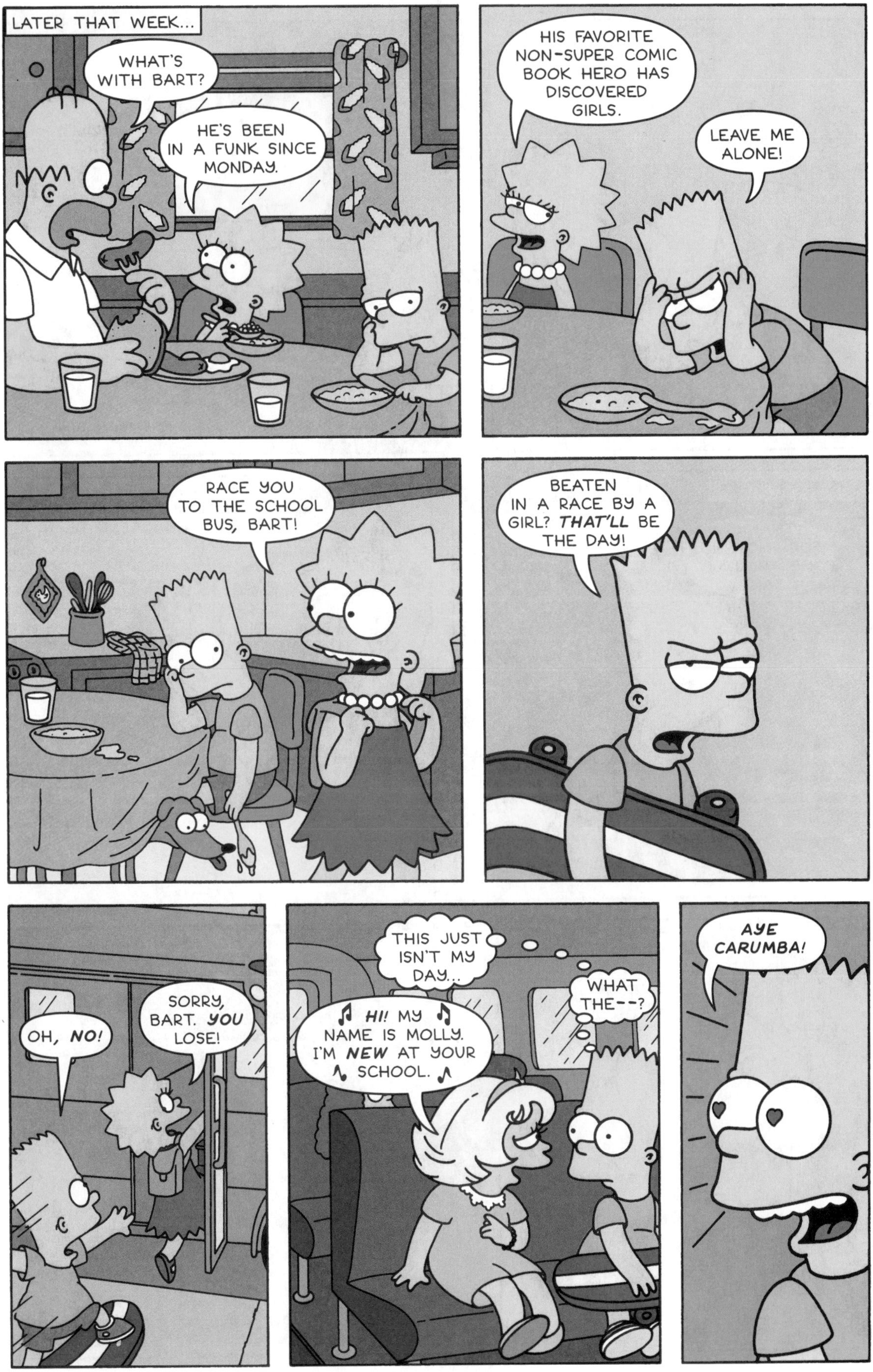
LATER THAT WEEK...
WHAT'S WITH BART?
HE'S BEEN IN A FUNK SINCE MONDAY.
HIS FAVORITE NON-SUPER COMIC BOOK HERO HAS DISCOVERED GIRLS.
LEAVE ME ALONE!
RACE YOU TO THE SCHOOL BUS, BART!
BEATEN IN A RACE BY A GIRL? THAT'LL BE THE DAY!
OH, NO!
SORRY, BART. YOU LOSE!
THIS JUST ISN'T MY DAY...
WHAT THE--?
♪ HI! MY ♪ NAME IS MOLLY. I'M NEW AT YOUR ♪ SCHOOL. ♪
AYE CARUMBA!

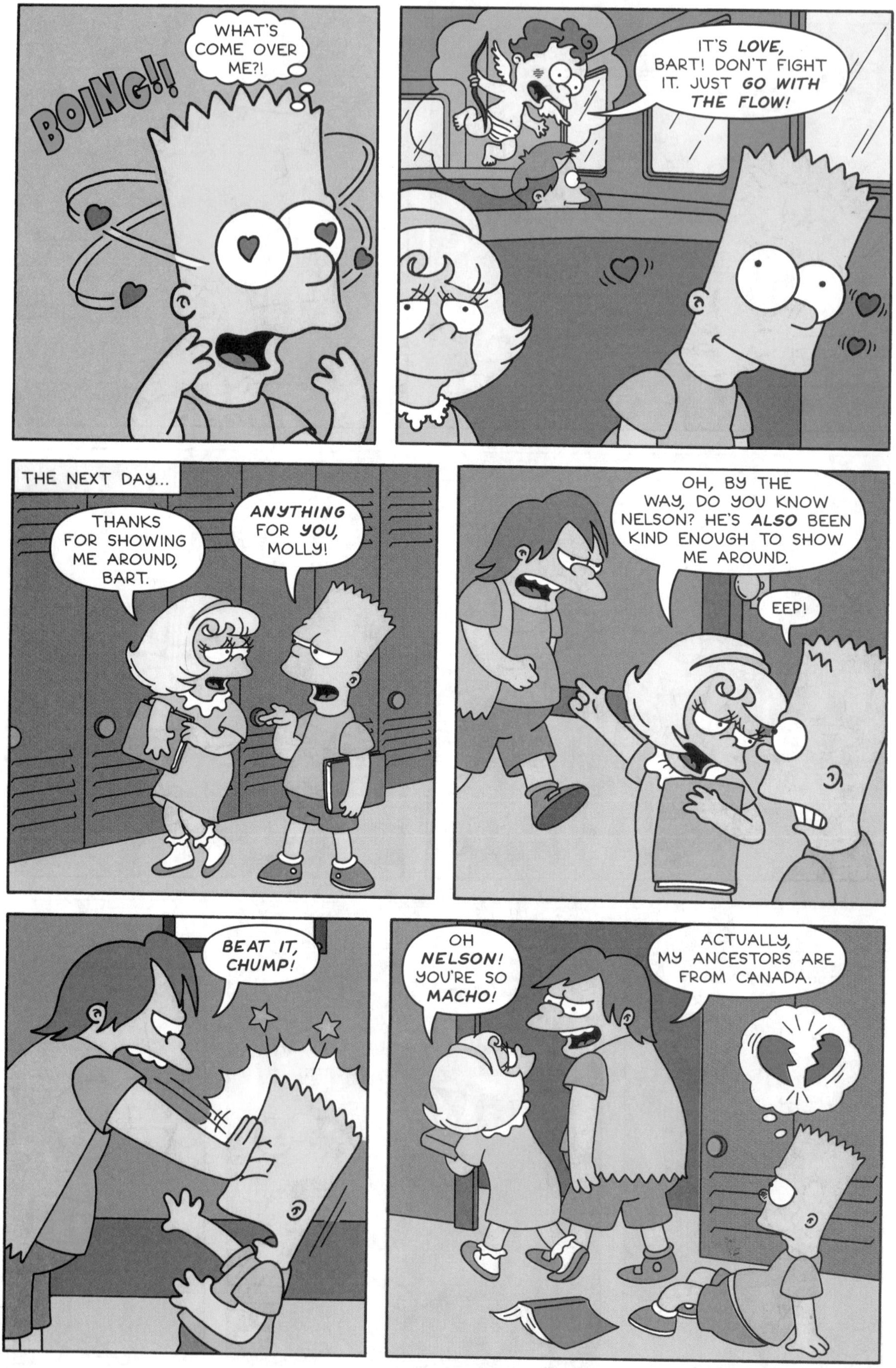
BOING!!
WHAT'S COME OVER ME?!
IT'S LOVE, BART! DON'T FIGHT IT. JUST GO WITH THE FLOW!
THE NEXT DAY...
THANKS FOR SHOWING ME AROUND, BART.
ANYTHING FOR YOU, MOLLY!
OH, BY THE WAY, DO YOU KNOW NELSON? HE'S ALSO BEEN KIND ENOUGH TO SHOW ME AROUND.
EEP!
BEAT IT, CHUMP!
OH NELSON! YOU'RE SO MACHO!
ACTUALLY, MY ANCESTORS ARE FROM CANADA.

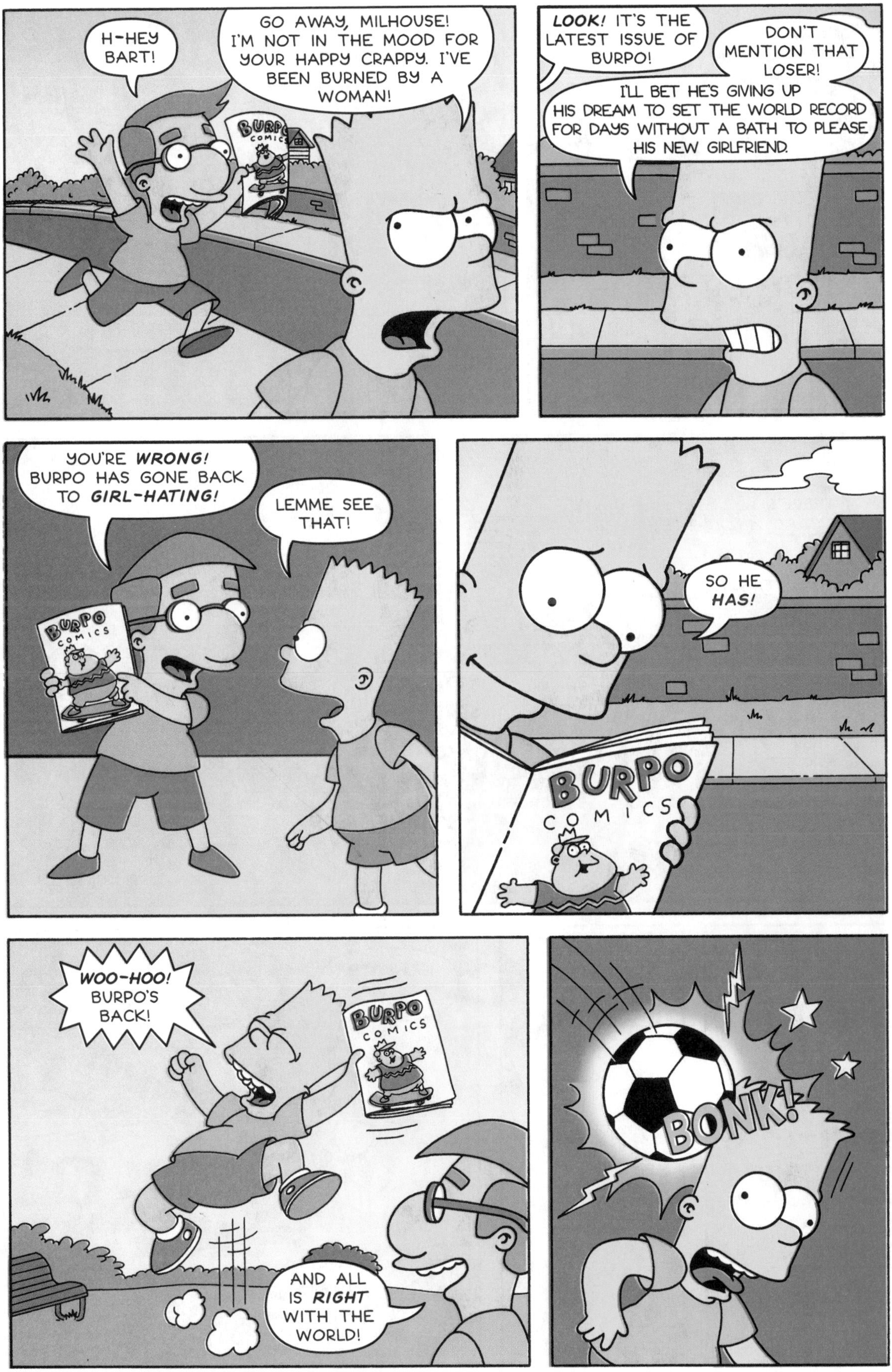
H-HEY BART!
GO AWAY, MILHOUSE! I'M NOT IN THE MOOD FOR YOUR HAPPY CRAPPY. I'VE BEEN BURNED BY A WOMAN!
BURPO COMICS
LOOK! IT'S THE LATEST ISSUE OF BURPO!
DON'T MENTION THAT LOSER!
I'LL BET HE'S GIVING UP HIS DREAM TO SET THE WORLD RECORD FOR DAYS WITHOUT A BATH TO PLEASE HIS NEW GIRLFRIEND.
YOU'RE WRONG! BURPO HAS GONE BACK TO GIRL-HATING!
LEMME SEE THAT!
BURPO COMICS
SO HE HAS!
BURPO COMICS
WOO-HOO! BURPO'S BACK!
BURPO COMICS
AND ALL IS RIGHT WITH THE WORLD!
BONK!

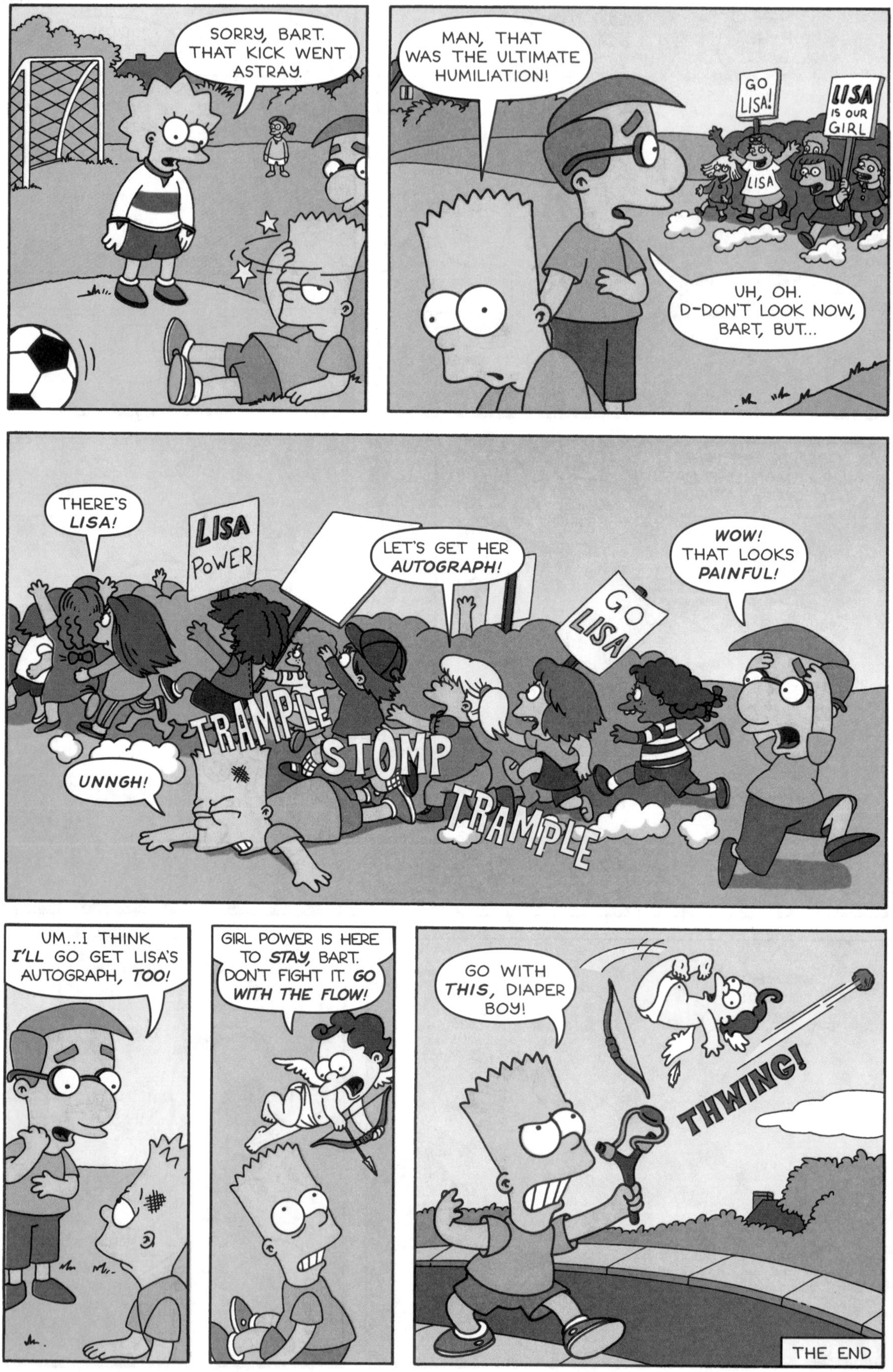
SORRY, BART. THAT KICK WENT ASTRAY.
MAN, THAT WAS THE ULTIMATE HUMILIATION!
GO LISA!
LISA IS OUR GIRL
LISA
UH, OH. D-DON'T LOOK NOW, BART, BUT...
THERE'S LISA!
LISA POWER
LET'S GET HER AUTOGRAPH!
GO LISA
WOW! THAT LOOKS PAINFUL!
TRAMPLE
STOMP
TRAMPLE
UNNGH!
UM...I THINK I'LL GO GET LISA'S AUTOGRAPH, TOO!
GIRL POWER IS HERE TO STAY, BART. DON'T FIGHT IT. GO WITH THE FLOW!
GO WITH THIS, DIAPER BOY!
THWING!
THE END

STORY GEORGE GLADIR

PENCILS CAROLINE KELLY

INKS MIKE ROTE

LETTERS KAREN BATES

COLORS BATES/VILLANUEVA

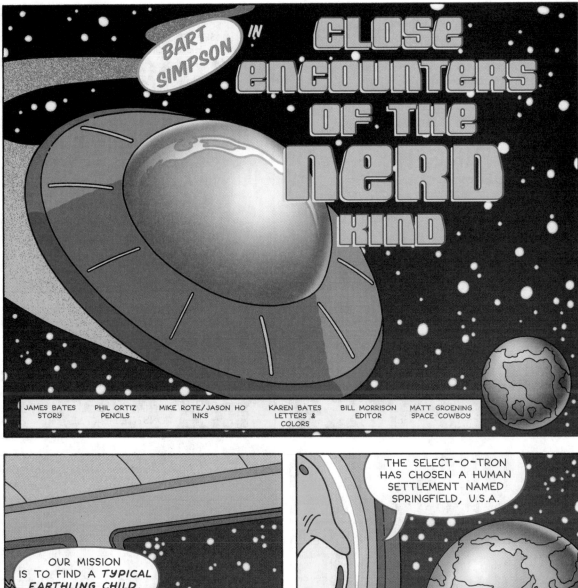

BART SIMPSON IN

CLOSE ENCOUNTERS OF THE NERD KIND

| JAMES BATES STORY | PHIL ORTIZ PENCILS | MIKE ROTE/JASON HO INKS | KAREN BATES LETTERS & COLORS | BILL MORRISON EDITOR | MATT GROENING SPACE COWBOY |

OUR MISSION IS TO FIND A *TYPICAL EARTHLING CHILD*, KANG.

GOOD! I COULD GO FOR A SNACK.

THE SELECT-O-TRON HAS CHOSEN A HUMAN SETTLEMENT NAMED SPRINGFIELD, U.S.A.

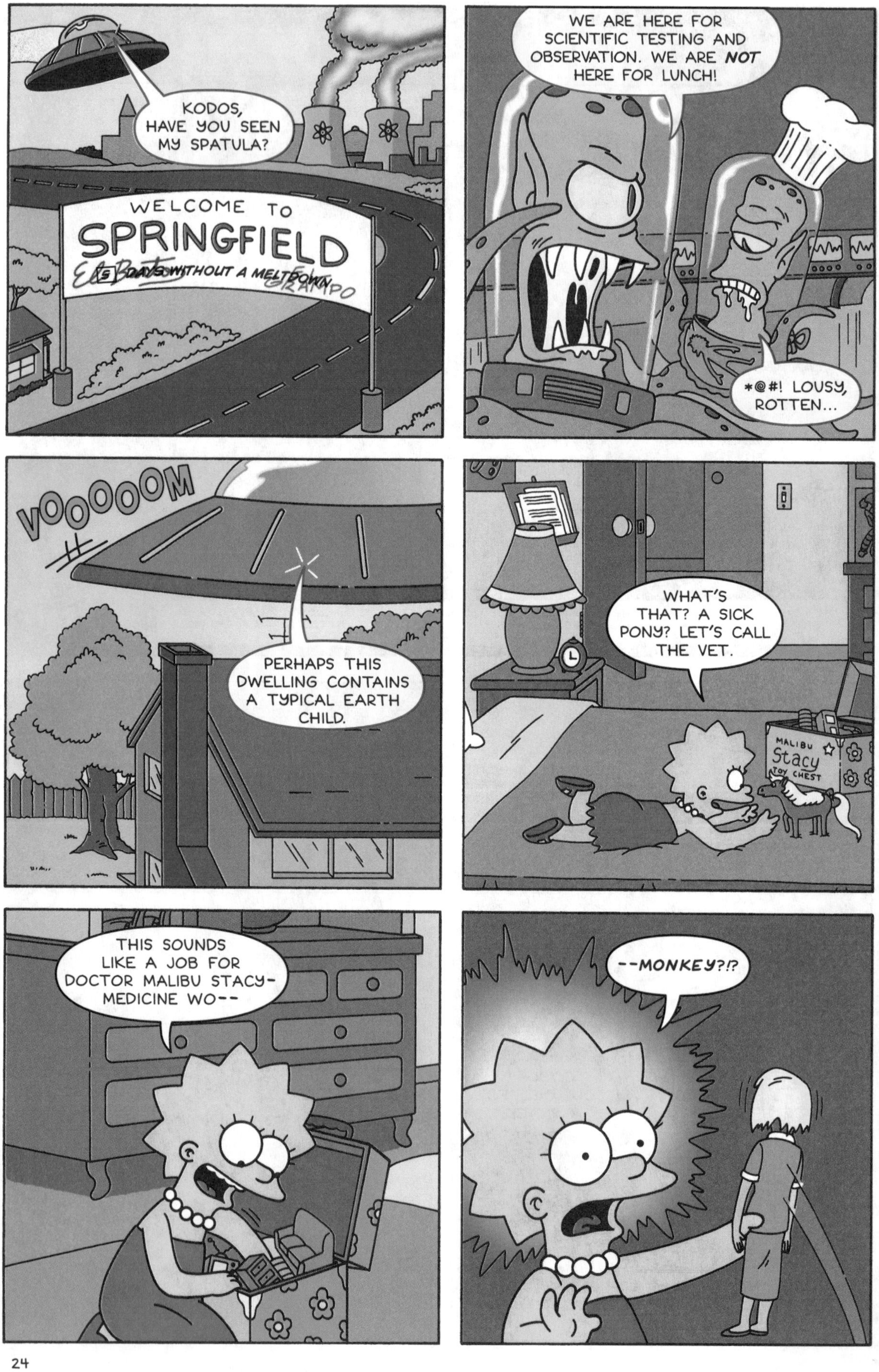
KODOS, HAVE YOU SEEN MY SPATULA?
WELCOME TO
SPRINGFIELD
5 DAYS WITHOUT A MELTDOWN
WE ARE HERE FOR SCIENTIFIC TESTING AND OBSERVATION. WE ARE **NOT** HERE FOR LUNCH!
*@#! LOUSY, ROTTEN...
VOOOOOM
PERHAPS THIS DWELLING CONTAINS A TYPICAL EARTH CHILD.
WHAT'S THAT? A SICK PONY? LET'S CALL THE VET.
MALIBU Stacy TOY CHEST
THIS SOUNDS LIKE A JOB FOR DOCTOR MALIBU STACY-MEDICINE WO--
--**MONKEY**?!?

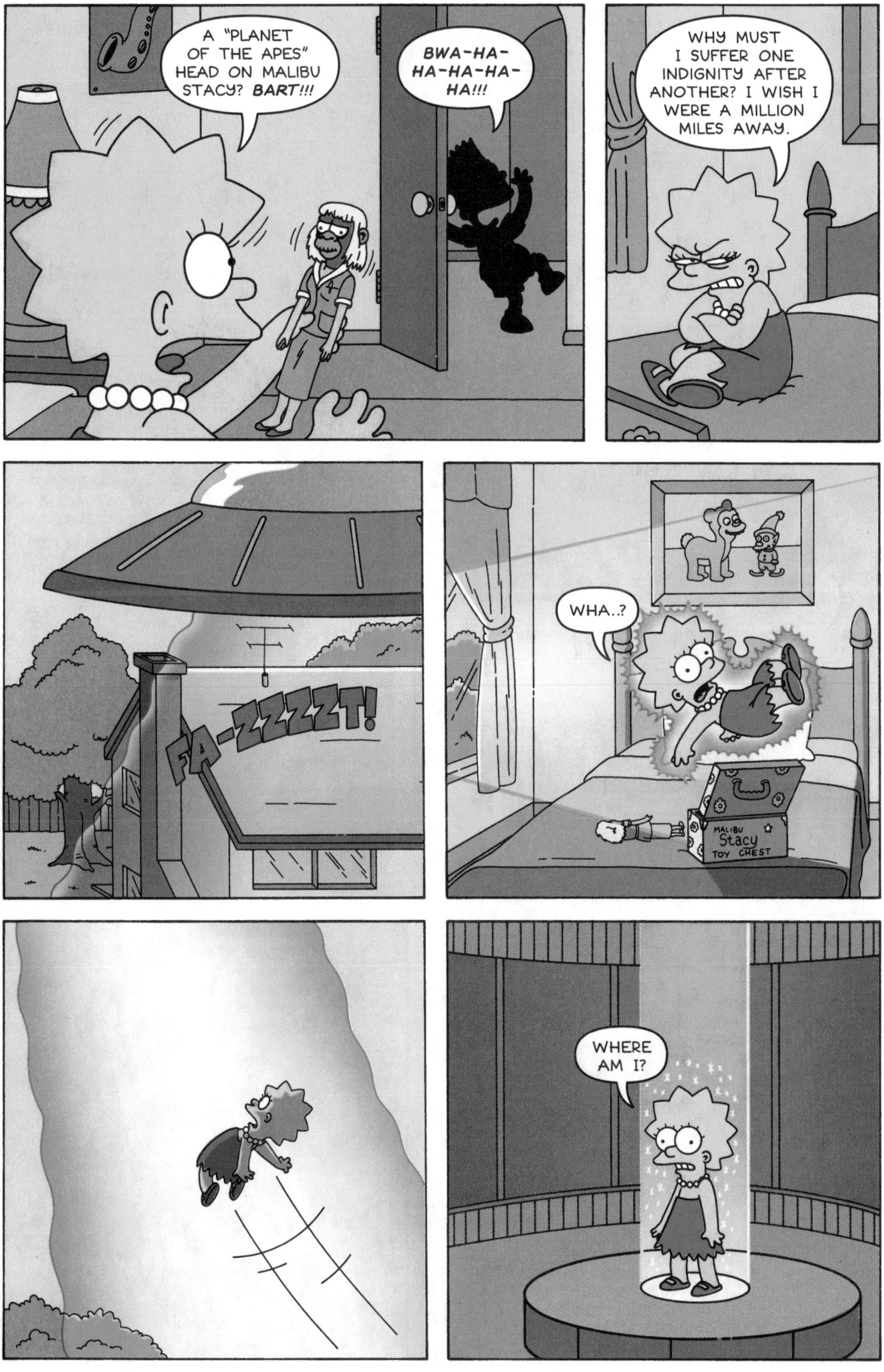
A "PLANET OF THE APES" HEAD ON MALIBU STACY? BART!!!
BWA-HA-HA-HA-HA-HA!!!
WHY MUST I SUFFER ONE INDIGNITY AFTER ANOTHER? I WISH I WERE A MILLION MILES AWAY.
FA-ZZZZT!
WHA..?
MALIBU Stacy TOY CHEST
WHERE AM I?

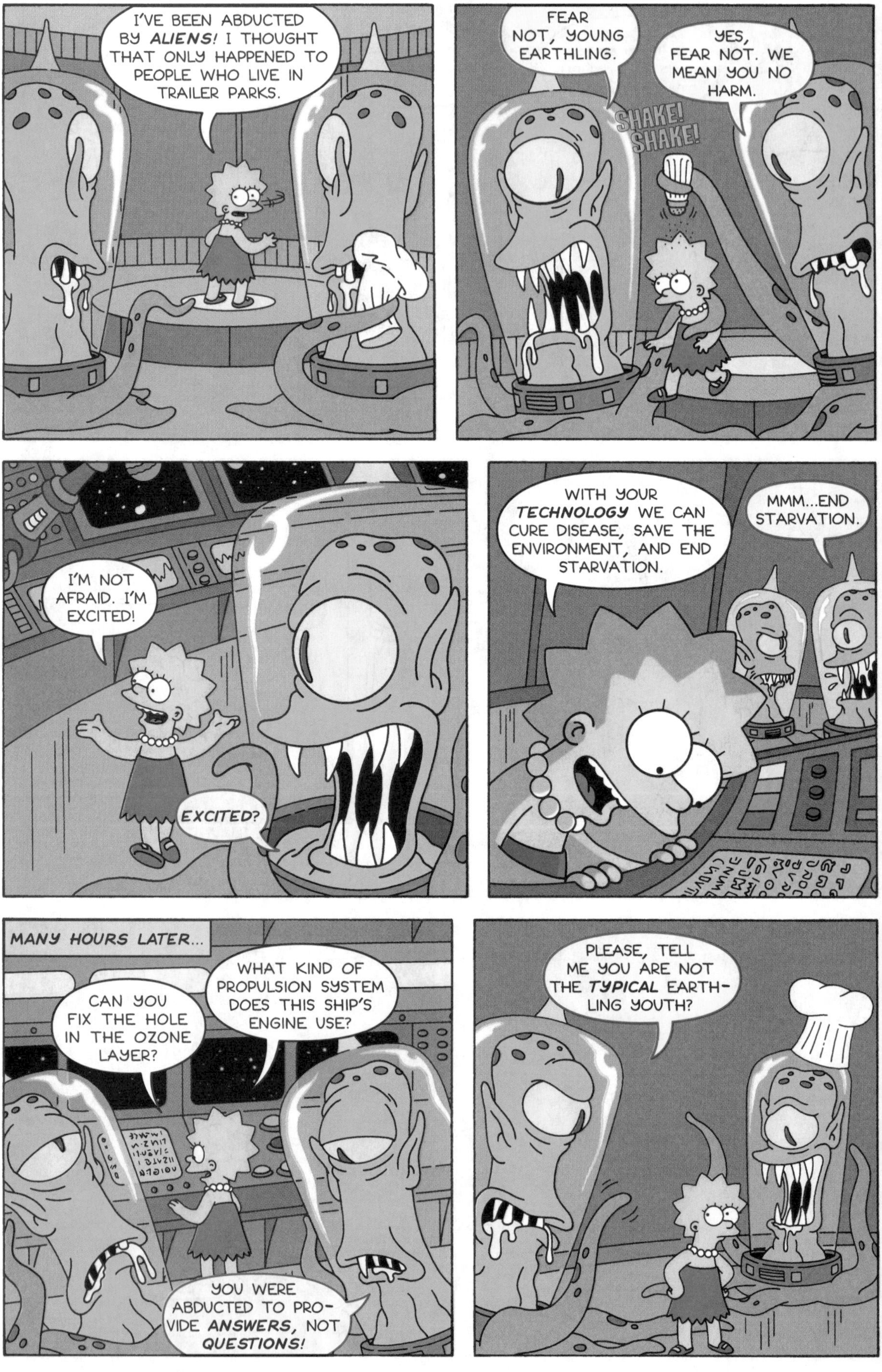

I'VE BEEN ABDUCTED BY ALIENS! I THOUGHT THAT ONLY HAPPENED TO PEOPLE WHO LIVE IN TRAILER PARKS.
FEAR NOT, YOUNG EARTHLING.
YES, FEAR NOT. WE MEAN YOU NO HARM.
SHAKE! SHAKE!
I'M NOT AFRAID. I'M EXCITED!
EXCITED?
WITH YOUR TECHNOLOGY WE CAN CURE DISEASE, SAVE THE ENVIRONMENT, AND END STARVATION.
MMM...END STARVATION.
MANY HOURS LATER...
CAN YOU FIX THE HOLE IN THE OZONE LAYER?
WHAT KIND OF PROPULSION SYSTEM DOES THIS SHIP'S ENGINE USE?
YOU WERE ABDUCTED TO PROVIDE ANSWERS, NOT QUESTIONS!
PLEASE, TELL ME YOU ARE NOT THE TYPICAL EARTHLING YOUTH?

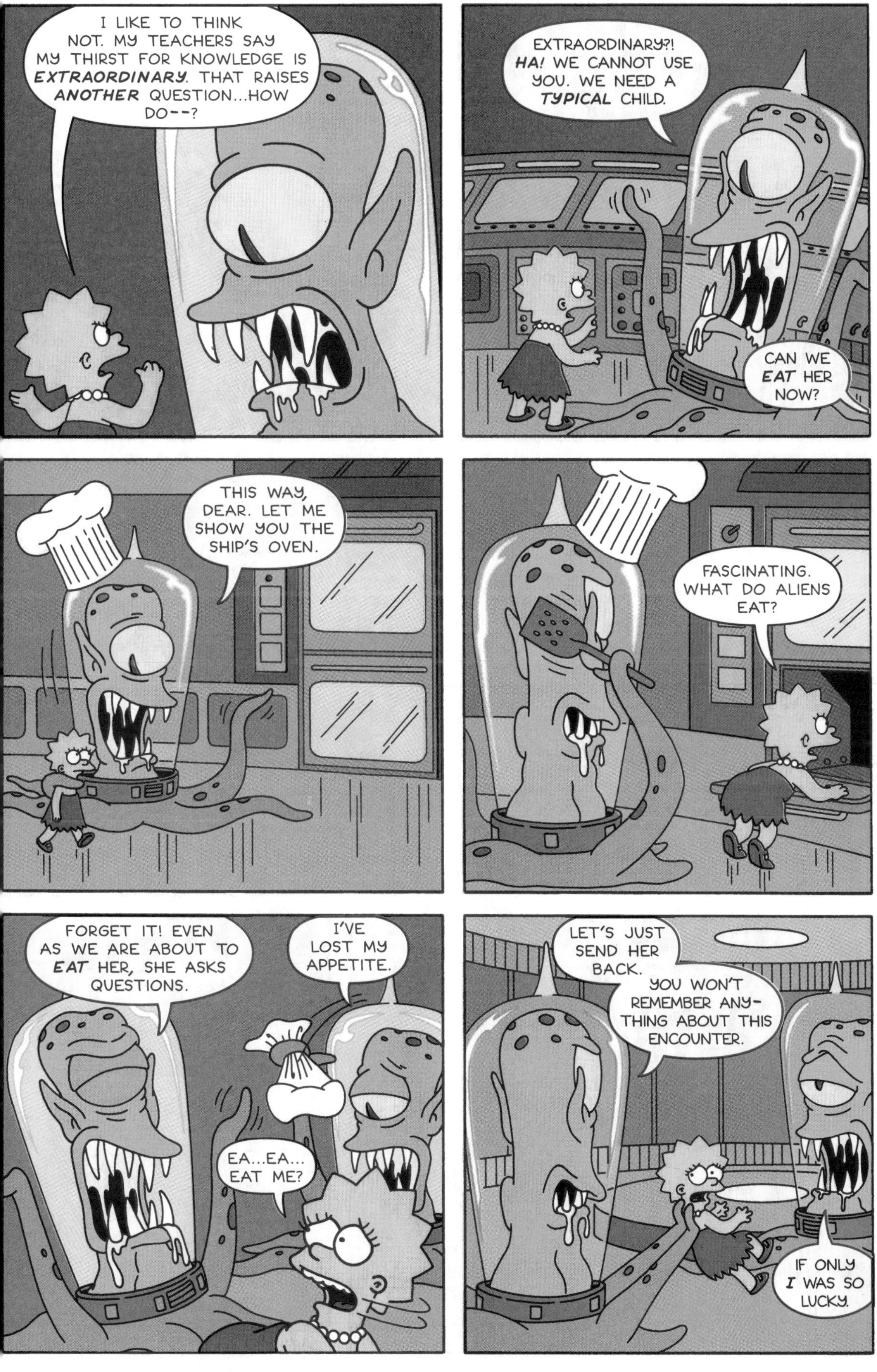
I LIKE TO THINK NOT. MY TEACHERS SAY MY THIRST FOR KNOWLEDGE IS **EXTRAORDINARY**. THAT RAISES **ANOTHER** QUESTION...HOW DO--?
EXTRAORDINARY?! **HA!** WE CANNOT USE YOU. WE NEED A **TYPICAL** CHILD.
CAN WE **EAT** HER NOW?
THIS WAY, DEAR. LET ME SHOW YOU THE SHIP'S OVEN.
FASCINATING. WHAT DO ALIENS EAT?
FORGET IT! EVEN AS WE ARE ABOUT TO **EAT** HER, SHE ASKS QUESTIONS.
I'VE LOST MY APPETITE.
EA...EA... EAT ME?
LET'S JUST SEND HER BACK.
YOU WON'T REMEMBER ANY-THING ABOUT THIS ENCOUNTER.
IF ONLY **I** WAS SO LUCKY.

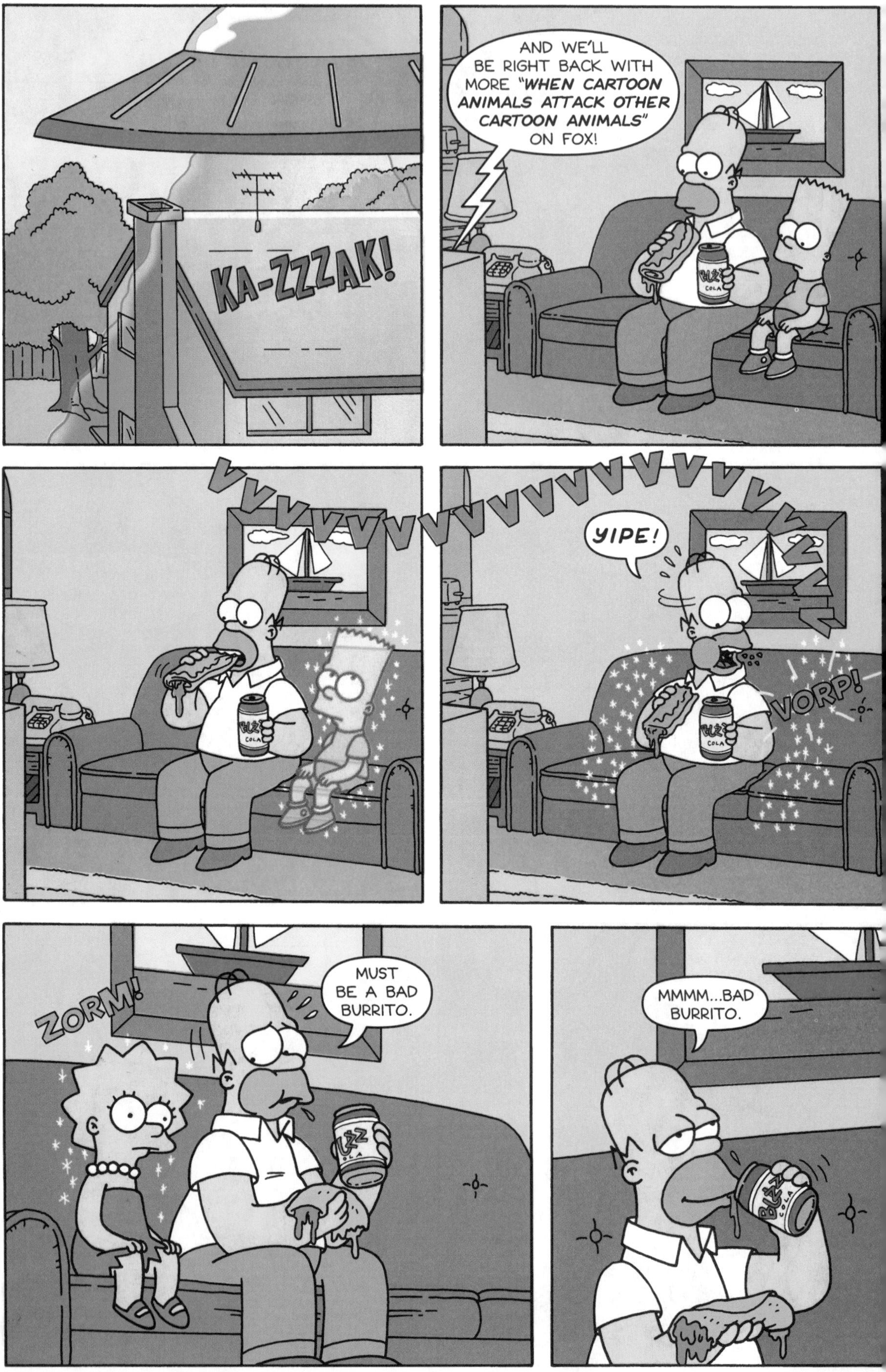
KA-ZZZAK!
AND WE'LL BE RIGHT BACK WITH MORE "WHEN CARTOON ANIMALS ATTACK OTHER CARTOON ANIMALS" ON FOX!
VVVVVVVVVVVVVVVVVVVVVV
YIPE!
VORP!
ZORM!
MUST BE A BAD BURRITO.
MMMM...BAD BURRITO.

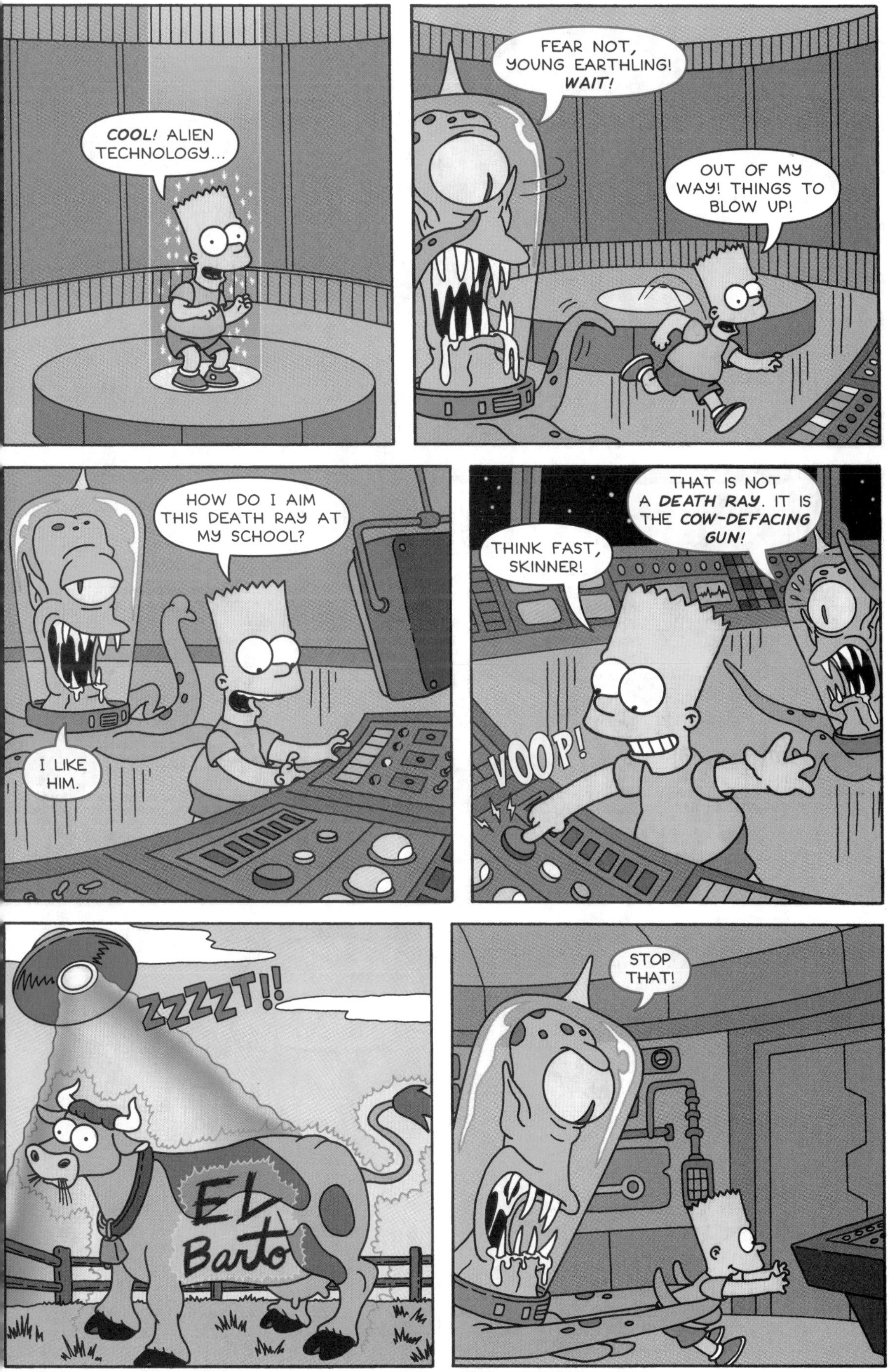
COOL! ALIEN TECHNOLOGY...
FEAR NOT, YOUNG EARTHLING! WAIT!
OUT OF MY WAY! THINGS TO BLOW UP!
HOW DO I AIM THIS DEATH RAY AT MY SCHOOL?
I LIKE HIM.
THINK FAST, SKINNER!
THAT IS NOT A DEATH RAY. IT IS THE COW-DEFACING GUN!
VOOP!
ZZZZT!!
EL Barto
STOP THAT!

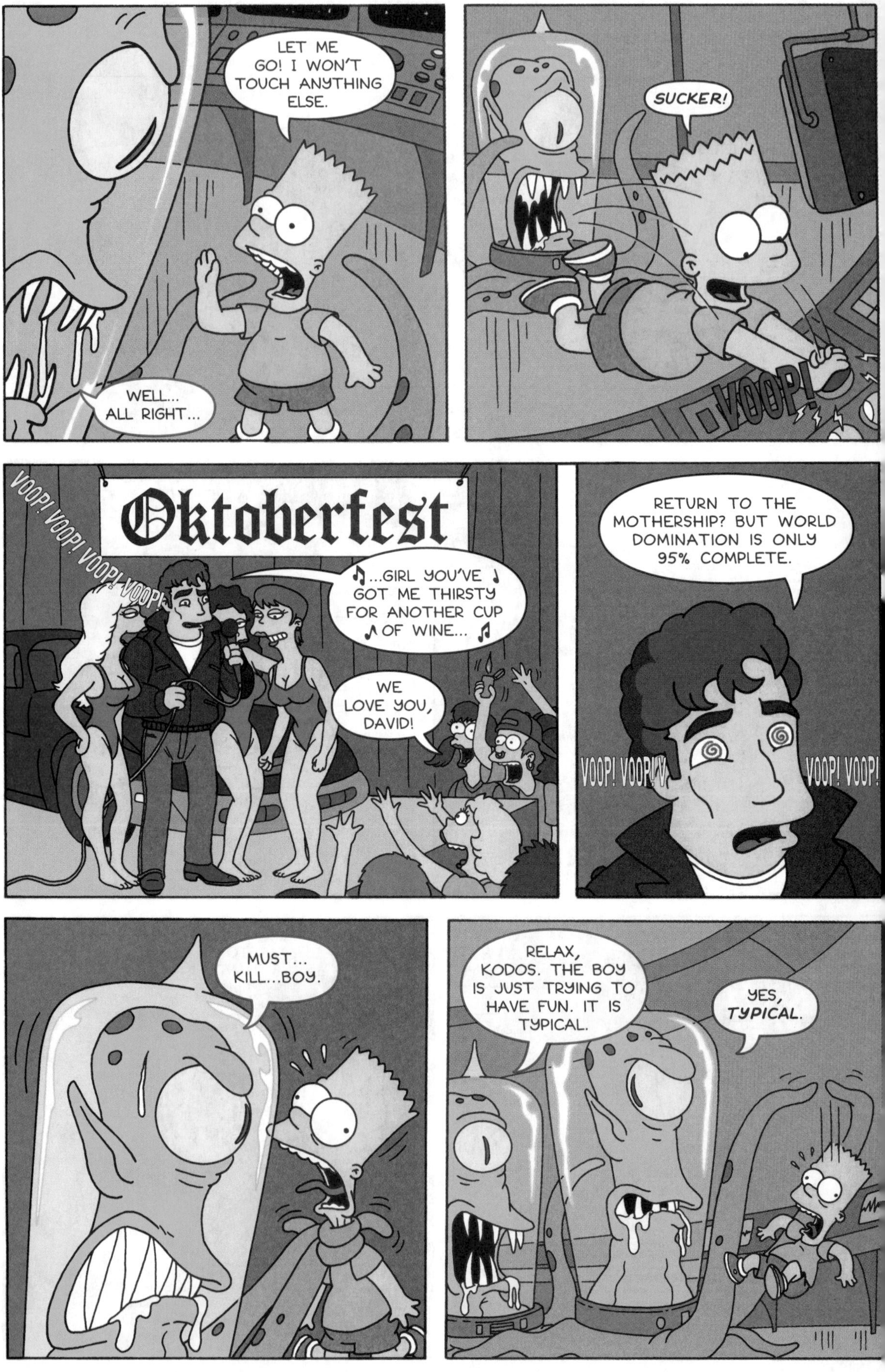
LET ME GO! I WON'T TOUCH ANYTHING ELSE.
WELL... ALL RIGHT...
SUCKER!
VOOP!
Oktoberfest
VOOP! VOOP! VOOP! VOOP!
♫ ...GIRL YOU'VE GOT ME THIRSTY FOR ANOTHER CUP OF WINE... ♫
WE LOVE YOU, DAVID!
RETURN TO THE MOTHERSHIP? BUT WORLD DOMINATION IS ONLY 95% COMPLETE.
VOOP! VOOP! V
VOOP! VOOP!
MUST... KILL...BOY.
RELAX, KODOS. THE BOY IS JUST TRYING TO HAVE FUN. IT IS TYPICAL.
YES, *TYPICAL*.

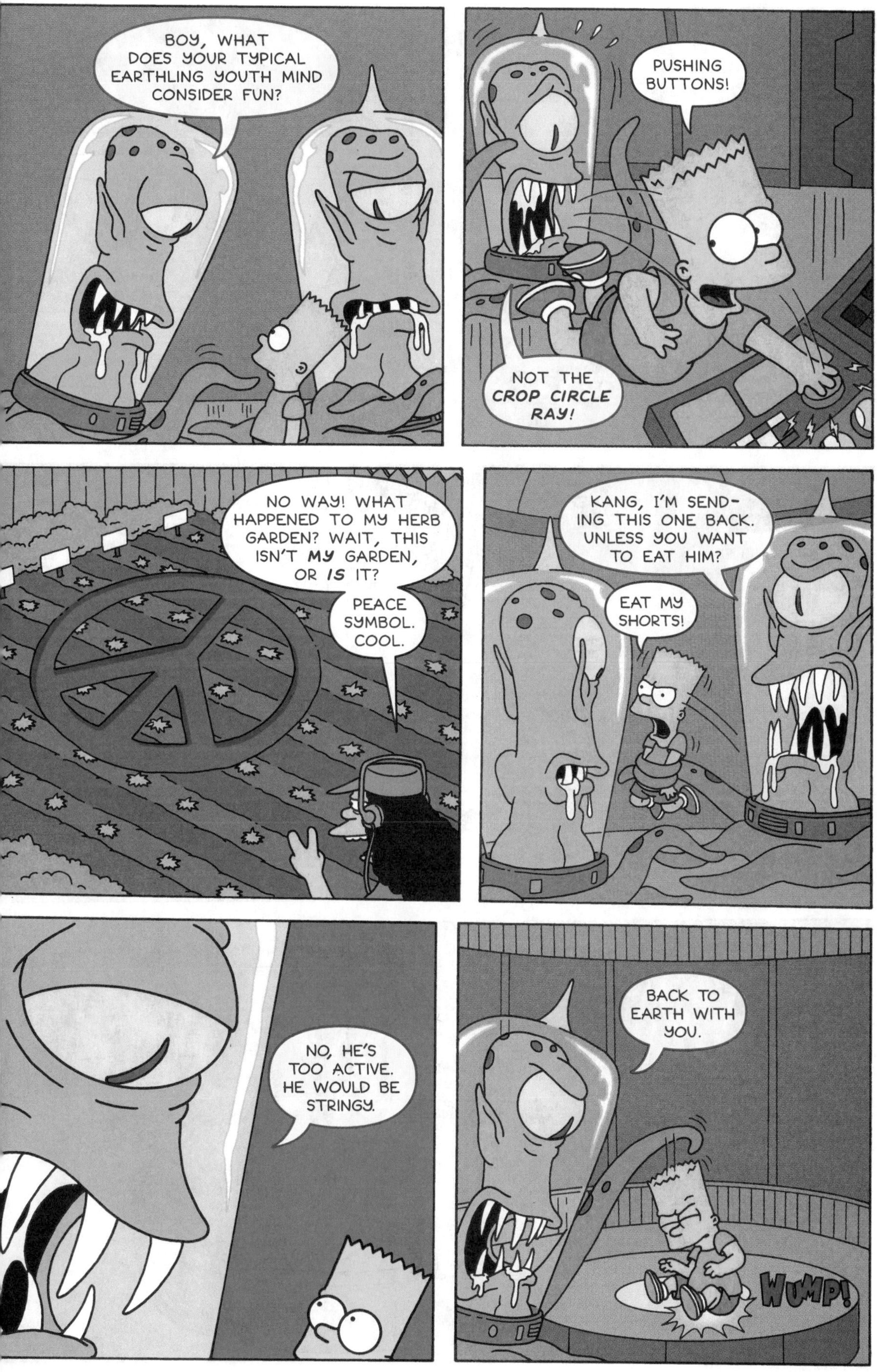
BOY, WHAT DOES YOUR TYPICAL EARTHLING YOUTH MIND CONSIDER FUN?
PUSHING BUTTONS!
NOT THE CROP CIRCLE RAY!
NO WAY! WHAT HAPPENED TO MY HERB GARDEN? WAIT, THIS ISN'T MY GARDEN, OR IS IT?
PEACE SYMBOL. COOL.
KANG, I'M SENDING THIS ONE BACK. UNLESS YOU WANT TO EAT HIM?
EAT MY SHORTS!
NO, HE'S TOO ACTIVE. HE WOULD BE STRINGY.
BACK TO EARTH WITH YOU.
WUMP!

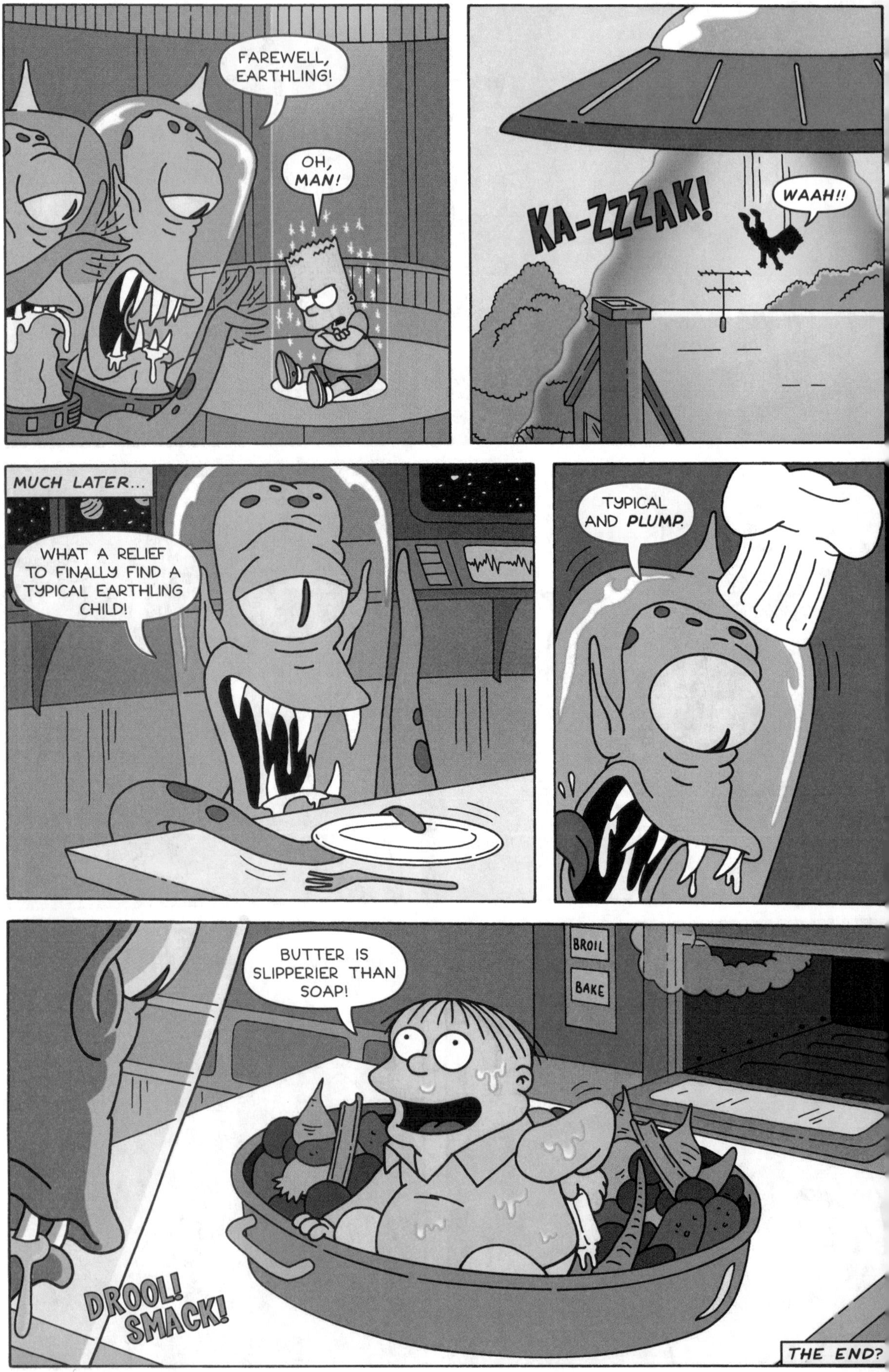
FAREWELL, EARTHLING!
OH, MAN!
KA-ZZZAK!
WAAH!!
MUCH LATER...
WHAT A RELIEF TO FINALLY FIND A TYPICAL EARTHLING CHILD!
TYPICAL AND PLUMP.
BUTTER IS SLIPPERIER THAN SOAP!
BROIL
BAKE
DROOL! SMACK!
THE END?

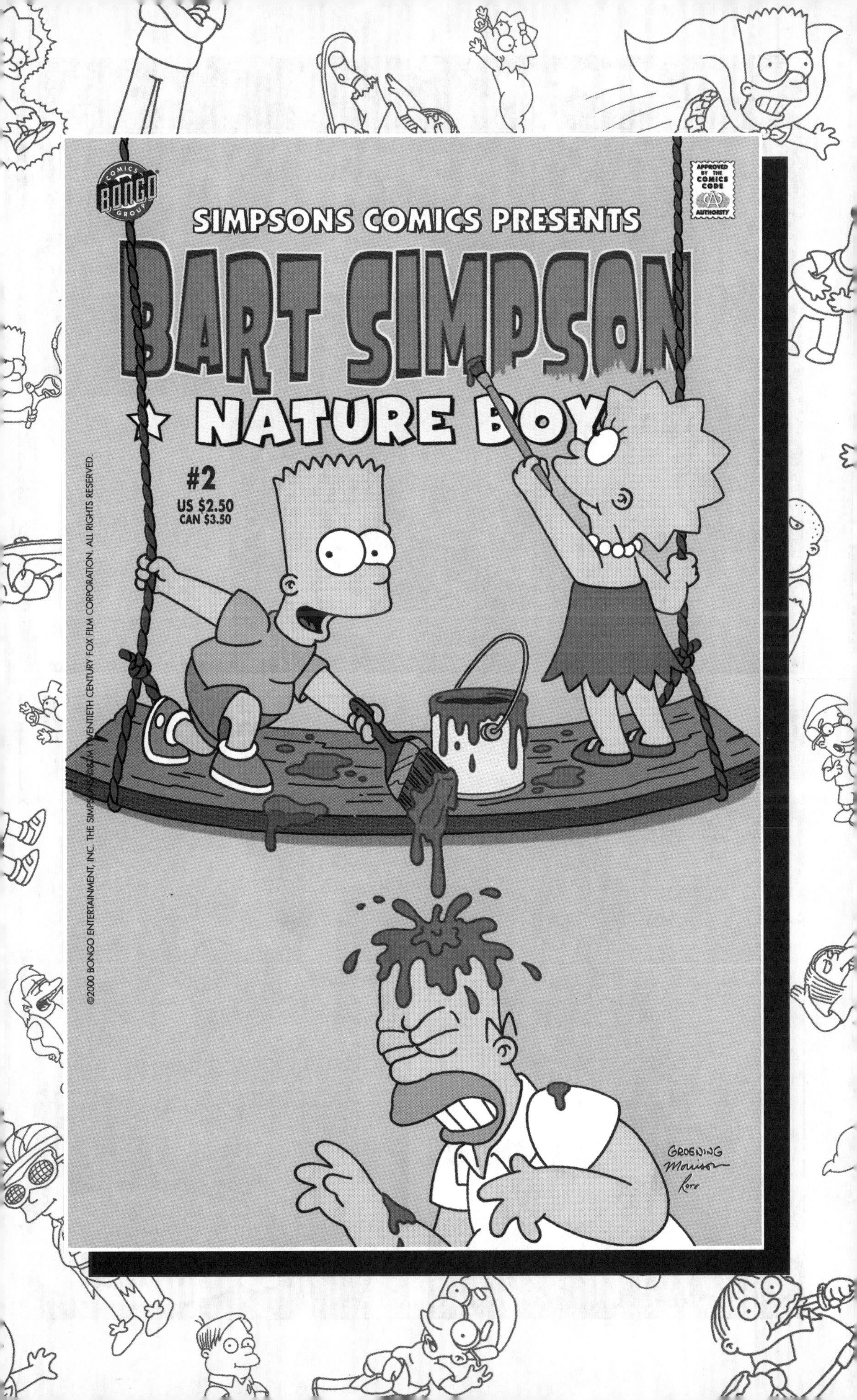
BONGO COMICS GROUP
APPROVED BY THE COMICS CODE AUTHORITY
SIMPSONS COMICS PRESENTS
BART SIMPSON
NATURE BOY
#2
US $2.50
CAN $3.50
©2000 BONGO ENTERTAINMENT, INC. THE SIMPSONS©&TM TWENTIETH CENTURY FOX FILM CORPORATION. ALL RIGHTS RESERVED.
GROENING
Morrison
Rote

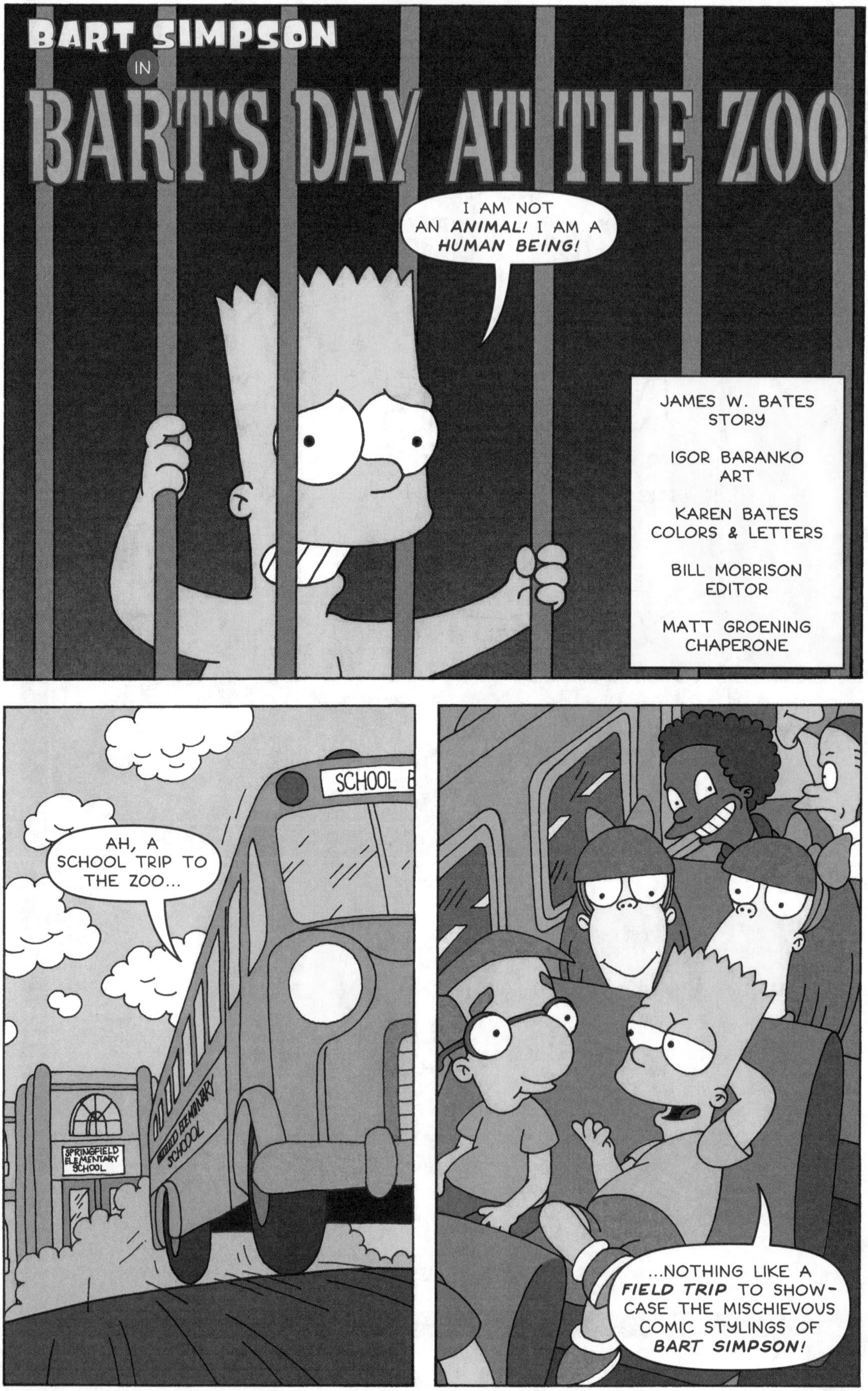
BART SIMPSON
IN
BART'S DAY AT THE ZOO
I AM NOT AN *ANIMAL!* I AM A *HUMAN BEING!*
JAMES W. BATES
STORY
IGOR BARANKO
ART
KAREN BATES
COLORS & LETTERS
BILL MORRISON
EDITOR
MATT GROENING
CHAPERONE
SCHOOL B
AH, A SCHOOL TRIP TO THE ZOO...
SPRINGFIELD ELEMENTARY SCHOOL
SPRINGFIELD ELEMENTARY SCHOOL
...NOTHING LIKE A *FIELD TRIP* TO SHOW-CASE THE MISCHIEVOUS COMIC STYLINGS OF *BART SIMPSON!*

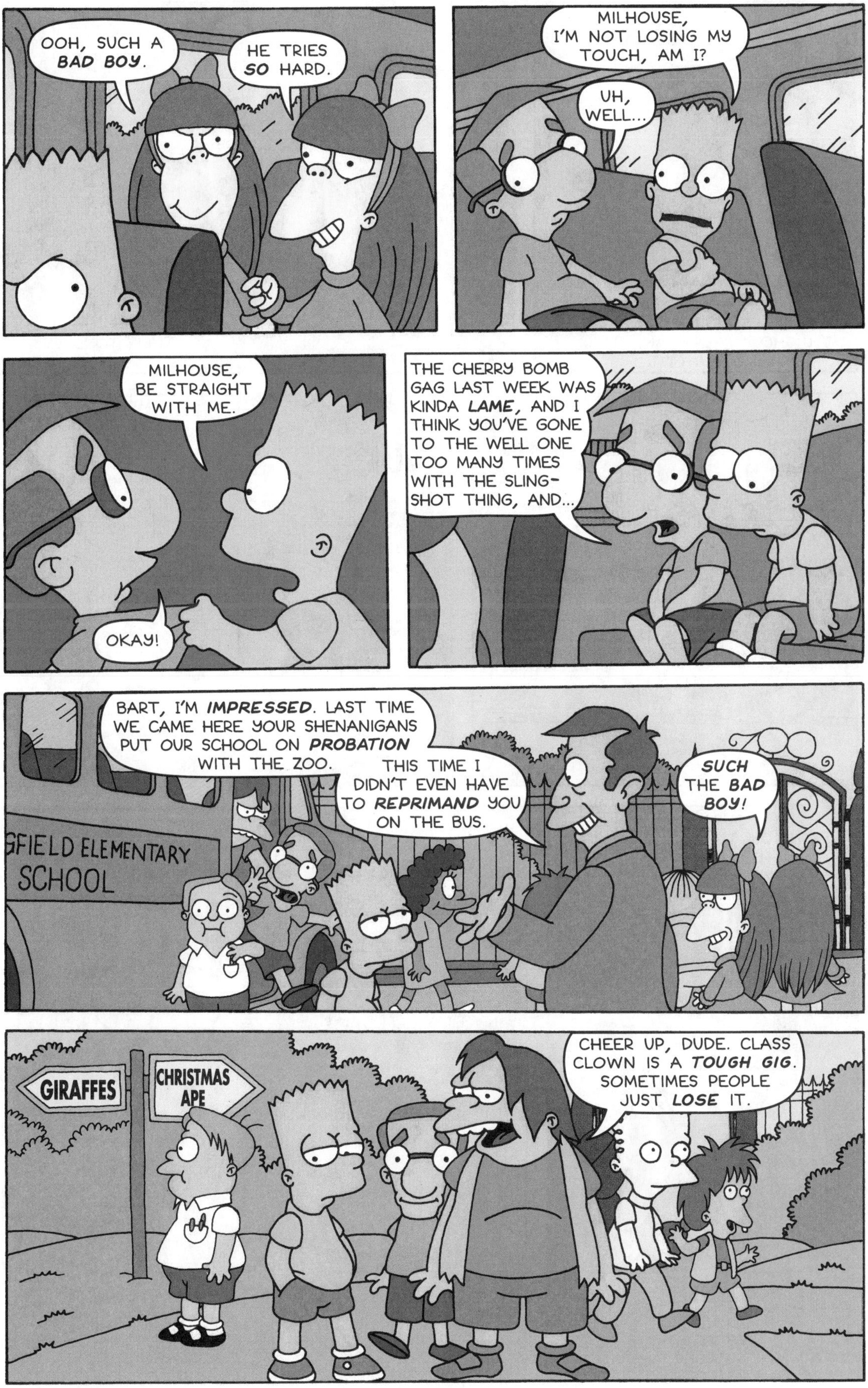
OOH, SUCH A BAD BOY.
HE TRIES SO HARD.
MILHOUSE, I'M NOT LOSING MY TOUCH, AM I?
UH, WELL...
MILHOUSE, BE STRAIGHT WITH ME.
OKAY!
THE CHERRY BOMB GAG LAST WEEK WAS KINDA LAME, AND I THINK YOU'VE GONE TO THE WELL ONE TOO MANY TIMES WITH THE SLING-SHOT THING, AND...
BART, I'M IMPRESSED. LAST TIME WE CAME HERE YOUR SHENANIGANS PUT OUR SCHOOL ON PROBATION WITH THE ZOO.
THIS TIME I DIDN'T EVEN HAVE TO REPRIMAND YOU ON THE BUS.
SUCH THE BAD BOY!
GFIELD ELEMENTARY SCHOOL
GIRAFFES
CHRISTMAS APE
CHEER UP, DUDE. CLASS CLOWN IS A TOUGH GIG. SOMETIMES PEOPLE JUST LOSE IT.

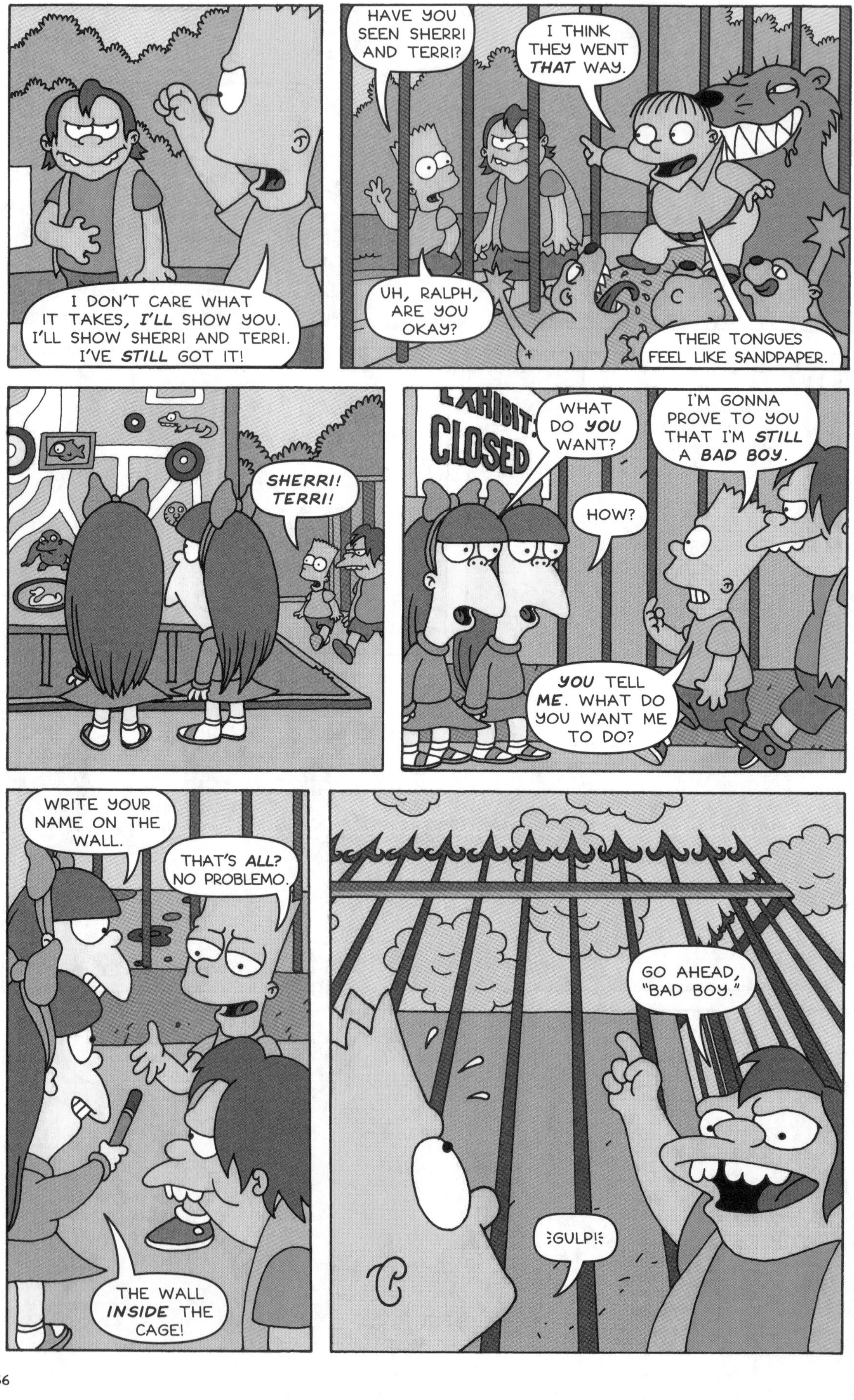
I DON'T CARE WHAT IT TAKES, I'LL SHOW YOU. I'LL SHOW SHERRI AND TERRI. I'VE STILL GOT IT!
HAVE YOU SEEN SHERRI AND TERRI?
I THINK THEY WENT THAT WAY.
UH, RALPH, ARE YOU OKAY?
THEIR TONGUES FEEL LIKE SANDPAPER.
SHERRI! TERRI!
EXHIBIT CLOSED
WHAT DO YOU WANT?
I'M GONNA PROVE TO YOU THAT I'M STILL A BAD BOY.
HOW?
YOU TELL ME. WHAT DO YOU WANT ME TO DO?
WRITE YOUR NAME ON THE WALL.
THAT'S ALL? NO PROBLEMO.
THE WALL INSIDE THE CAGE!
GO AHEAD, "BAD BOY."
GULP!

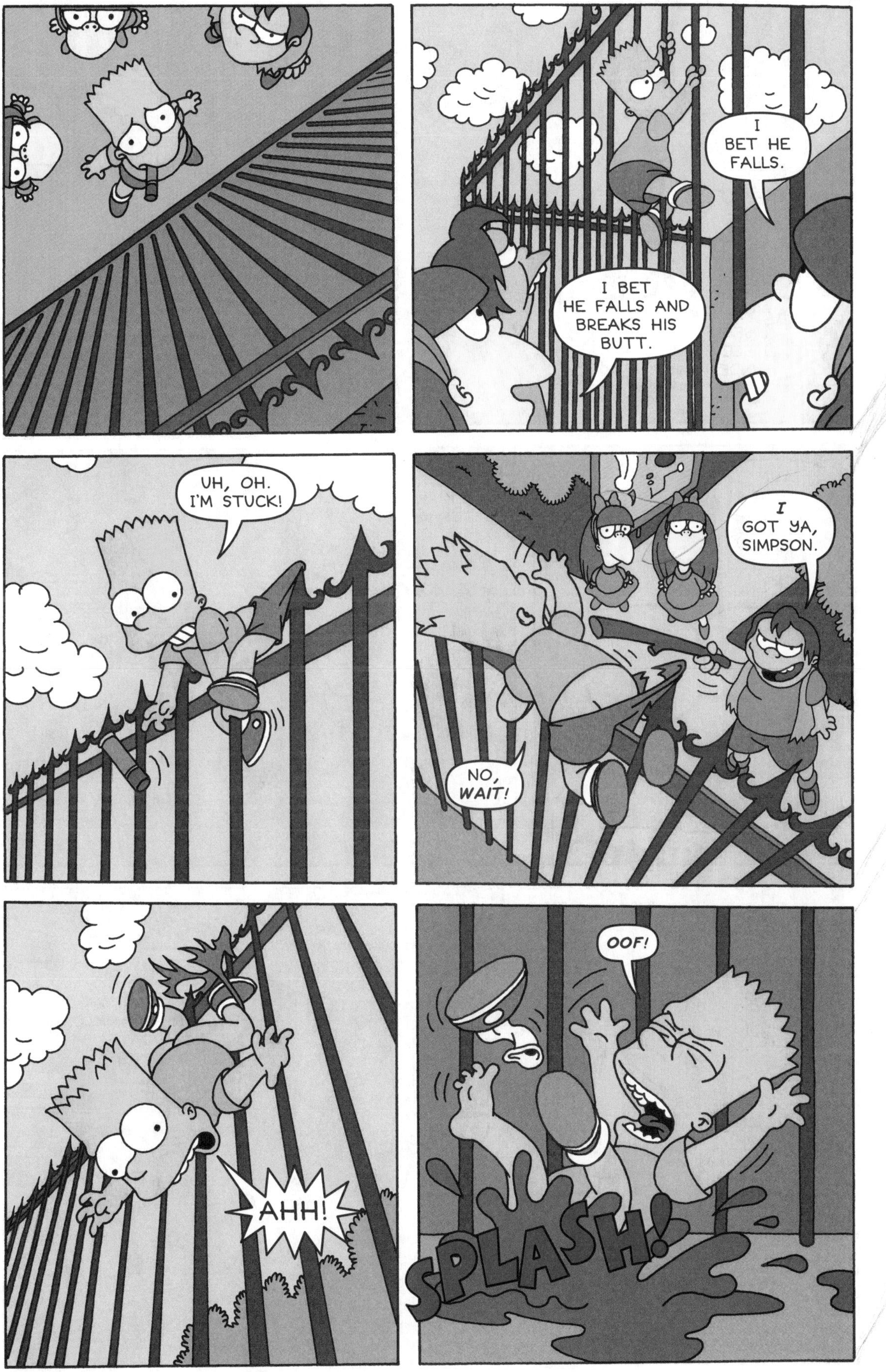
I BET HE FALLS.
I BET HE FALLS AND BREAKS HIS BUTT.
UH, OH. I'M STUCK!
I GOT YA, SIMPSON.
NO, WAIT!
AHH!
OOF!
SPLASH!

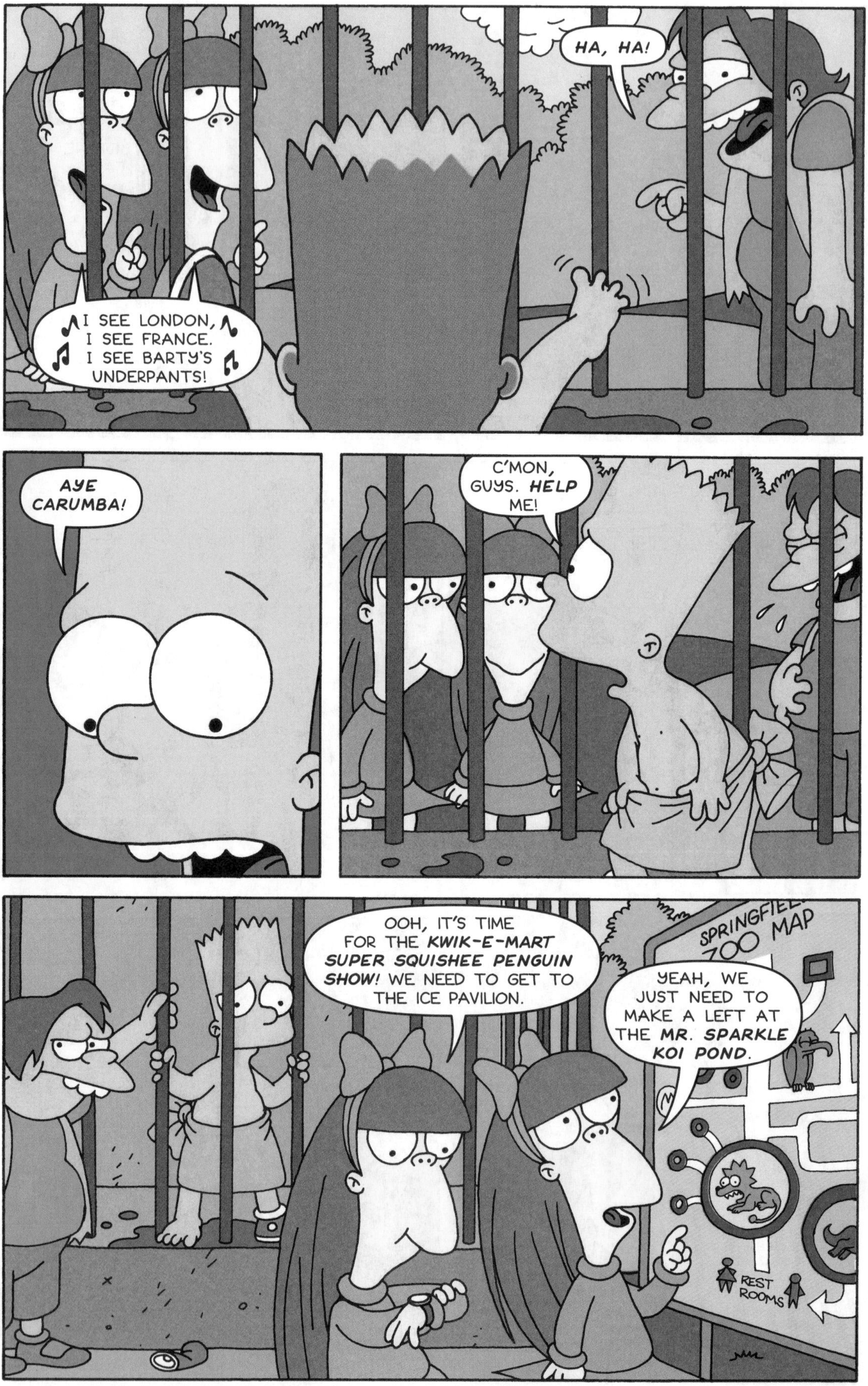
HA, HA!
I SEE LONDON, I SEE FRANCE. I SEE BARTY'S UNDERPANTS!
AYE CARUMBA!
C'MON, GUYS. HELP ME!
OOH, IT'S TIME FOR THE KWIK-E-MART SUPER SQUISHEE PENGUIN SHOW! WE NEED TO GET TO THE ICE PAVILION.
YEAH, WE JUST NEED TO MAKE A LEFT AT THE MR. SPARKLE KOI POND.
ZOO MAP
REST ROOMS

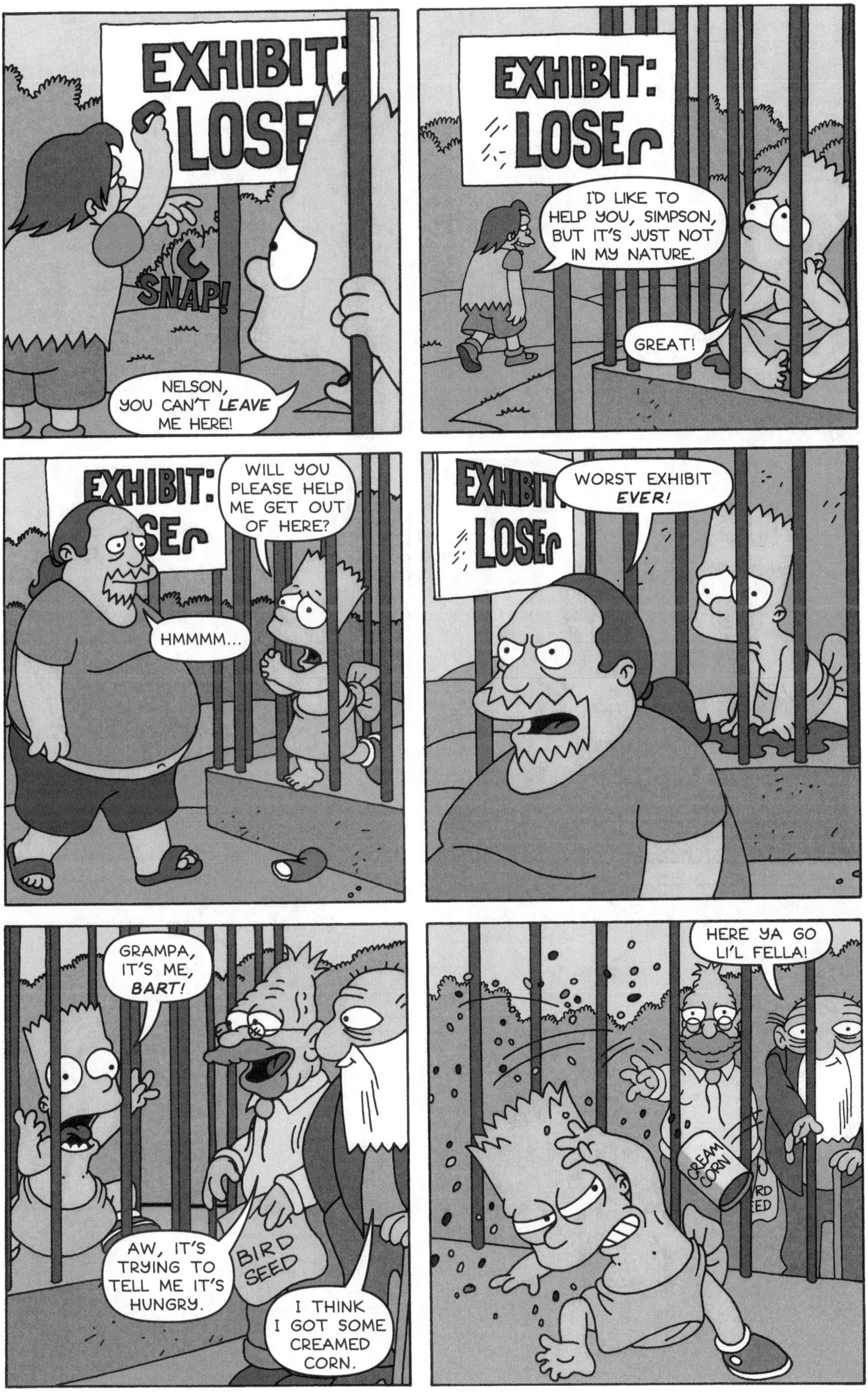
EXHIBIT:
LOSE
SNAP!
NELSON, YOU CAN'T *LEAVE* ME HERE!
EXHIBIT:
LOSE
I'D LIKE TO HELP YOU, SIMPSON, BUT IT'S JUST NOT IN MY NATURE.
GREAT!
EXHIBIT:
WILL YOU PLEASE HELP ME GET OUT OF HERE?
HMMMM...
LOSE
WORST EXHIBIT *EVER!*
GRAMPA, IT'S ME, *BART!*
AW, IT'S TRYING TO TELL ME IT'S HUNGRY.
BIRD SEED
I THINK I GOT SOME CREAMED CORN.
HERE YA GO LI'L FELLA!
CREAM CORN

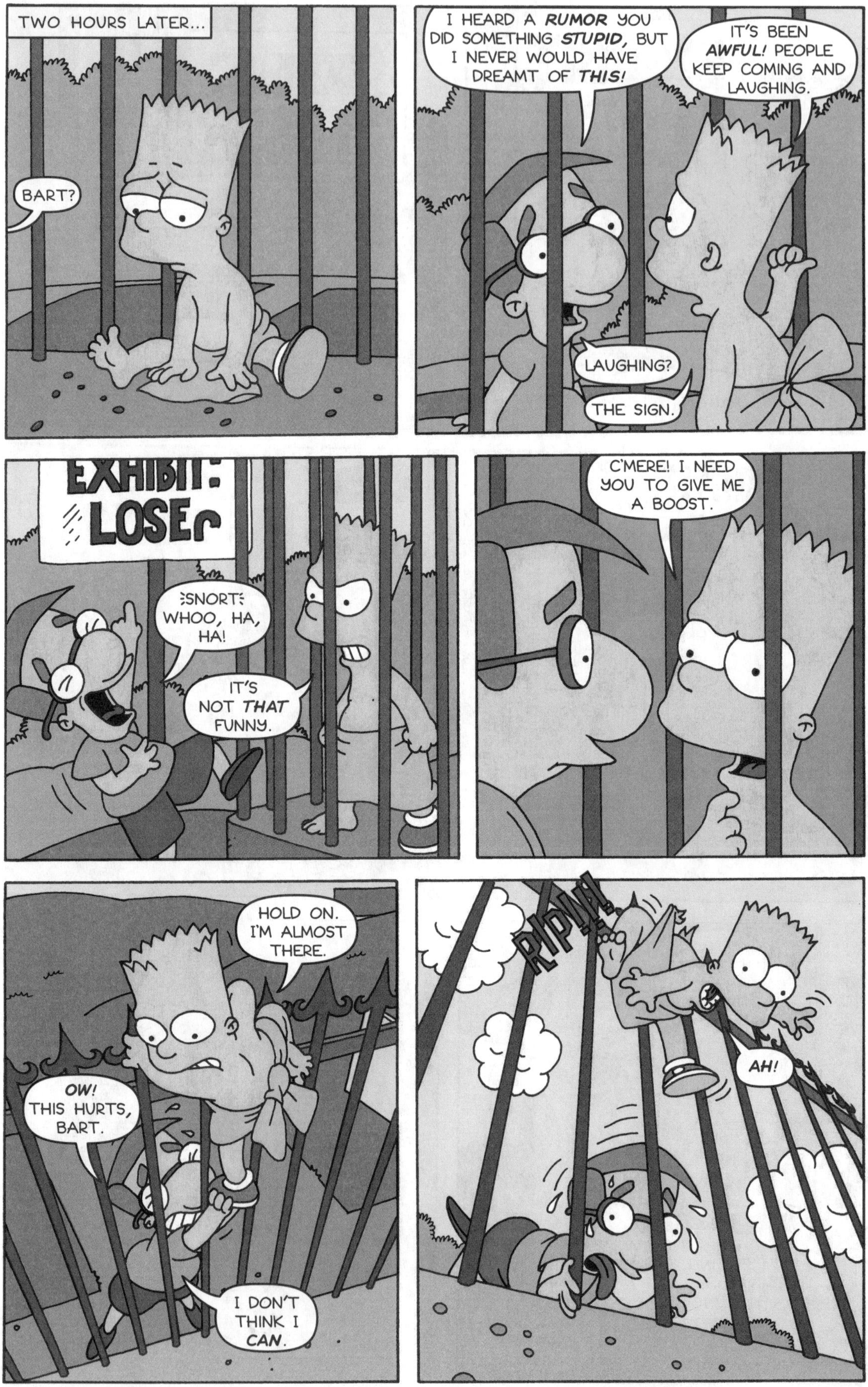
TWO HOURS LATER...
BART?
I HEARD A RUMOR YOU DID SOMETHING STUPID, BUT I NEVER WOULD HAVE DREAMT OF THIS!
IT'S BEEN AWFUL! PEOPLE KEEP COMING AND LAUGHING.
LAUGHING?
THE SIGN.
EXHIBIT: LOSE
SNORT WHOO, HA, HA!
IT'S NOT THAT FUNNY.
C'MERE! I NEED YOU TO GIVE ME A BOOST.
HOLD ON. I'M ALMOST THERE.
OW! THIS HURTS, BART.
I DON'T THINK I CAN.
RIP!!!
AH!

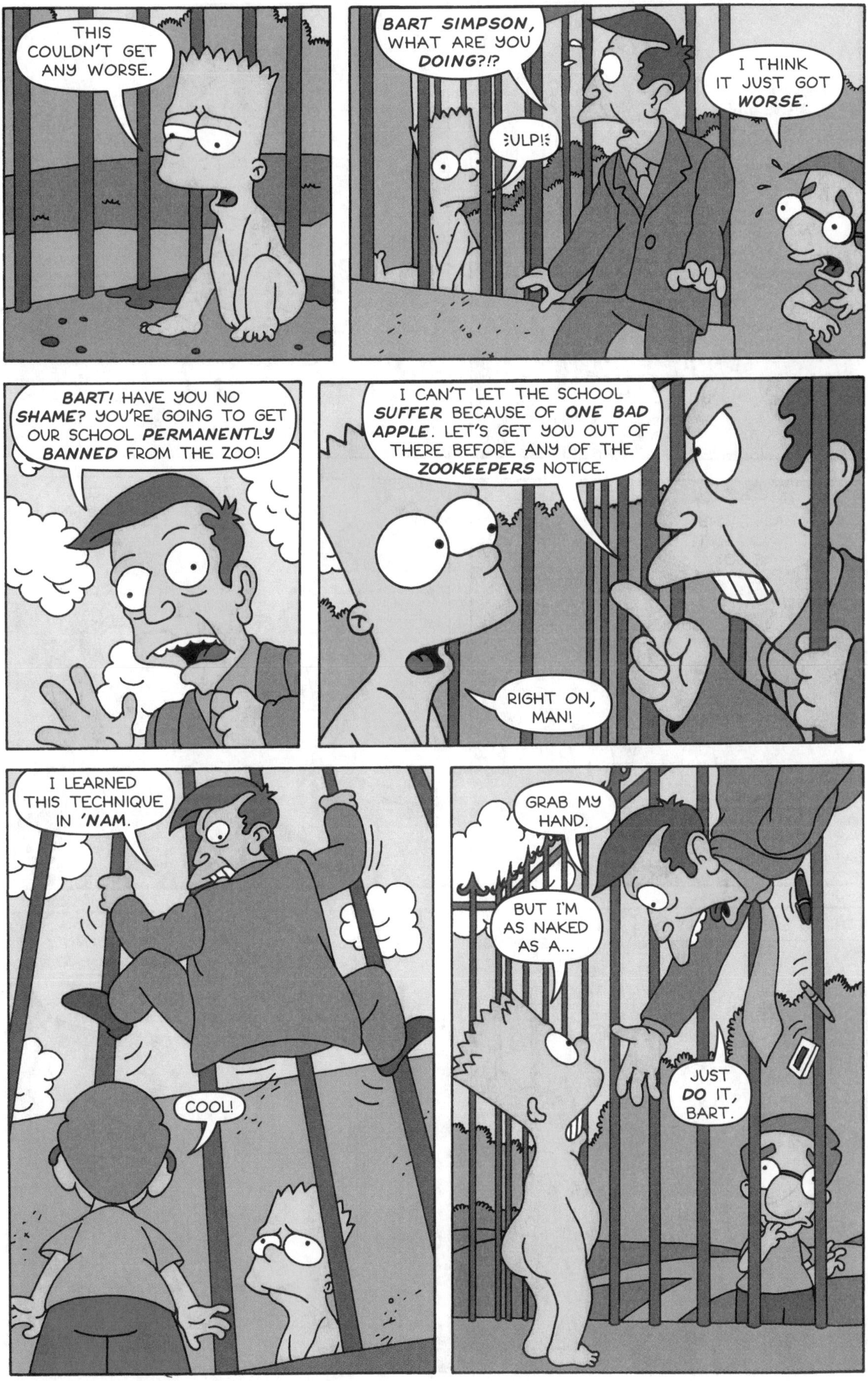
THIS COULDN'T GET ANY WORSE.
BART SIMPSON, WHAT ARE YOU DOING?!?
ULP!
I THINK IT JUST GOT WORSE.
BART! HAVE YOU NO SHAME? YOU'RE GOING TO GET OUR SCHOOL PERMANENTLY BANNED FROM THE ZOO!
I CAN'T LET THE SCHOOL SUFFER BECAUSE OF ONE BAD APPLE. LET'S GET YOU OUT OF THERE BEFORE ANY OF THE ZOOKEEPERS NOTICE.
RIGHT ON, MAN!
I LEARNED THIS TECHNIQUE IN 'NAM.
COOL!
GRAB MY HAND.
BUT I'M AS NAKED AS A...
JUST DO IT, BART.

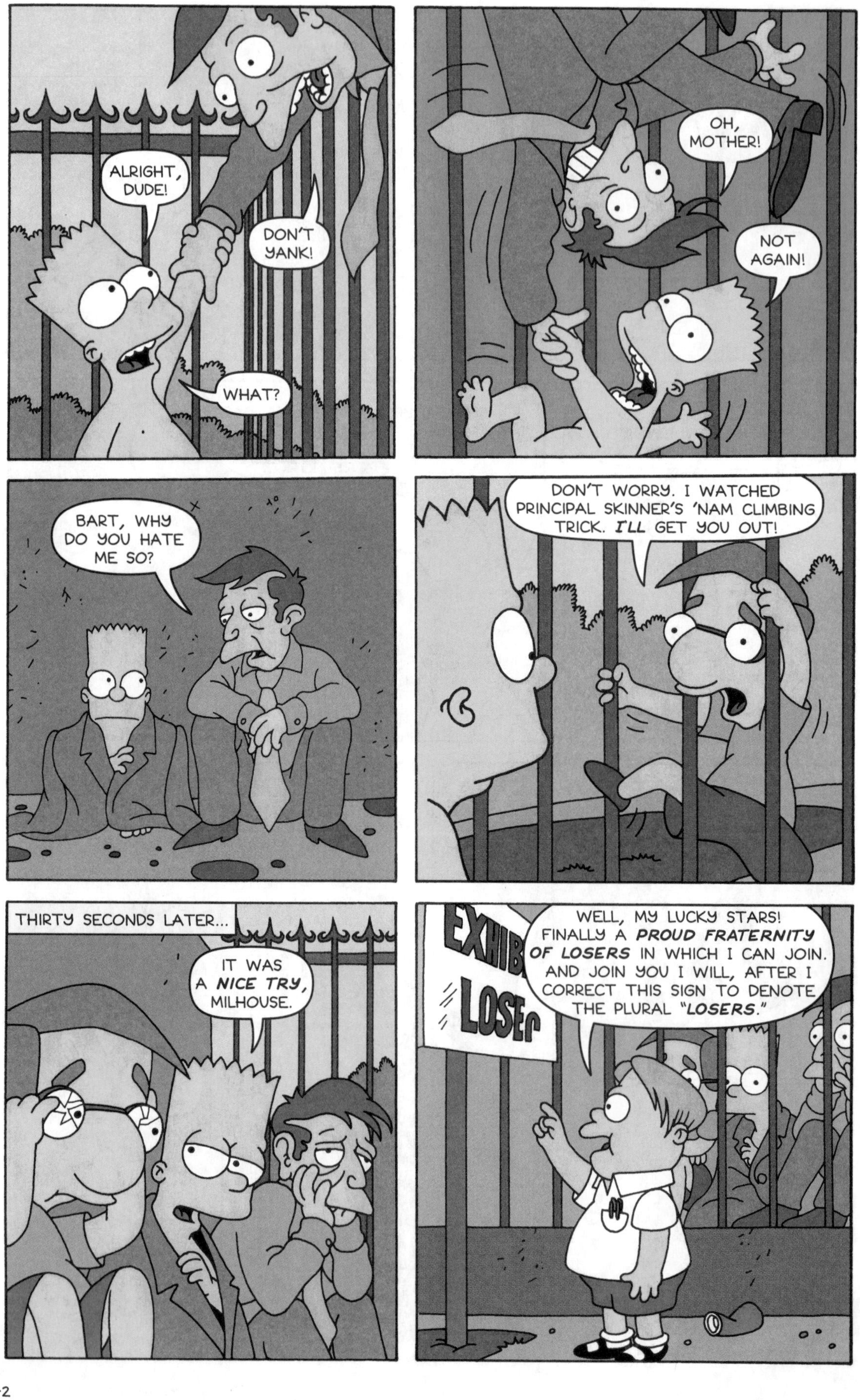
ALRIGHT, DUDE!
DON'T YANK!
WHAT?
OH, MOTHER!
NOT AGAIN!
BART, WHY DO YOU HATE ME SO?
DON'T WORRY. I WATCHED PRINCIPAL SKINNER'S 'NAM CLIMBING TRICK. *I'LL* GET YOU OUT!
THIRTY SECONDS LATER...
IT WAS A *NICE TRY*, MILHOUSE.
WELL, MY LUCKY STARS! FINALLY A ***PROUD FRATERNITY OF LOSERS*** IN WHICH I CAN JOIN. AND JOIN YOU I WILL, AFTER I CORRECT THIS SIGN TO DENOTE THE PLURAL "***LOSERS***."

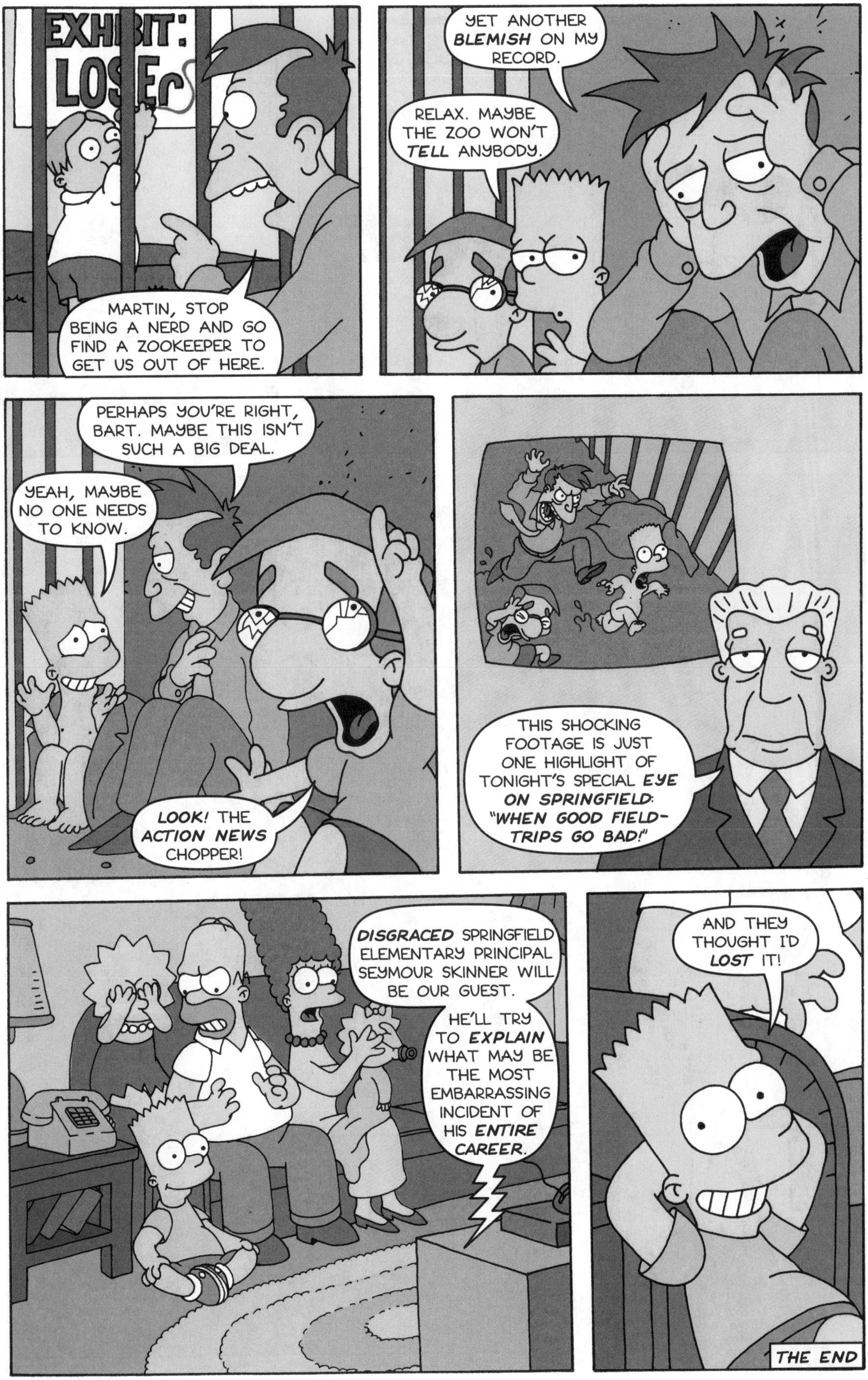
EXHIBIT: LOSErs
MARTIN, STOP BEING A NERD AND GO FIND A ZOOKEEPER TO GET US OUT OF HERE.
YET ANOTHER BLEMISH ON MY RECORD.
RELAX. MAYBE THE ZOO WON'T TELL ANYBODY.
PERHAPS YOU'RE RIGHT, BART. MAYBE THIS ISN'T SUCH A BIG DEAL.
YEAH, MAYBE NO ONE NEEDS TO KNOW.
LOOK! THE ACTION NEWS CHOPPER!
THIS SHOCKING FOOTAGE IS JUST ONE HIGHLIGHT OF TONIGHT'S SPECIAL EYE ON SPRINGFIELD: "WHEN GOOD FIELD-TRIPS GO BAD!"
DISGRACED SPRINGFIELD ELEMENTARY PRINCIPAL SEYMOUR SKINNER WILL BE OUR GUEST.
HE'LL TRY TO EXPLAIN WHAT MAY BE THE MOST EMBARRASSING INCIDENT OF HIS ENTIRE CAREER.
AND THEY THOUGHT I'D LOST IT!
THE END

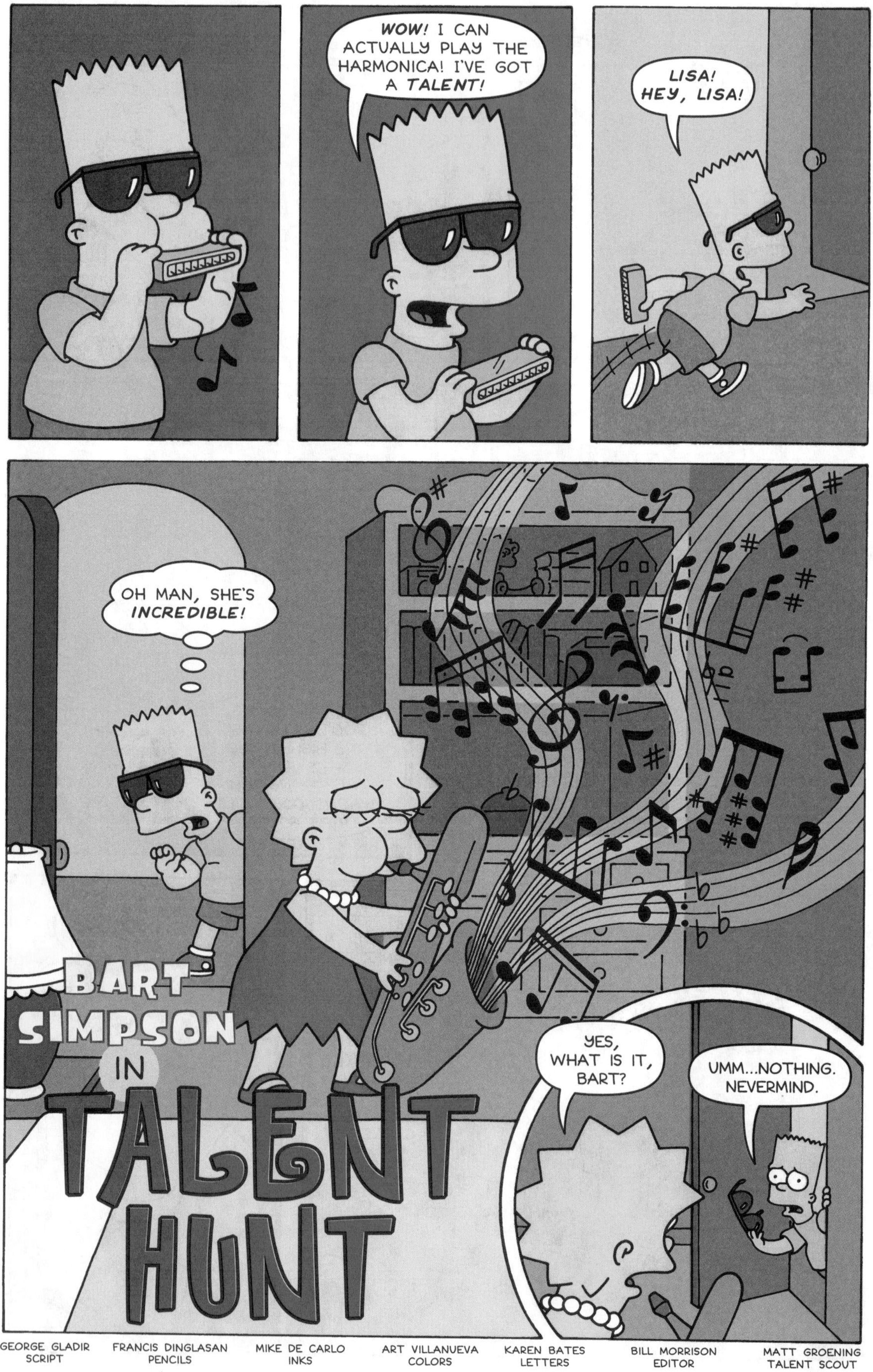
WOW! I CAN ACTUALLY PLAY THE HARMONICA! I'VE GOT A TALENT!
LISA! HEY, LISA!
OH MAN, SHE'S INCREDIBLE!
BART SIMPSON IN
TALENT HUNT
YES, WHAT IS IT, BART?
UMM...NOTHING. NEVERMIND.

GEORGE GLADIR SCRIPT
FRANCIS DINGLASAN PENCILS
MIKE DE CARLO INKS
ART VILLANUEVA COLORS
KAREN BATES LETTERS
BILL MORRISON EDITOR
MATT GROENING TALENT SCOUT

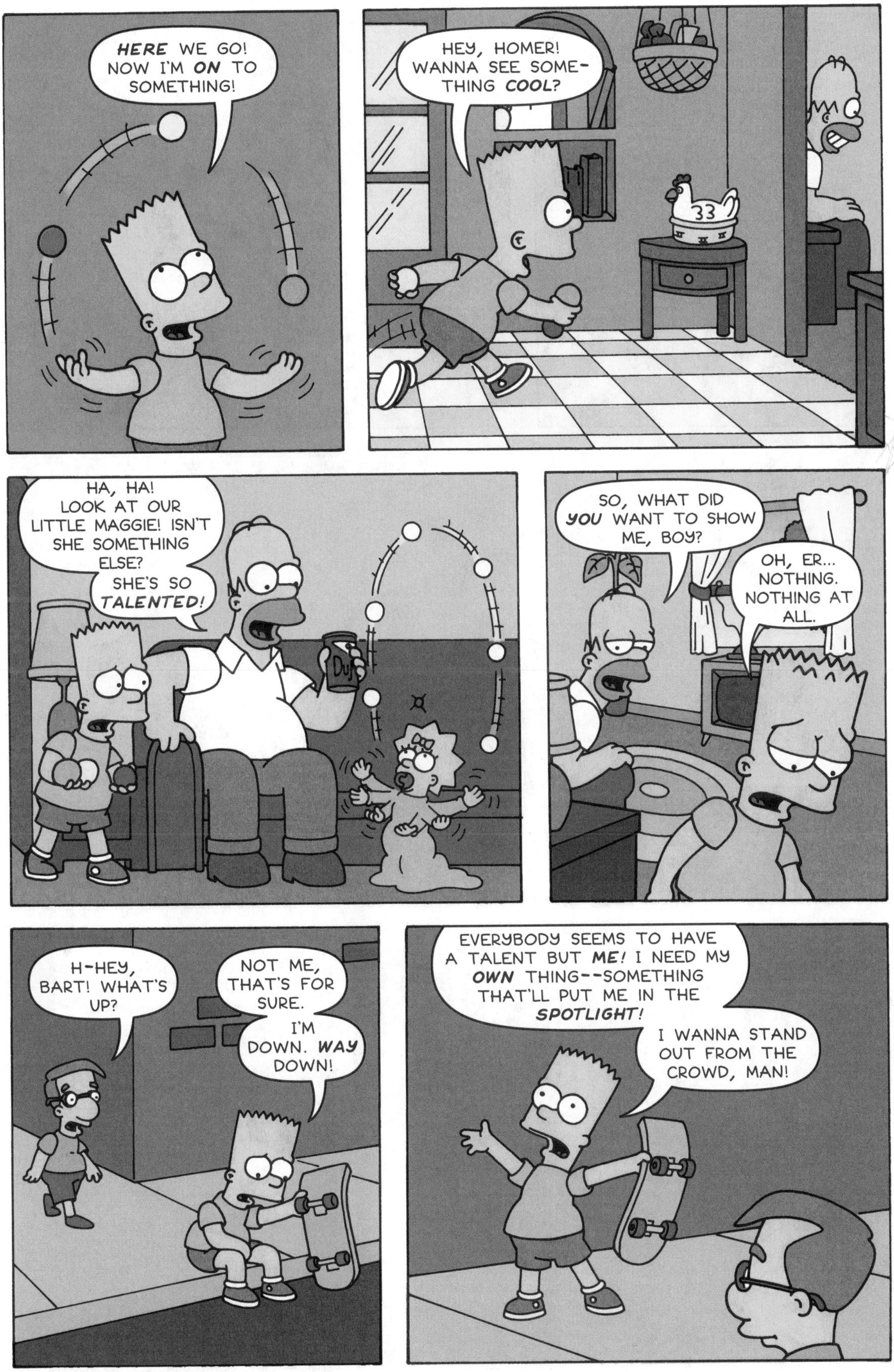
HERE WE GO! NOW I'M ON TO SOMETHING!
HEY, HOMER! WANNA SEE SOME-THING COOL?
HA, HA! LOOK AT OUR LITTLE MAGGIE! ISN'T SHE SOMETHING ELSE?
SHE'S SO TALENTED!
SO, WHAT DID YOU WANT TO SHOW ME, BOY?
OH, ER... NOTHING. NOTHING AT ALL.
H-HEY, BART! WHAT'S UP?
NOT ME, THAT'S FOR SURE.
I'M DOWN. WAY DOWN!
EVERYBODY SEEMS TO HAVE A TALENT BUT ME! I NEED MY OWN THING--SOMETHING THAT'LL PUT ME IN THE SPOTLIGHT!
I WANNA STAND OUT FROM THE CROWD, MAN!

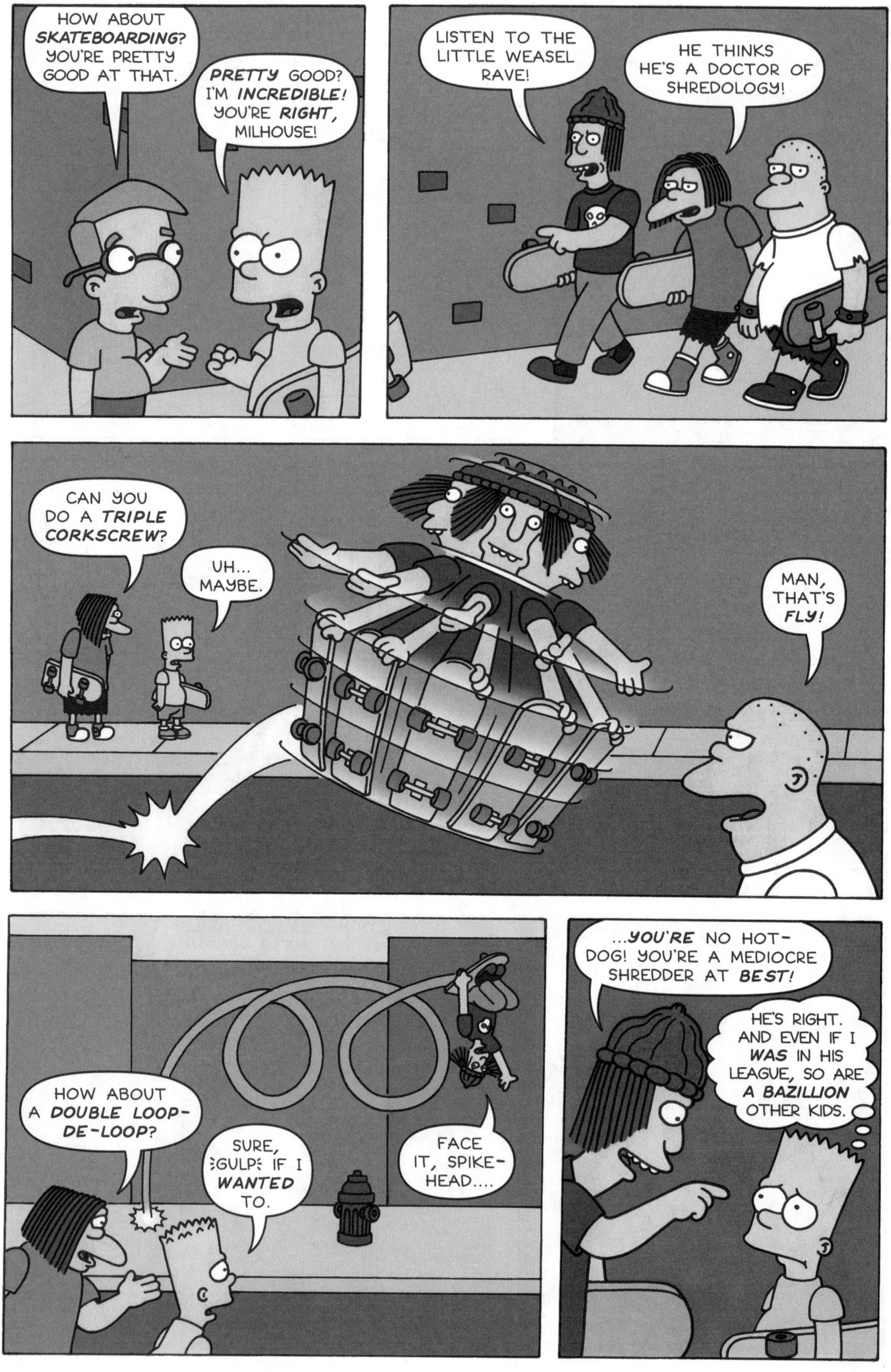
HOW ABOUT SKATEBOARDING? YOU'RE PRETTY GOOD AT THAT.
PRETTY GOOD? I'M INCREDIBLE! YOU'RE RIGHT, MILHOUSE!
LISTEN TO THE LITTLE WEASEL RAVE!
HE THINKS HE'S A DOCTOR OF SHREDOLOGY!
CAN YOU DO A TRIPLE CORKSCREW?
UH... MAYBE.
MAN, THAT'S FLY!
HOW ABOUT A DOUBLE LOOP-DE-LOOP?
SURE, GULP IF I WANTED TO.
FACE IT, SPIKE-HEAD....
...YOU'RE NO HOT-DOG! YOU'RE A MEDIOCRE SHREDDER AT BEST!
HE'S RIGHT. AND EVEN IF I WAS IN HIS LEAGUE, SO ARE A BAZILLION OTHER KIDS.

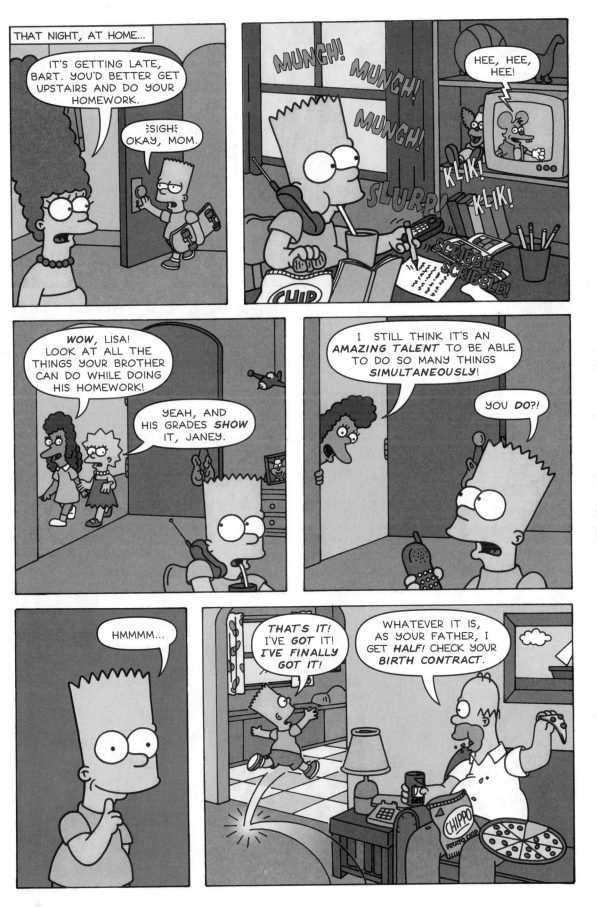

THAT NIGHT, AT HOME...

IT'S GETTING LATE, BART. YOU'D BETTER GET UPSTAIRS AND DO YOUR HOMEWORK.

∶SIGH∶ OKAY, MOM.

MUNCH! MUNCH! MUNCH!

SLURP!

KLIK! KLIK!

HEE, HEE, HEE!

SCRIBBLE! SCRIBBLE!

CHIP

WOW, LISA! LOOK AT ALL THE THINGS YOUR BROTHER CAN DO WHILE DOING HIS HOMEWORK!

YEAH, AND HIS GRADES SHOW IT, JANEY.

I STILL THINK IT'S AN AMAZING TALENT TO BE ABLE TO DO SO MANY THINGS SIMULTANEOUSLY!

YOU DO?!

HMMMM...

THAT'S IT! I'VE GOT IT! I'VE FINALLY GOT IT!

WHATEVER IT IS, AS YOUR FATHER, I GET HALF! CHECK YOUR BIRTH CONTRACT.

CHIPPO POTATO CHIPS

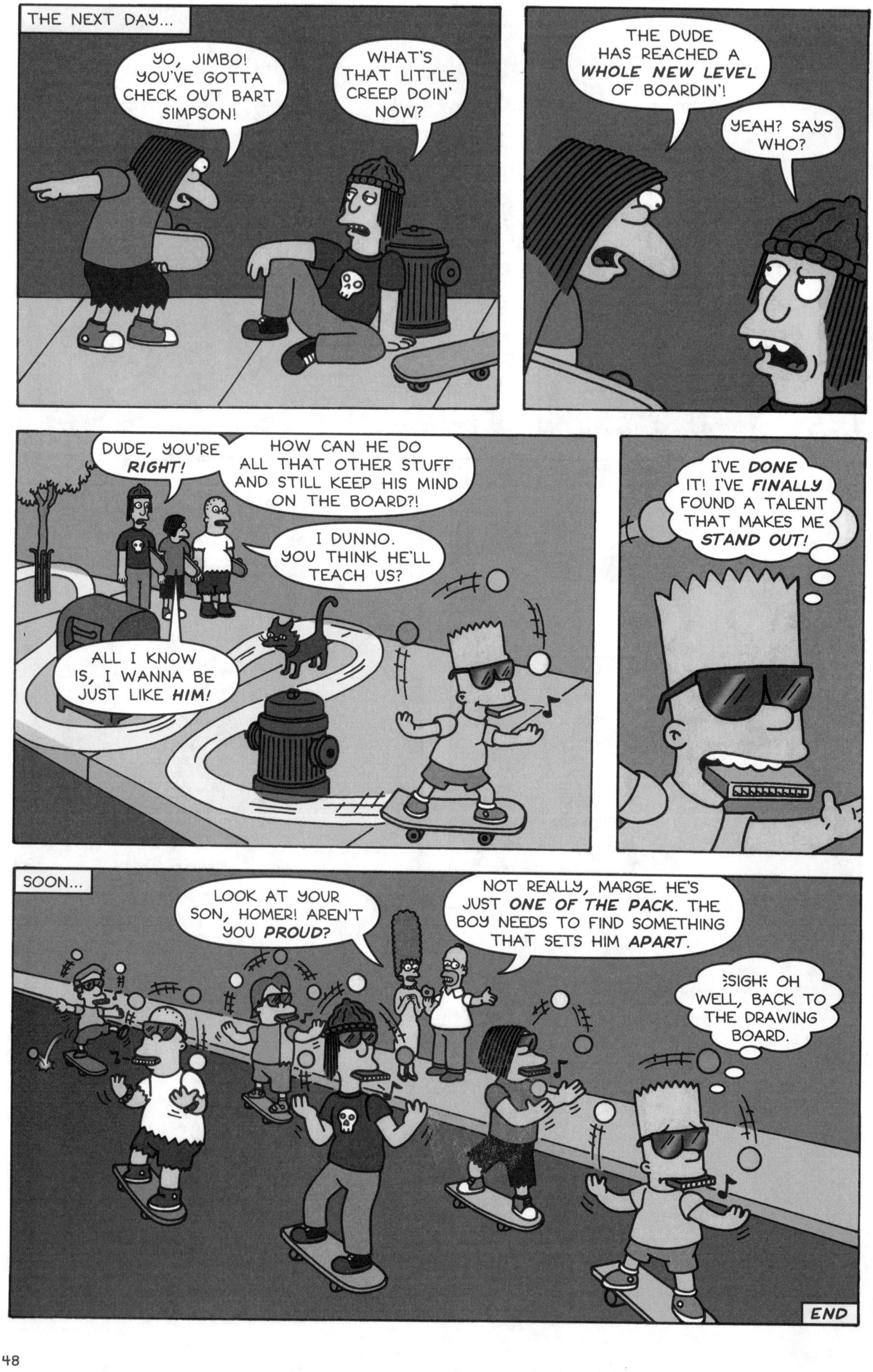
THE NEXT DAY...
YO, JIMBO! YOU'VE GOTTA CHECK OUT BART SIMPSON!
WHAT'S THAT LITTLE CREEP DOIN' NOW?
THE DUDE HAS REACHED A ***WHOLE NEW LEVEL*** OF BOARDIN'!
YEAH? SAYS WHO?
DUDE, YOU'RE ***RIGHT!***
HOW CAN HE DO ALL THAT OTHER STUFF AND STILL KEEP HIS MIND ON THE BOARD?!
I DUNNO. YOU THINK HE'LL TEACH US?
ALL I KNOW IS, I WANNA BE JUST LIKE ***HIM!***
I'VE ***DONE*** IT! I'VE ***FINALLY*** FOUND A TALENT THAT MAKES ME ***STAND OUT!***
SOON...
LOOK AT YOUR SON, HOMER! AREN'T YOU ***PROUD?***
NOT REALLY, MARGE. HE'S JUST ***ONE OF THE PACK***. THE BOY NEEDS TO FIND SOMETHING THAT SETS HIM ***APART***.
:SIGH: OH WELL, BACK TO THE DRAWING BOARD.
END

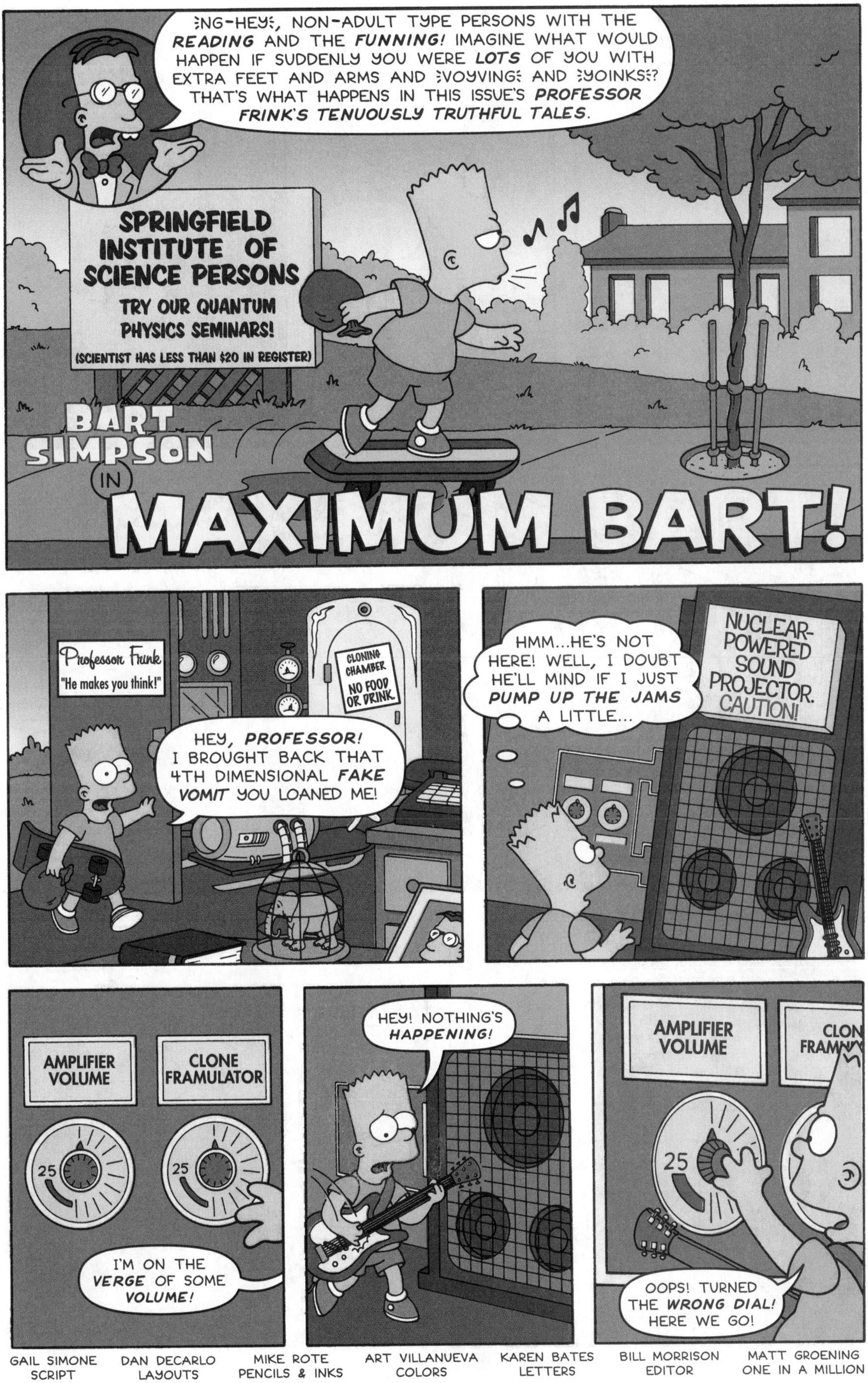
NG-HEY, NON-ADULT TYPE PERSONS WITH THE READING AND THE FUNNING! IMAGINE WHAT WOULD HAPPEN IF SUDDENLY YOU WERE LOTS OF YOU WITH EXTRA FEET AND ARMS AND VOYVING AND YOINKS? THAT'S WHAT HAPPENS IN THIS ISSUE'S PROFESSOR FRINK'S TENUOUSLY TRUTHFUL TALES.
SPRINGFIELD INSTITUTE OF SCIENCE PERSONS
TRY OUR QUANTUM PHYSICS SEMINARS!
(SCIENTIST HAS LESS THAN $20 IN REGISTER)
BART SIMPSON IN
MAXIMUM BART!
Professor Frink
"He makes you think!"
CLONING CHAMBER
NO FOOD OR DRINK.
HEY, PROFESSOR! I BROUGHT BACK THAT 4TH DIMENSIONAL FAKE VOMIT YOU LOANED ME!
HMM...HE'S NOT HERE! WELL, I DOUBT HE'LL MIND IF I JUST PUMP UP THE JAMS A LITTLE...
NUCLEAR-POWERED SOUND PROJECTOR. CAUTION!
AMPLIFIER VOLUME
CLONE FRAMULATOR
25
25
I'M ON THE VERGE OF SOME VOLUME!
HEY! NOTHING'S HAPPENING!
AMPLIFIER VOLUME
25
OOPS! TURNED THE WRONG DIAL! HERE WE GO!

GAIL SIMONE SCRIPT | DAN DECARLO LAYOUTS | MIKE ROTE PENCILS & INKS | ART VILLANUEVA COLORS | KAREN BATES LETTERS | BILL MORRISON EDITOR | MATT GROENING ONE IN A MILLION

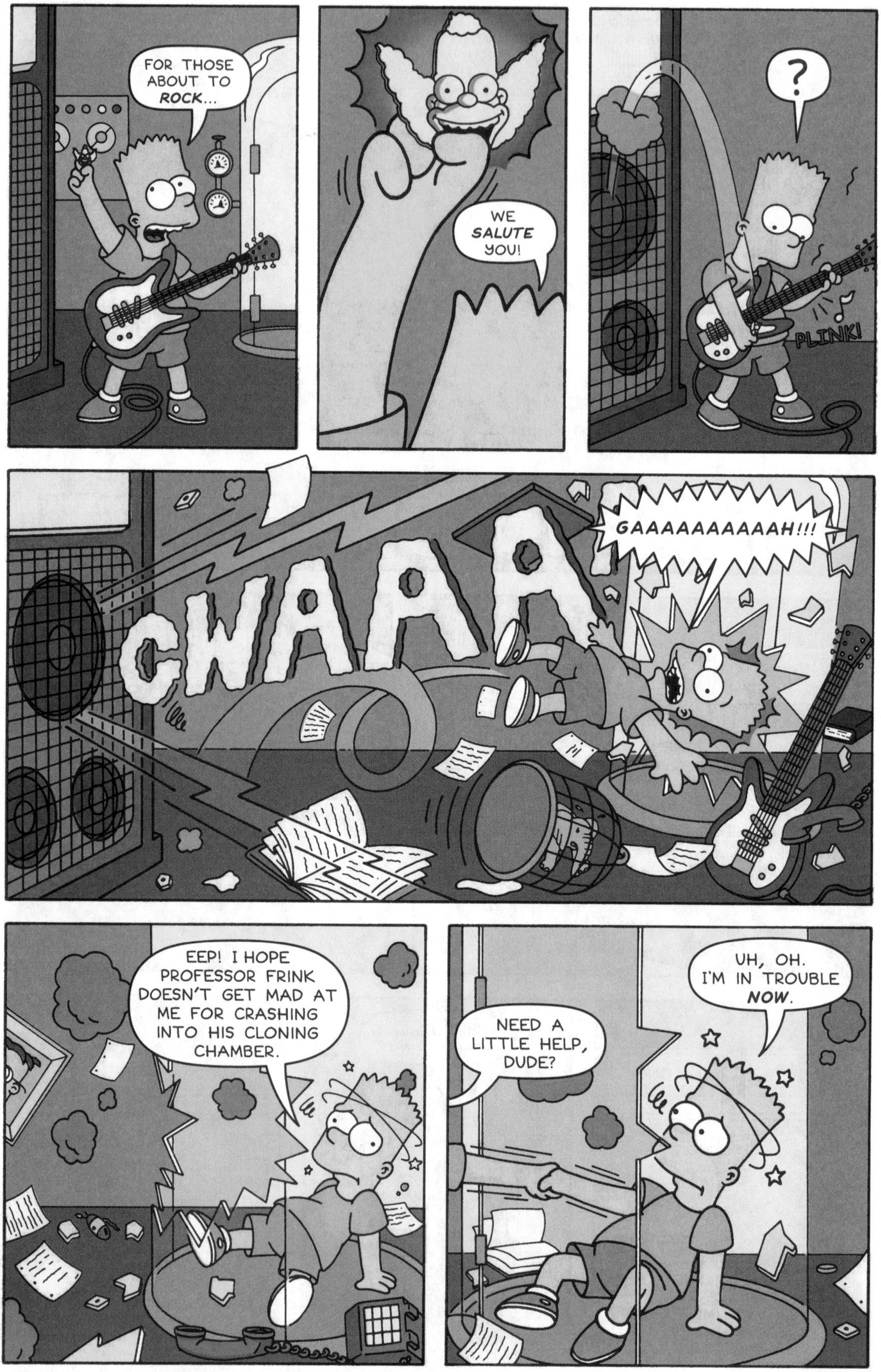
FOR THOSE ABOUT TO ROCK...
WE SALUTE YOU!
?
PLINK!
CWAAA
GAAAAAAAAAAH!!!
EEP! I HOPE PROFESSOR FRINK DOESN'T GET MAD AT ME FOR CRASHING INTO HIS CLONING CHAMBER.
NEED A LITTLE HELP, DUDE?
UH, OH. I'M IN TROUBLE NOW.

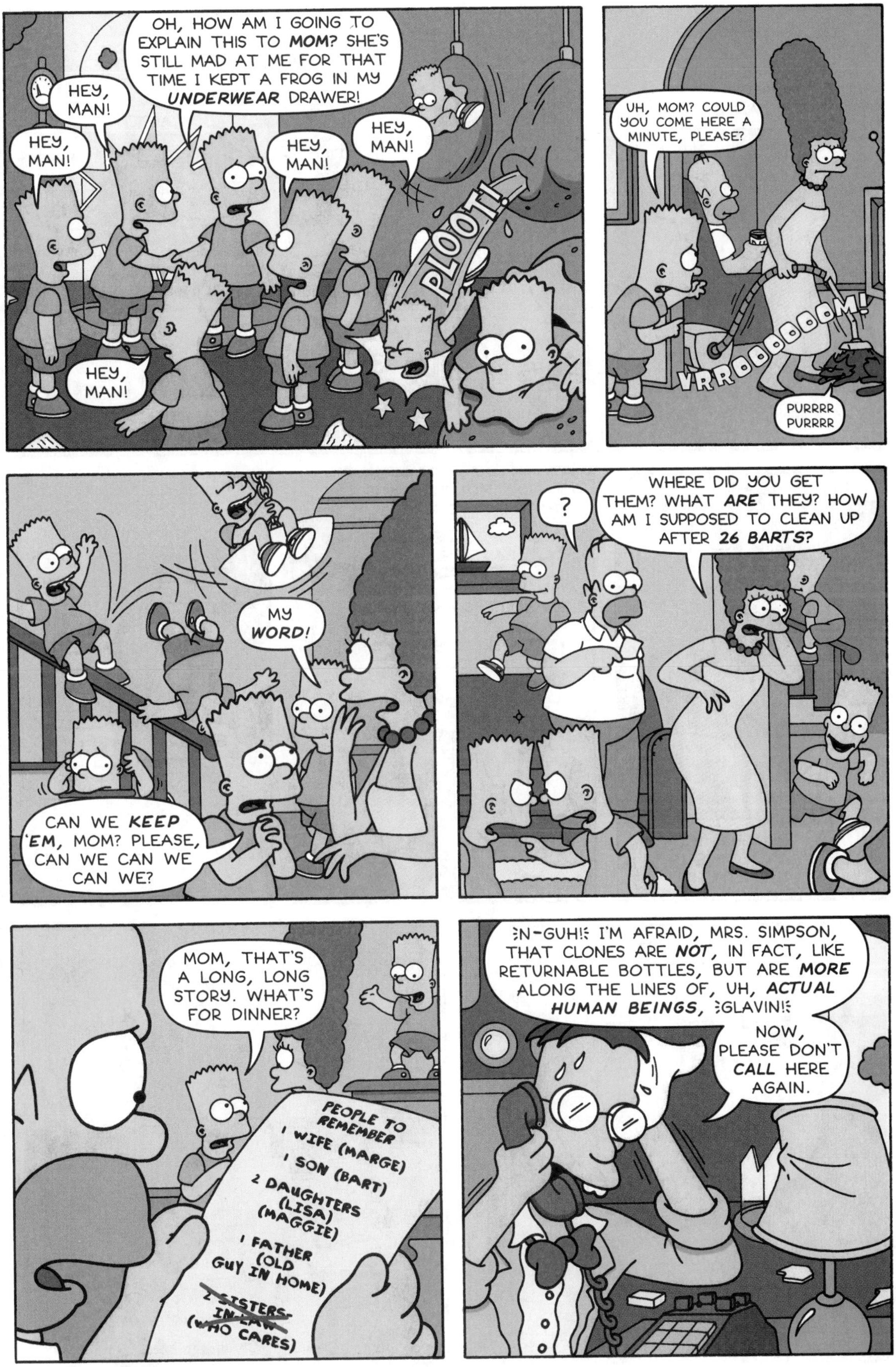
OH, HOW AM I GOING TO EXPLAIN THIS TO MOM? SHE'S STILL MAD AT ME FOR THAT TIME I KEPT A FROG IN MY UNDERWEAR DRAWER!
HEY, MAN!
HEY, MAN!
HEY, MAN!
HEY, MAN!
HEY, MAN!
PLOOT!
UH, MOM? COULD YOU COME HERE A MINUTE, PLEASE?
VRROOOOOOOOM!
PURRRR PURRRR
MY WORD!
CAN WE KEEP 'EM, MOM? PLEASE, CAN WE CAN WE CAN WE?
?
WHERE DID YOU GET THEM? WHAT ARE THEY? HOW AM I SUPPOSED TO CLEAN UP AFTER 26 BARTS?
MOM, THAT'S A LONG, LONG STORY. WHAT'S FOR DINNER?
PEOPLE TO REMEMBER
1 WIFE (MARGE)
1 SON (BART)
2 DAUGHTERS (LISA) (MAGGIE)
1 FATHER (OLD GUY IN HOME)
2 SISTERS-IN-LAW (WHO CARES)
N-GUH! I'M AFRAID, MRS. SIMPSON, THAT CLONES ARE NOT, IN FACT, LIKE RETURNABLE BOTTLES, BUT ARE MORE ALONG THE LINES OF, UH, ACTUAL HUMAN BEINGS, GLAVIN!
NOW, PLEASE DON'T CALL HERE AGAIN.

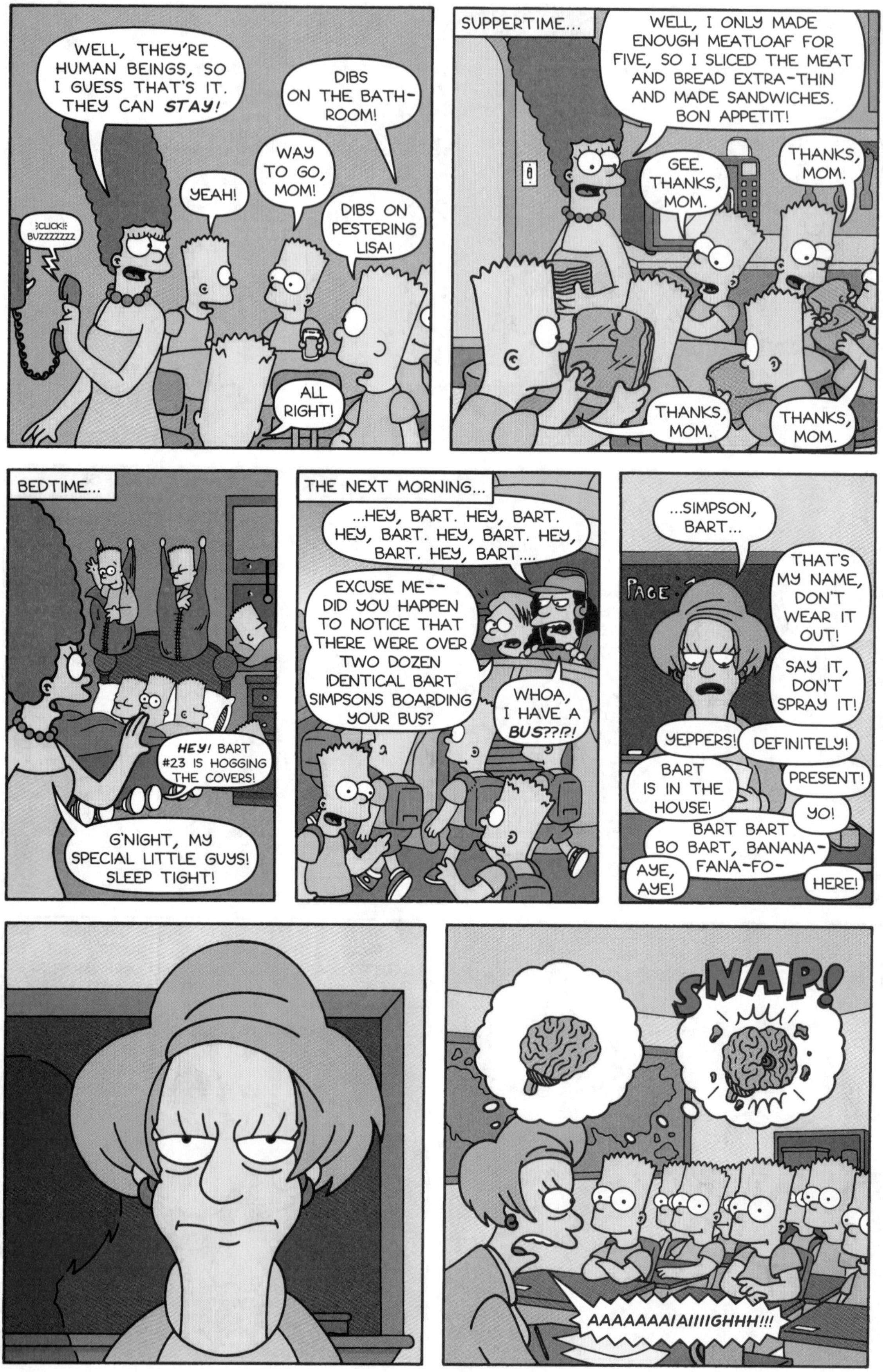

WELL, THEY'RE HUMAN BEINGS, SO I GUESS THAT'S IT. THEY CAN *STAY*!
⋮CLICK!⋮ BUZZZZZZZ
YEAH!
WAY TO GO, MOM!
DIBS ON THE BATH-ROOM!
DIBS ON PESTERING LISA!
ALL RIGHT!
SUPPERTIME...
WELL, I ONLY MADE ENOUGH MEATLOAF FOR FIVE, SO I SLICED THE MEAT AND BREAD EXTRA-THIN AND MADE SANDWICHES. BON APPETIT!
GEE. THANKS, MOM.
THANKS, MOM.
THANKS, MOM.
THANKS, MOM.
BEDTIME...
HEY! BART #23 IS HOGGING THE COVERS!
G'NIGHT, MY SPECIAL LITTLE GUYS! SLEEP TIGHT!
THE NEXT MORNING...
...HEY, BART. HEY, BART. HEY, BART. HEY, BART. HEY, BART. HEY, BART....
EXCUSE ME-- DID YOU HAPPEN TO NOTICE THAT THERE WERE OVER TWO DOZEN IDENTICAL BART SIMPSONS BOARDING YOUR BUS?
WHOA, I HAVE A *BUS*??!?!
...SIMPSON, BART...
PAGE 1
THAT'S MY NAME, DON'T WEAR IT OUT!
SAY IT, DON'T SPRAY IT!
YEPPERS!
DEFINITELY!
BART IS IN THE HOUSE!
PRESENT!
YO!
BART BART BO BART, BANANA-FANA-FO-
AYE, AYE!
HERE!
SNAP!
AAAAAAAIAIIIIGHHH!!!

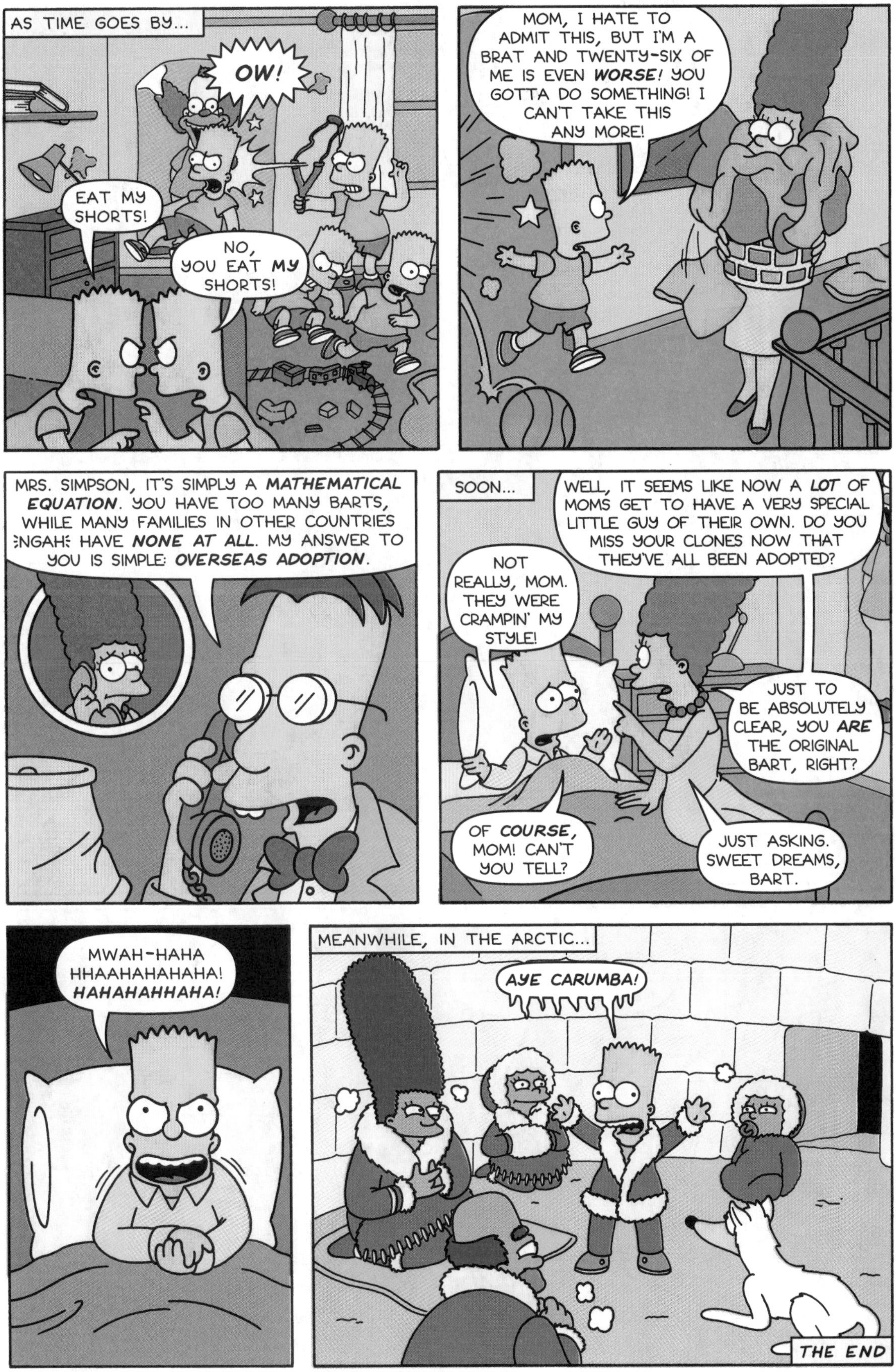
AS TIME GOES BY...
OW!
EAT MY SHORTS!
NO, YOU EAT MY SHORTS!
MOM, I HATE TO ADMIT THIS, BUT I'M A BRAT AND TWENTY-SIX OF ME IS EVEN WORSE! YOU GOTTA DO SOMETHING! I CAN'T TAKE THIS ANY MORE!
MRS. SIMPSON, IT'S SIMPLY A MATHEMATICAL EQUATION. YOU HAVE TOO MANY BARTS, WHILE MANY FAMILIES IN OTHER COUNTRIES ;NGAH; HAVE NONE AT ALL. MY ANSWER TO YOU IS SIMPLE: OVERSEAS ADOPTION.
SOON...
WELL, IT SEEMS LIKE NOW A LOT OF MOMS GET TO HAVE A VERY SPECIAL LITTLE GUY OF THEIR OWN. DO YOU MISS YOUR CLONES NOW THAT THEY'VE ALL BEEN ADOPTED?
NOT REALLY, MOM. THEY WERE CRAMPIN' MY STYLE!
JUST TO BE ABSOLUTELY CLEAR, YOU ARE THE ORIGINAL BART, RIGHT?
OF COURSE, MOM! CAN'T YOU TELL?
JUST ASKING. SWEET DREAMS, BART.
MWAH-HAHA HHAAAHAHAHAHA! HAHAHAHHAHA!
MEANWHILE, IN THE ARCTIC...
AYE CARUMBA!
THE END

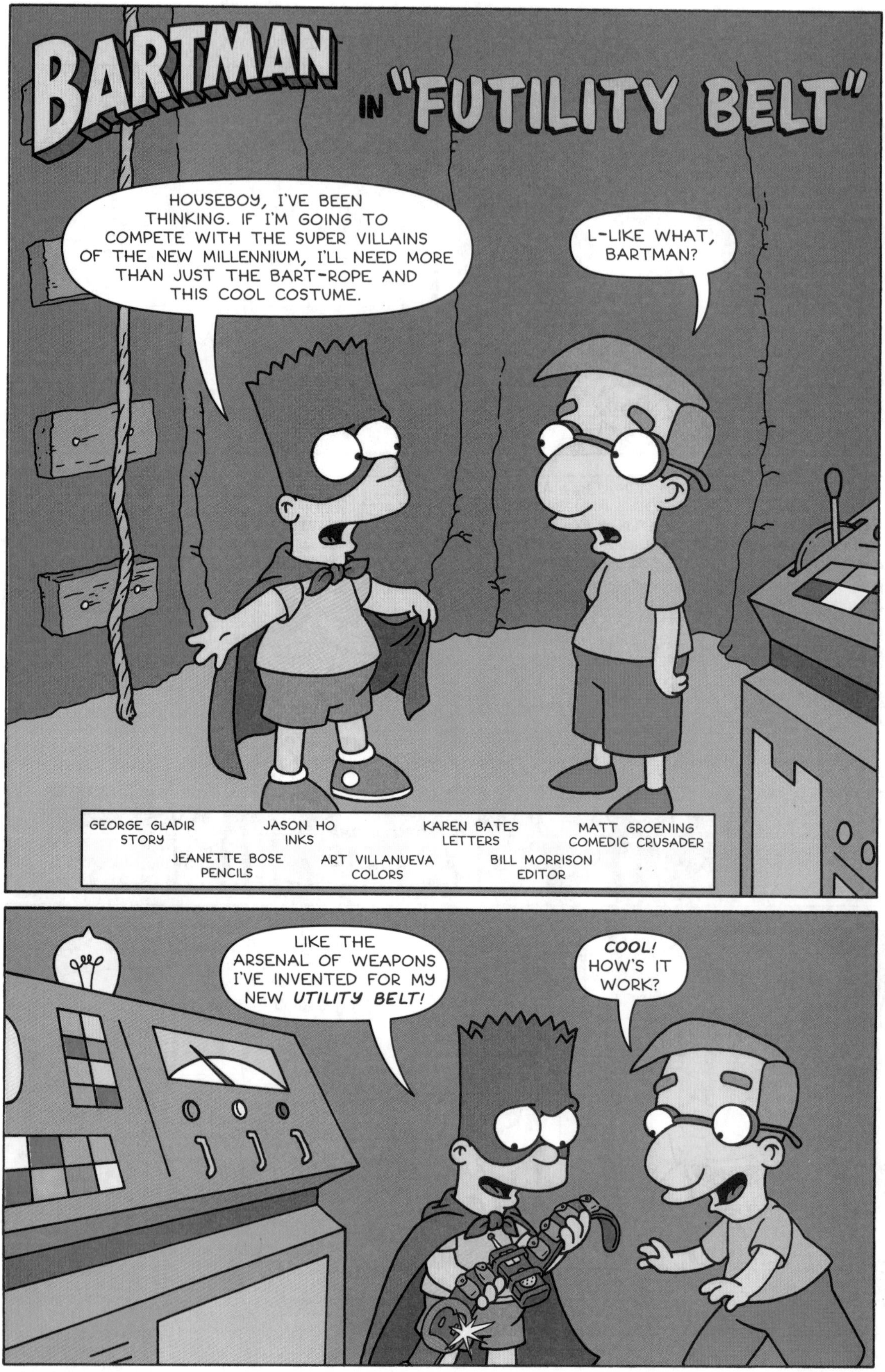
BARTMAN IN "FUTILITY BELT"
HOUSEBOY, I'VE BEEN THINKING. IF I'M GOING TO COMPETE WITH THE SUPER VILLAINS OF THE NEW MILLENNIUM, I'LL NEED MORE THAN JUST THE BART-ROPE AND THIS COOL COSTUME.
L-LIKE WHAT, BARTMAN?
GEORGE GLADIR STORY
JEANETTE BOSE PENCILS
JASON HO INKS
ART VILLANUEVA COLORS
KAREN BATES LETTERS
BILL MORRISON EDITOR
MATT GROENING COMEDIC CRUSADER
LIKE THE ARSENAL OF WEAPONS I'VE INVENTED FOR MY NEW *UTILITY BELT*!
COOL! HOW'S IT WORK?

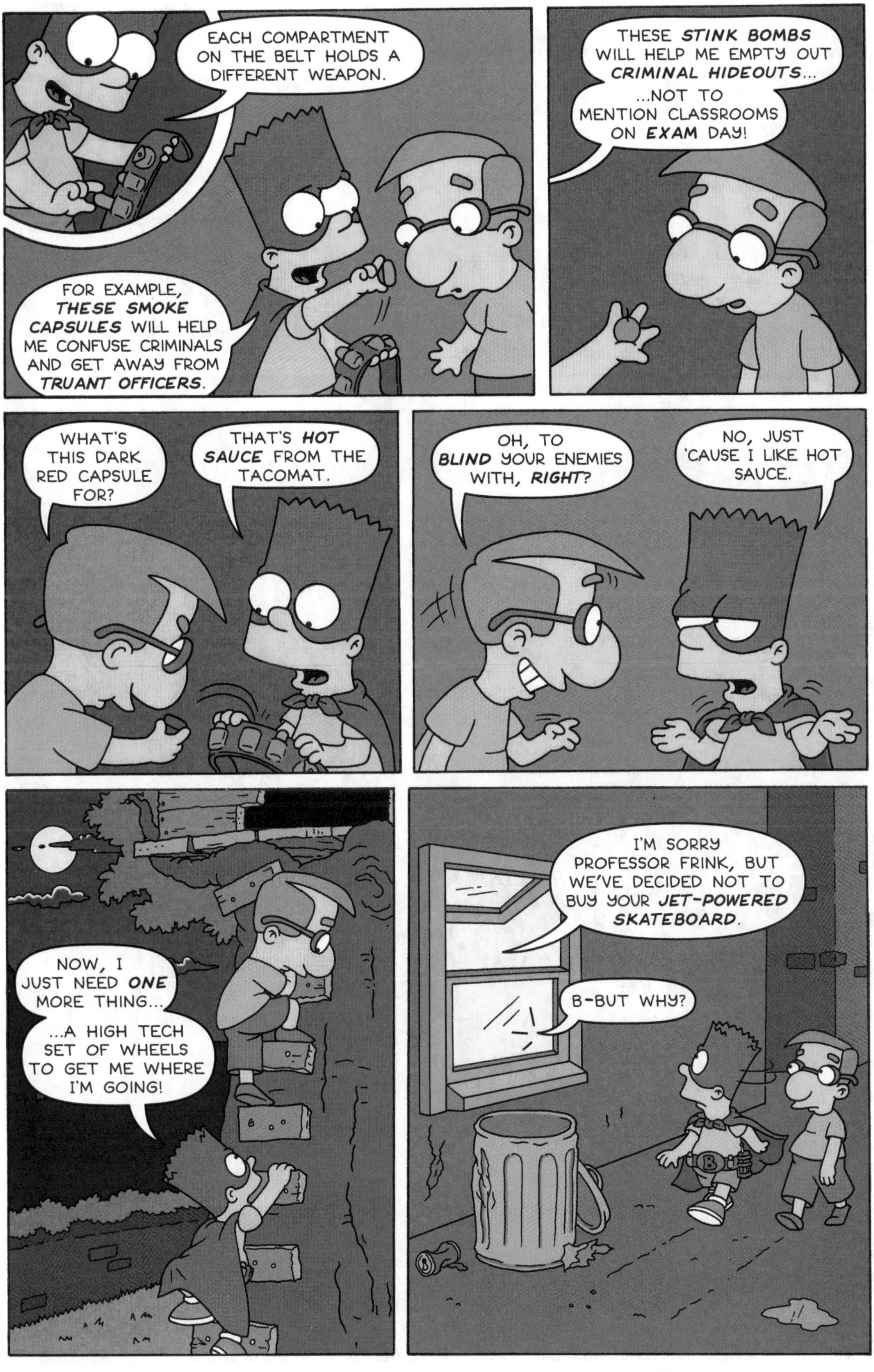
EACH COMPARTMENT ON THE BELT HOLDS A DIFFERENT WEAPON.
FOR EXAMPLE, THESE SMOKE CAPSULES WILL HELP ME CONFUSE CRIMINALS AND GET AWAY FROM TRUANT OFFICERS.
THESE STINK BOMBS WILL HELP ME EMPTY OUT CRIMINAL HIDEOUTS...
...NOT TO MENTION CLASSROOMS ON EXAM DAY!
WHAT'S THIS DARK RED CAPSULE FOR?
THAT'S HOT SAUCE FROM THE TACOMAT.
OH, TO BLIND YOUR ENEMIES WITH, RIGHT?
NO, JUST 'CAUSE I LIKE HOT SAUCE.
NOW, I JUST NEED ONE MORE THING...
...A HIGH TECH SET OF WHEELS TO GET ME WHERE I'M GOING!
I'M SORRY PROFESSOR FRINK, BUT WE'VE DECIDED NOT TO BUY YOUR JET-POWERED SKATEBOARD.
B-BUT WHY?

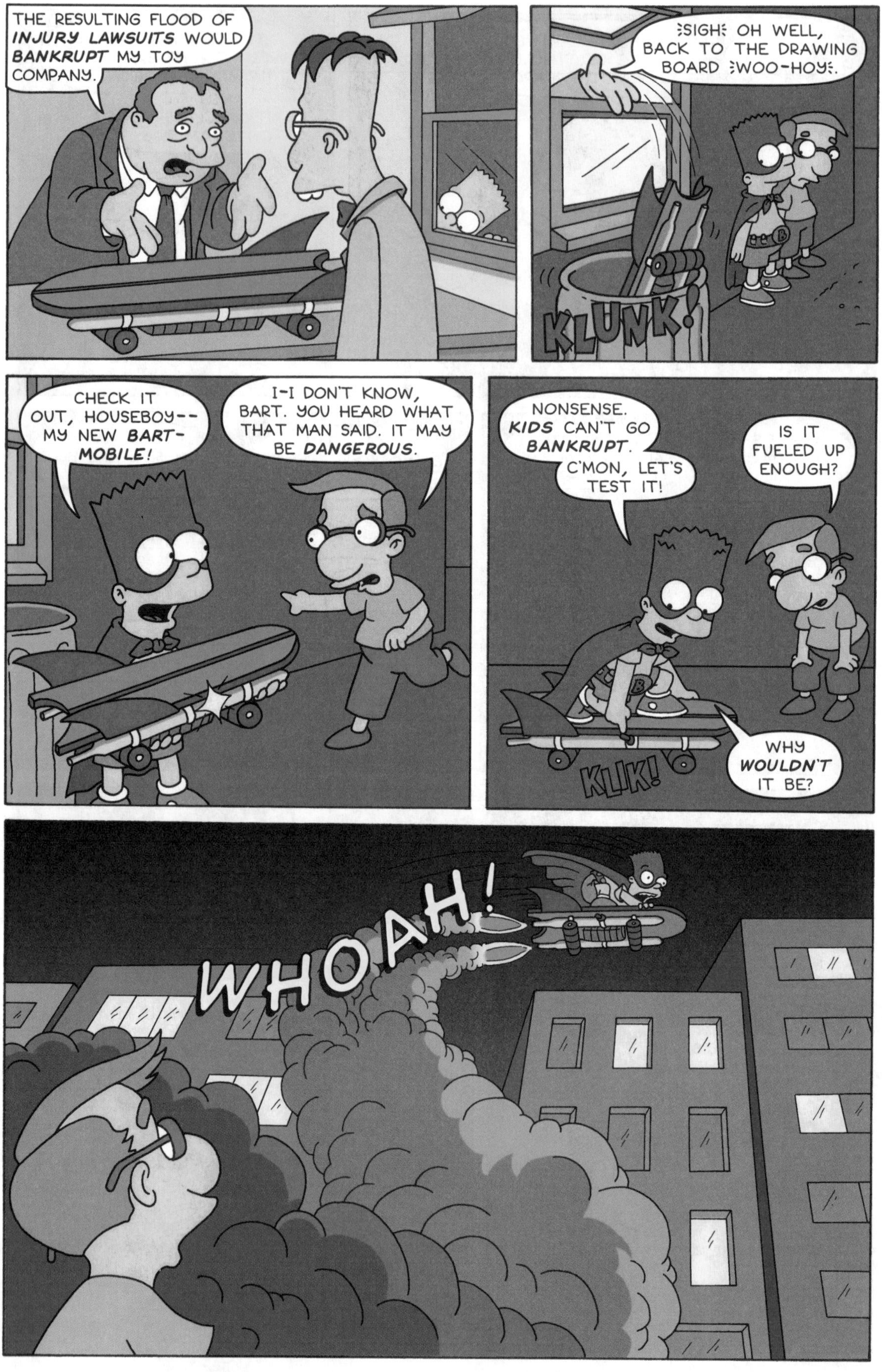
THE RESULTING FLOOD OF INJURY LAWSUITS WOULD BANKRUPT MY TOY COMPANY.
:SIGH: OH WELL, BACK TO THE DRAWING BOARD :WOO-HOY:.
KLUNK!
CHECK IT OUT, HOUSEBOY-- MY NEW BART-MOBILE!
I-I DON'T KNOW, BART. YOU HEARD WHAT THAT MAN SAID. IT MAY BE DANGEROUS.
NONSENSE. KIDS CAN'T GO BANKRUPT.
C'MON, LET'S TEST IT!
IS IT FUELED UP ENOUGH?
WHY WOULDN'T IT BE?
KLIK!
WHOAH!

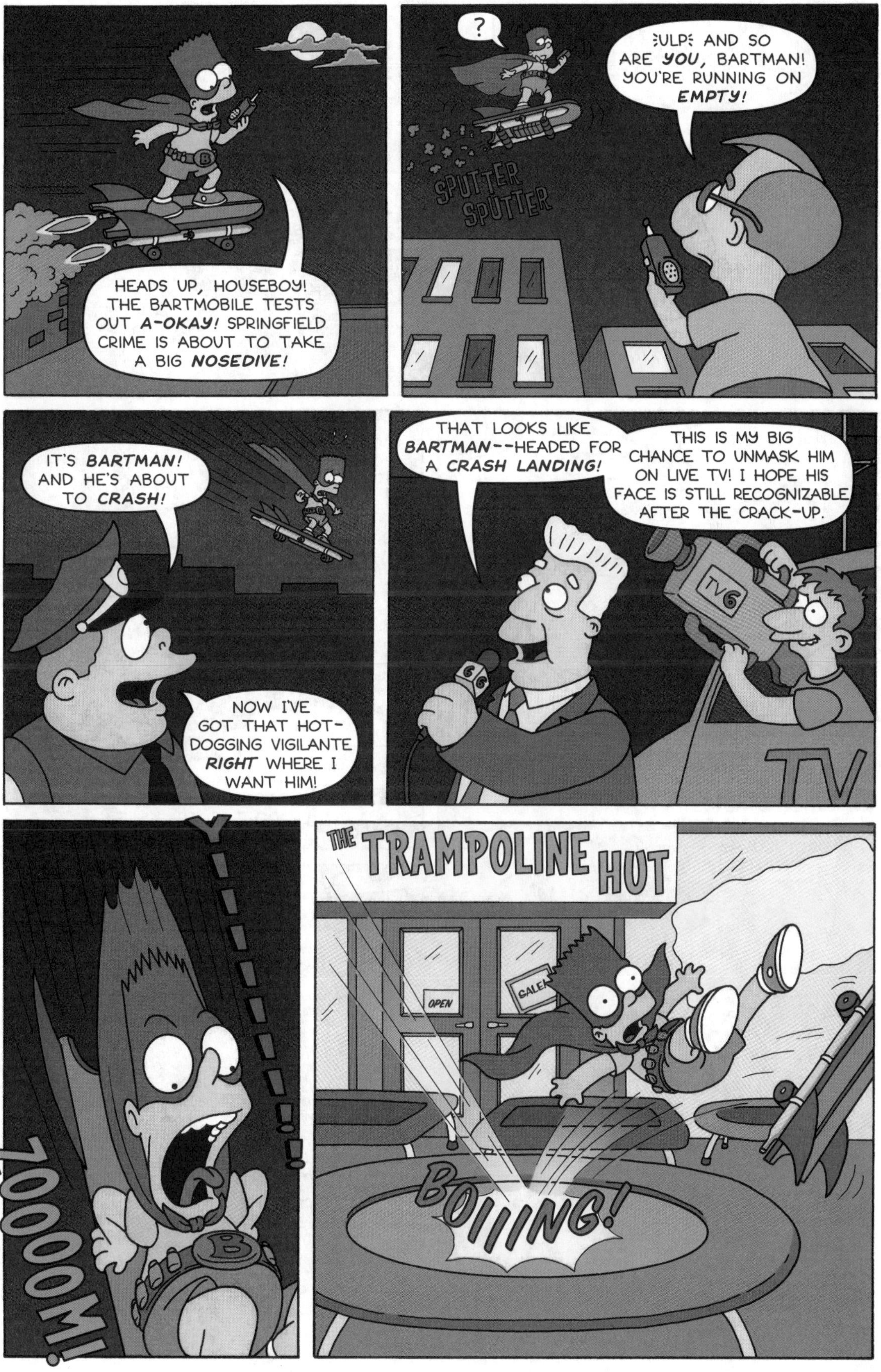
HEADS UP, HOUSEBOY! THE BARTMOBILE TESTS OUT **A-OKAY**! SPRINGFIELD CRIME IS ABOUT TO TAKE A BIG **NOSEDIVE**!
?
SPUTTER SPUTTER
:ULP: AND SO ARE **YOU**, BARTMAN! YOU'RE RUNNING ON **EMPTY**!
IT'S **BARTMAN**! AND HE'S ABOUT TO **CRASH**!
NOW I'VE GOT THAT HOT-DOGGING VIGILANTE **RIGHT** WHERE I WANT HIM!
THAT LOOKS LIKE **BARTMAN**--HEADED FOR A **CRASH LANDING**!
THIS IS MY BIG CHANCE TO UNMASK HIM ON LIVE TV! I HOPE HIS FACE IS STILL RECOGNIZABLE AFTER THE CRACK-UP.
TV6
TV
ZOOOOM!
THE TRAMPOLINE HUT
OPEN
SALE
BOIIING!

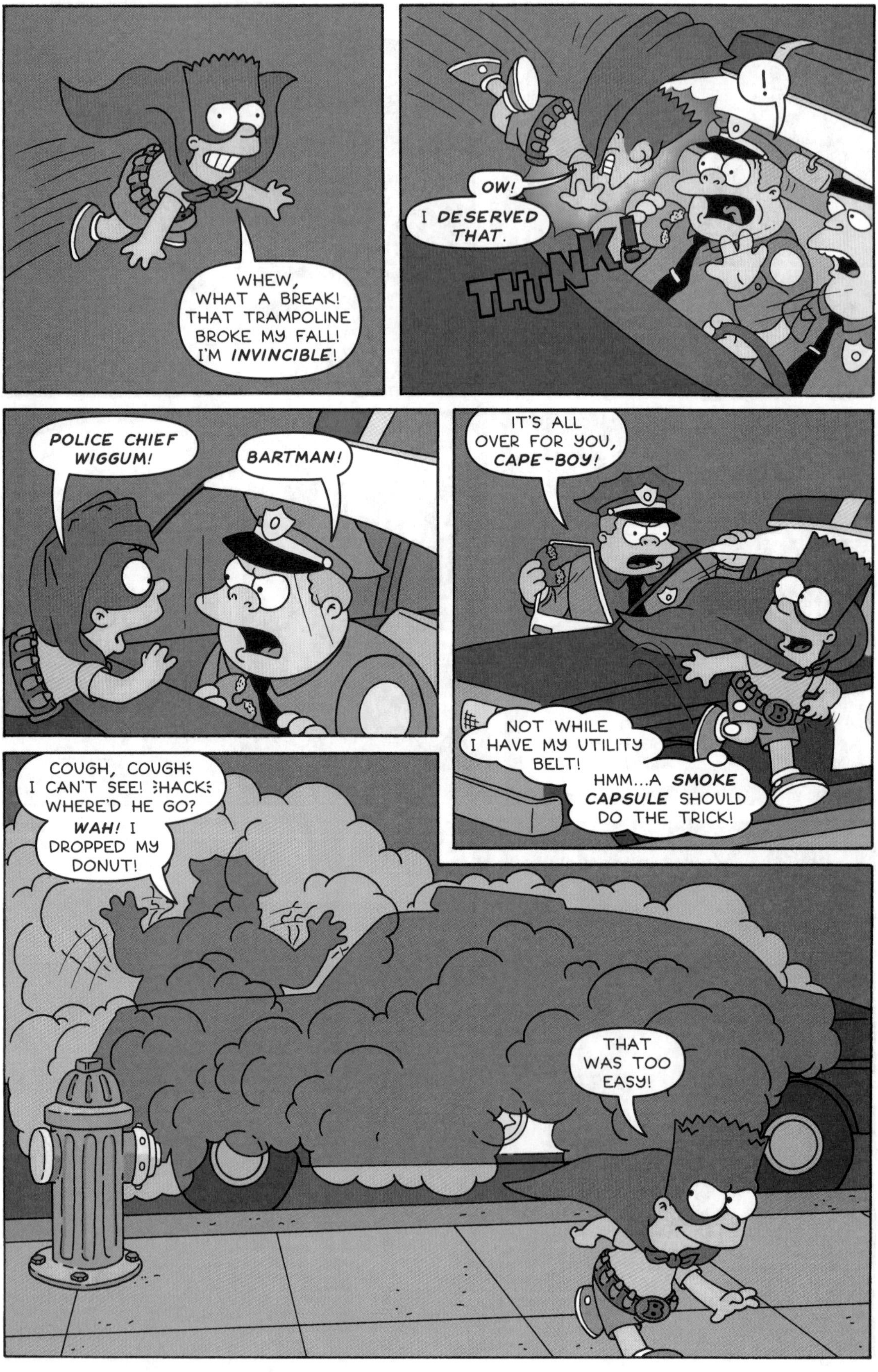
WHEW, WHAT A BREAK! THAT TRAMPOLINE BROKE MY FALL! I'M INVINCIBLE!
!
OW! I DESERVED THAT.
THUNK!
POLICE CHIEF WIGGUM!
BARTMAN!
IT'S ALL OVER FOR YOU, CAPE-BOY!
NOT WHILE I HAVE MY UTILITY BELT!
HMM...A SMOKE CAPSULE SHOULD DO THE TRICK!
COUGH, COUGH! I CAN'T SEE! HACK! WHERE'D HE GO? WAH! I DROPPED MY DONUT!
THAT WAS TOO EASY!

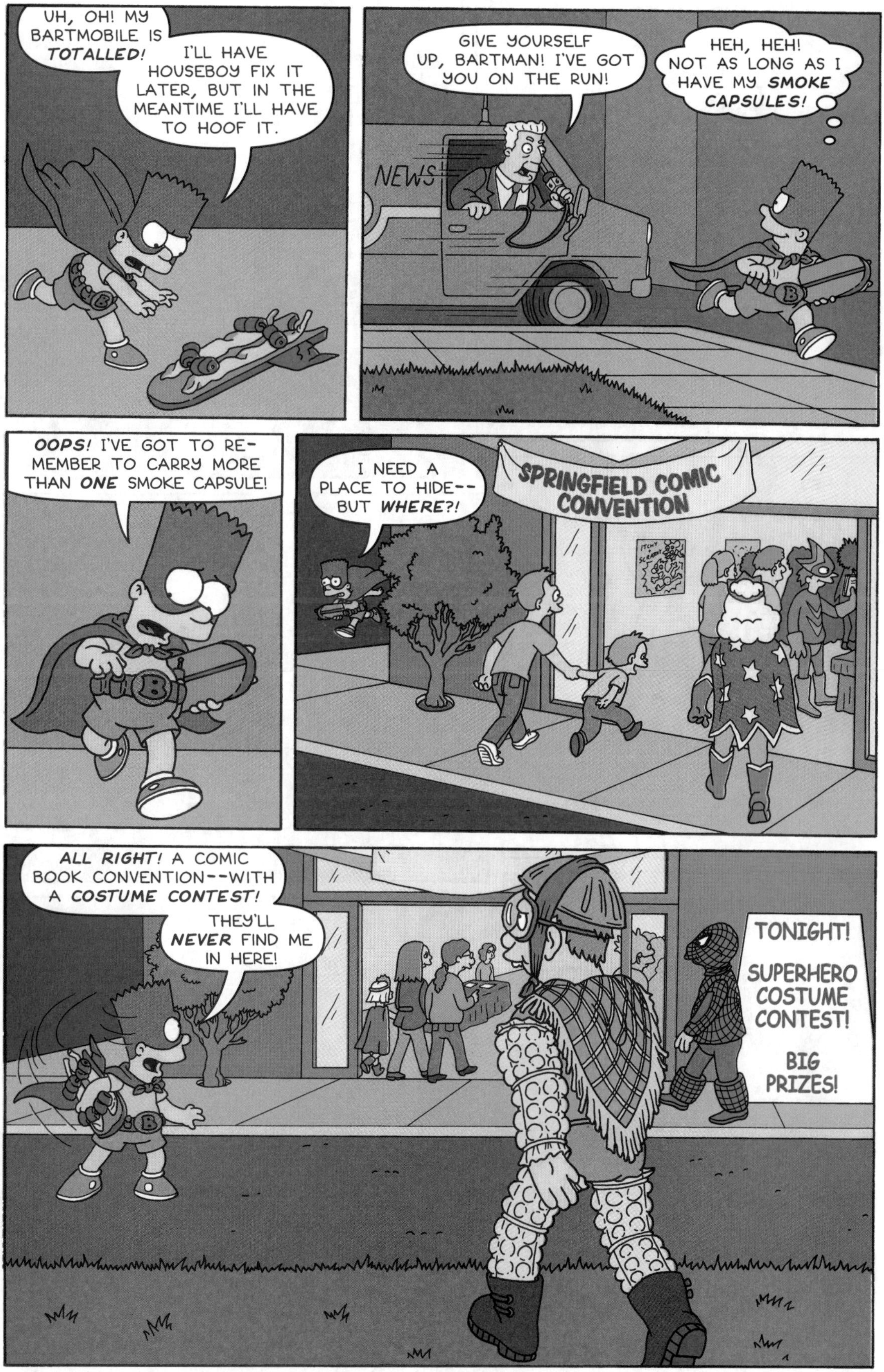
UH, OH! MY BARTMOBILE IS TOTALLED!
I'LL HAVE HOUSEBOY FIX IT LATER, BUT IN THE MEANTIME I'LL HAVE TO HOOF IT.
NEWS
GIVE YOURSELF UP, BARTMAN! I'VE GOT YOU ON THE RUN!
HEH, HEH! NOT AS LONG AS I HAVE MY SMOKE CAPSULES!
OOPS! I'VE GOT TO REMEMBER TO CARRY MORE THAN ONE SMOKE CAPSULE!
I NEED A PLACE TO HIDE--BUT WHERE?!
SPRINGFIELD COMIC CONVENTION
ALL RIGHT! A COMIC BOOK CONVENTION--WITH A COSTUME CONTEST!
THEY'LL NEVER FIND ME IN HERE!
TONIGHT!
SUPERHERO COSTUME CONTEST!
BIG PRIZES!

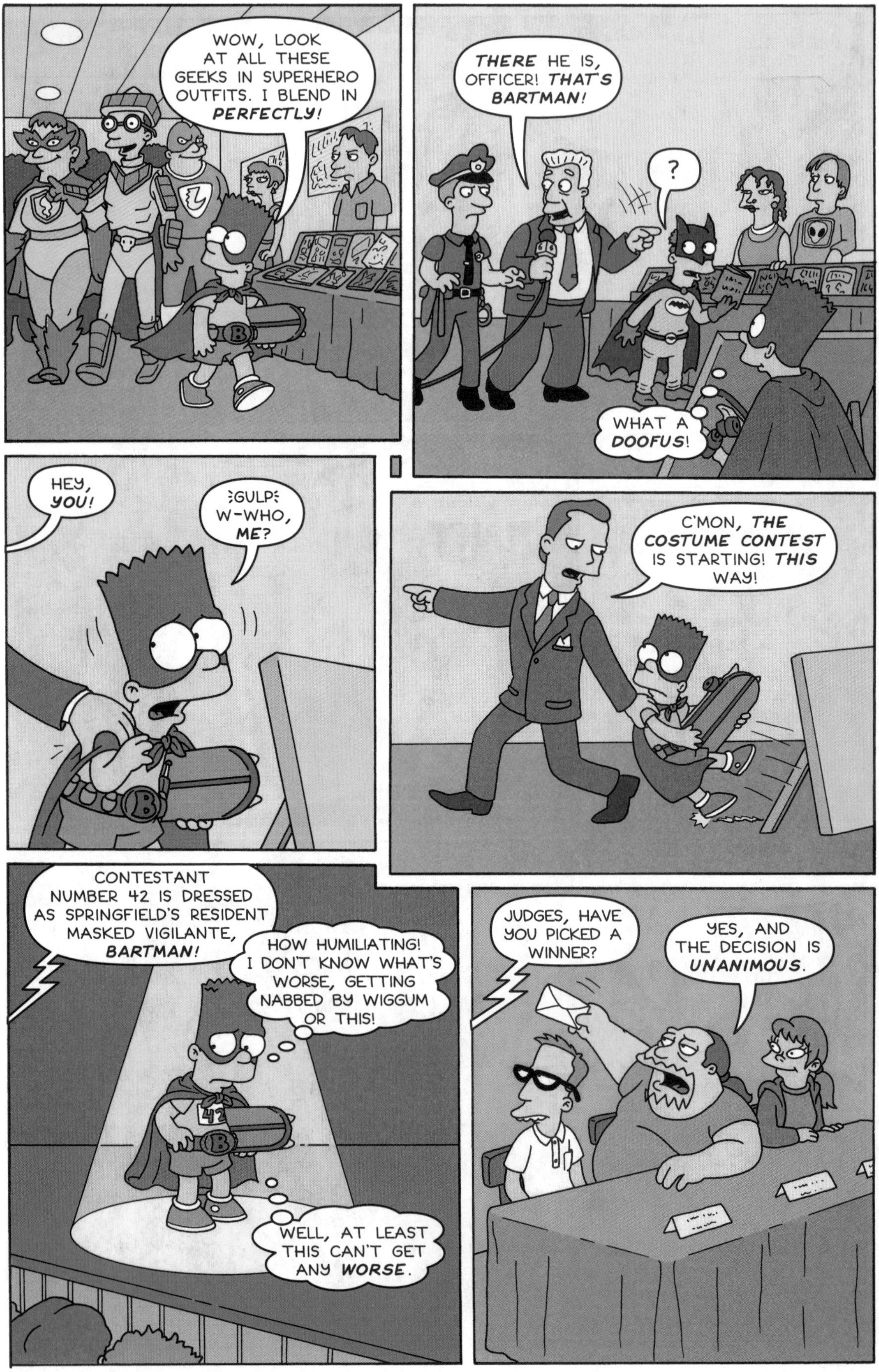
WOW, LOOK AT ALL THESE GEEKS IN SUPERHERO OUTFITS. I BLEND IN PERFECTLY!
THERE HE IS, OFFICER! THAT'S BARTMAN!
?
WHAT A DOOFUS!
HEY, YOU!
GULP W-WHO, ME?
C'MON, THE COSTUME CONTEST IS STARTING! THIS WAY!
CONTESTANT NUMBER 42 IS DRESSED AS SPRINGFIELD'S RESIDENT MASKED VIGILANTE, BARTMAN!
HOW HUMILIATING! I DON'T KNOW WHAT'S WORSE, GETTING NABBED BY WIGGUM OR THIS!
WELL, AT LEAST THIS CAN'T GET ANY WORSE.
JUDGES, HAVE YOU PICKED A WINNER?
YES, AND THE DECISION IS UNANIMOUS.

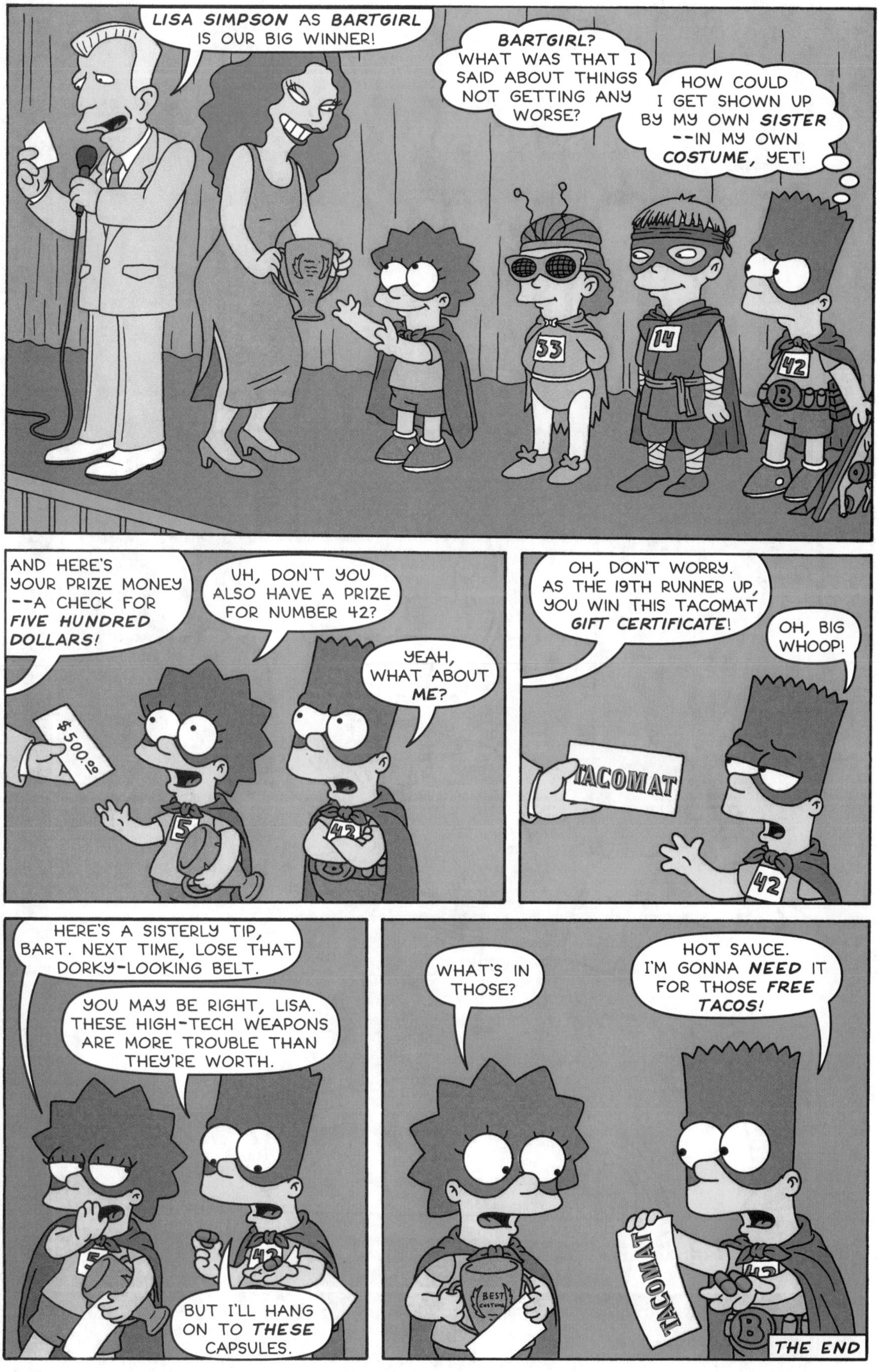
LISA SIMPSON AS BARTGIRL IS OUR BIG WINNER!
BARTGIRL? WHAT WAS THAT I SAID ABOUT THINGS NOT GETTING ANY WORSE?
HOW COULD I GET SHOWN UP BY MY OWN SISTER --IN MY OWN COSTUME, YET!
33
14
42
B
AND HERE'S YOUR PRIZE MONEY --A CHECK FOR FIVE HUNDRED DOLLARS!
UH, DON'T YOU ALSO HAVE A PRIZE FOR NUMBER 42?
YEAH, WHAT ABOUT ME?
$500.00
5
42
OH, DON'T WORRY. AS THE 19TH RUNNER UP, YOU WIN THIS TACOMAT GIFT CERTIFICATE!
OH, BIG WHOOP!
TACOMAT
42
HERE'S A SISTERLY TIP, BART. NEXT TIME, LOSE THAT DORKY-LOOKING BELT.
YOU MAY BE RIGHT, LISA. THESE HIGH-TECH WEAPONS ARE MORE TROUBLE THAN THEY'RE WORTH.
BUT I'LL HANG ON TO THESE CAPSULES.
WHAT'S IN THOSE?
HOT SAUCE. I'M GONNA NEED IT FOR THOSE FREE TACOS!
TACOMAT
B
THE END

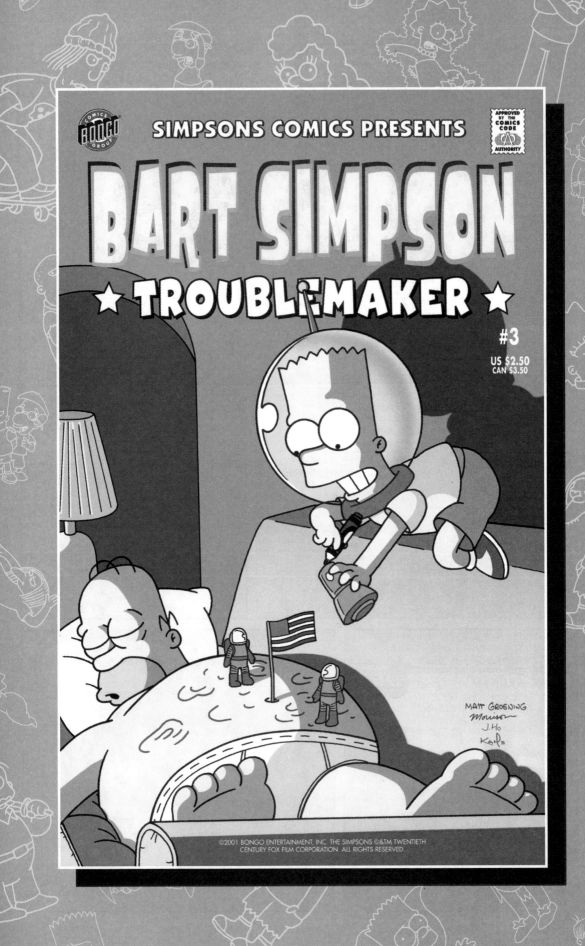

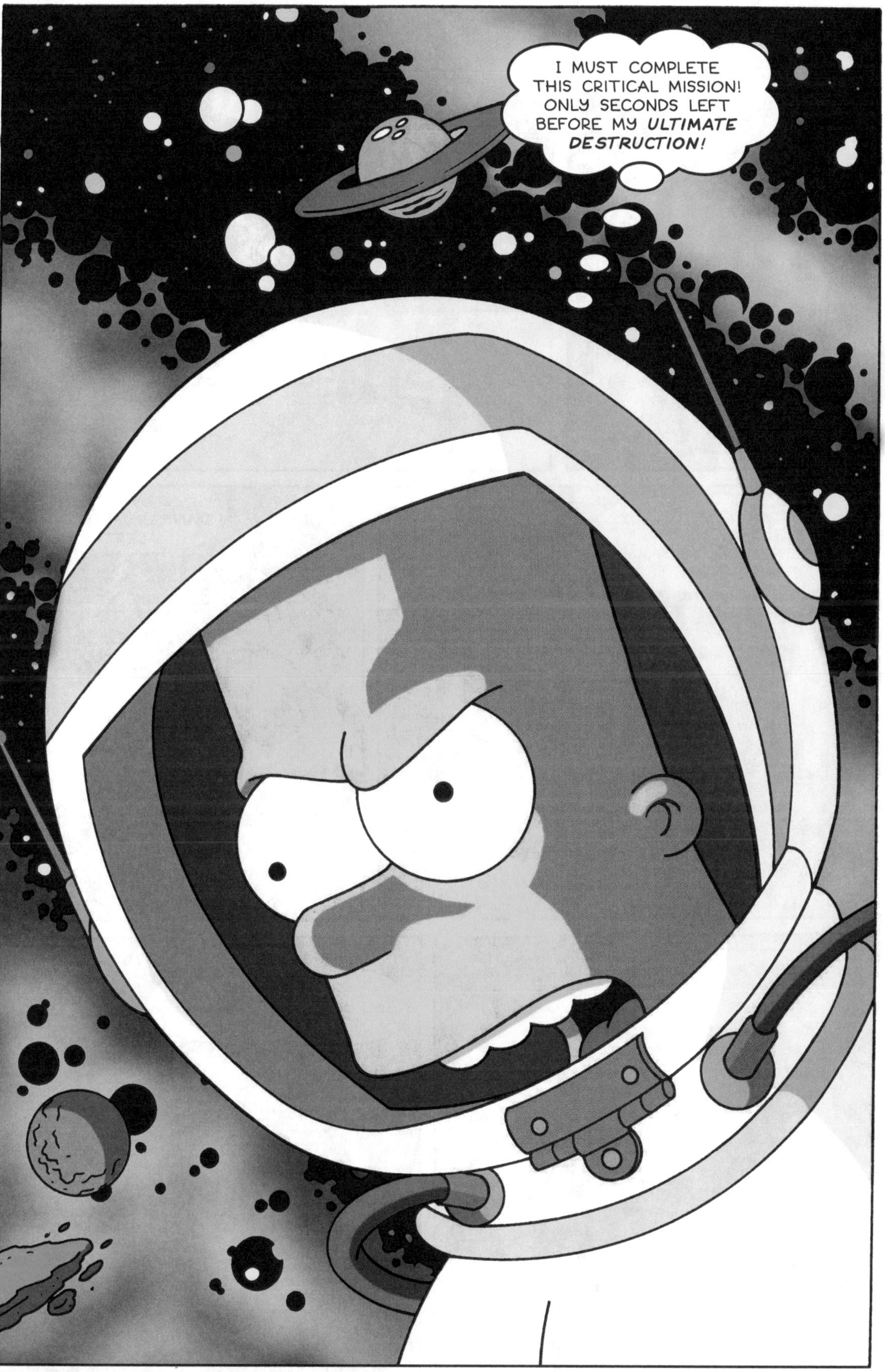
I MUST COMPLETE THIS CRITICAL MISSION! ONLY SECONDS LEFT BEFORE MY *ULTIMATE DESTRUCTION!*

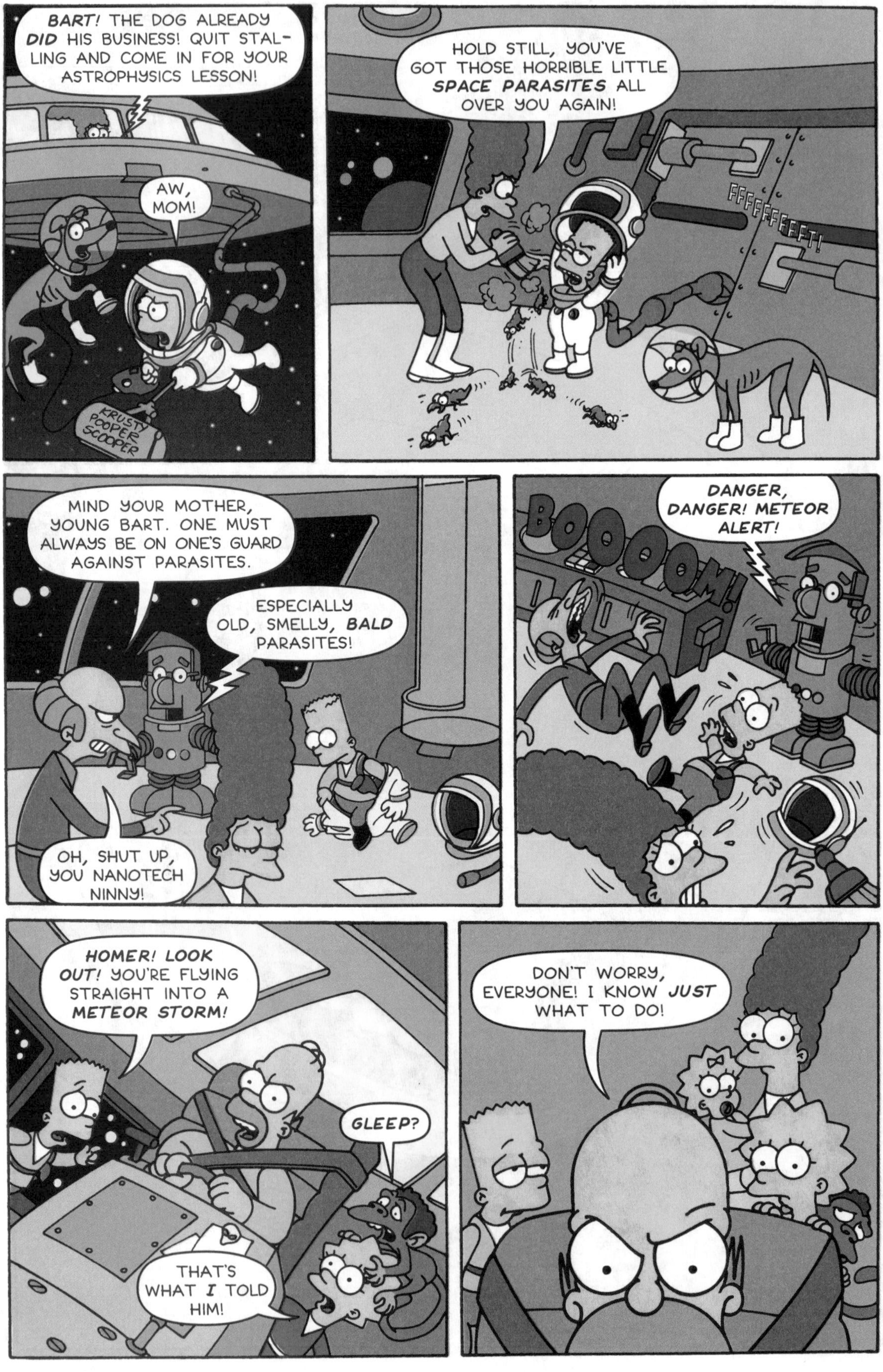
BART! THE DOG ALREADY DID HIS BUSINESS! QUIT STALLING AND COME IN FOR YOUR ASTROPHYSICS LESSON!
AW, MOM!
KRUSTY POOPER SCOOPER
HOLD STILL, YOU'VE GOT THOSE HORRIBLE LITTLE SPACE PARASITES ALL OVER YOU AGAIN!
FFFFFFFFFFT!
MIND YOUR MOTHER, YOUNG BART. ONE MUST ALWAYS BE ON ONE'S GUARD AGAINST PARASITES.
ESPECIALLY OLD, SMELLY, BALD PARASITES!
OH, SHUT UP, YOU NANOTECH NINNY!
BOOOOM!
DANGER, DANGER! METEOR ALERT!
HOMER! LOOK OUT! YOU'RE FLYING STRAIGHT INTO A METEOR STORM!
GLEEP?
THAT'S WHAT I TOLD HIM!
DON'T WORRY, EVERYONE! I KNOW JUST WHAT TO DO!

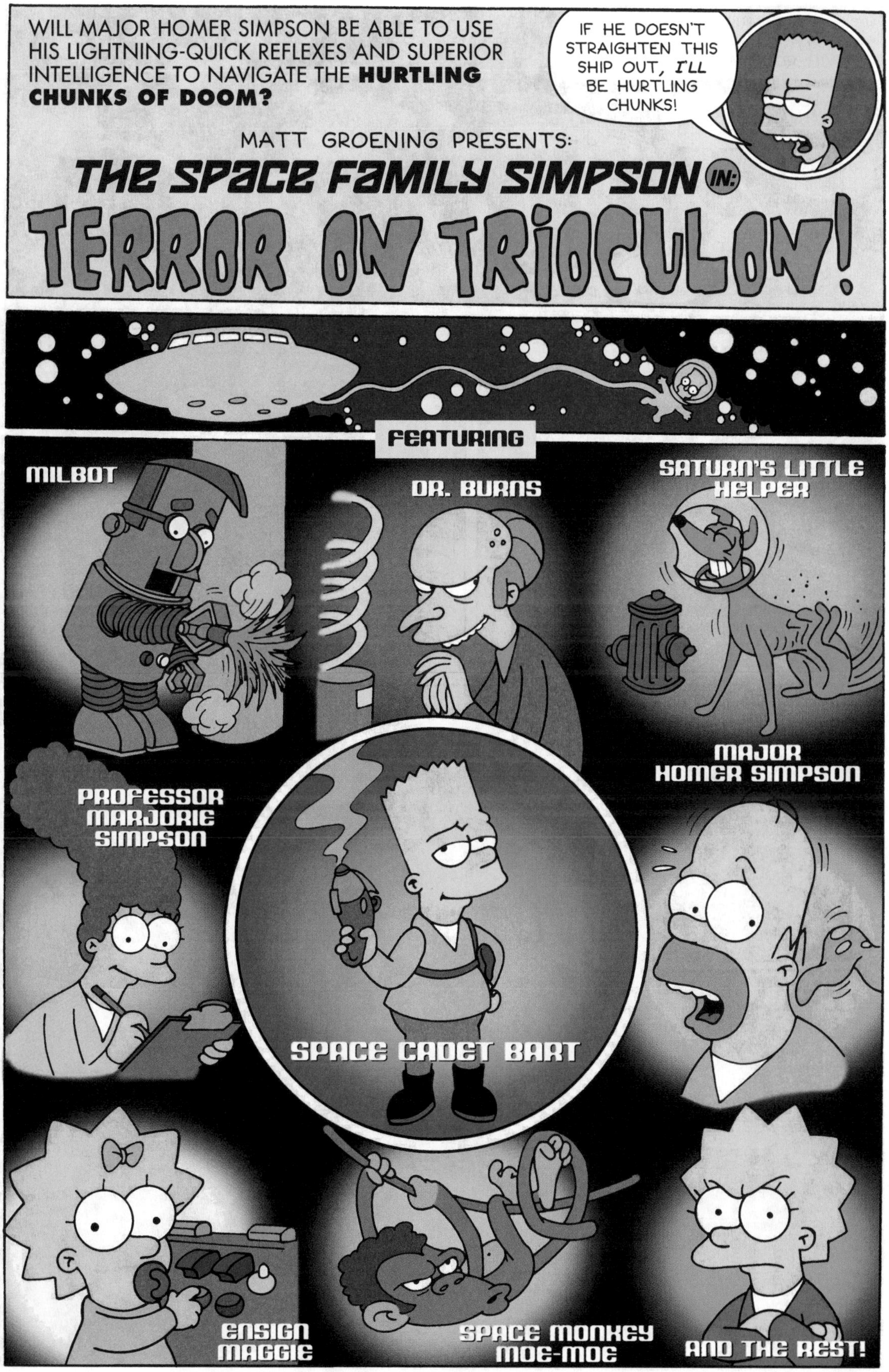

WILL MAJOR HOMER SIMPSON BE ABLE TO USE HIS LIGHTNING-QUICK REFLEXES AND SUPERIOR INTELLIGENCE TO NAVIGATE THE **HURTLING CHUNKS OF DOOM?**
IF HE DOESN'T STRAIGHTEN THIS SHIP OUT, *I'LL* BE HURTLING CHUNKS!
MATT GROENING PRESENTS:
THE SPACE FAMILY SIMPSON IN:
TERROR ON TRIOCULON!
FEATURING
MILBOT
DR. BURNS
SATURN'S LITTLE HELPER
PROFESSOR MARJORIE SIMPSON
MAJOR HOMER SIMPSON
SPACE CADET BART
ENSIGN MAGGIE
SPACE MONKEY MOE-MOE
AND THE REST!

GAIL SIMONE SPACE COMMUNICATIONS · JOHN COSTANZA ASTRO-PENCILS & BLACK HOLE INKS · ART VILLANUEVA COSMIC COLORS · KAREN BATES LIGHTSPEED LETTERS · BILL MORRISON HYPER-EDITS

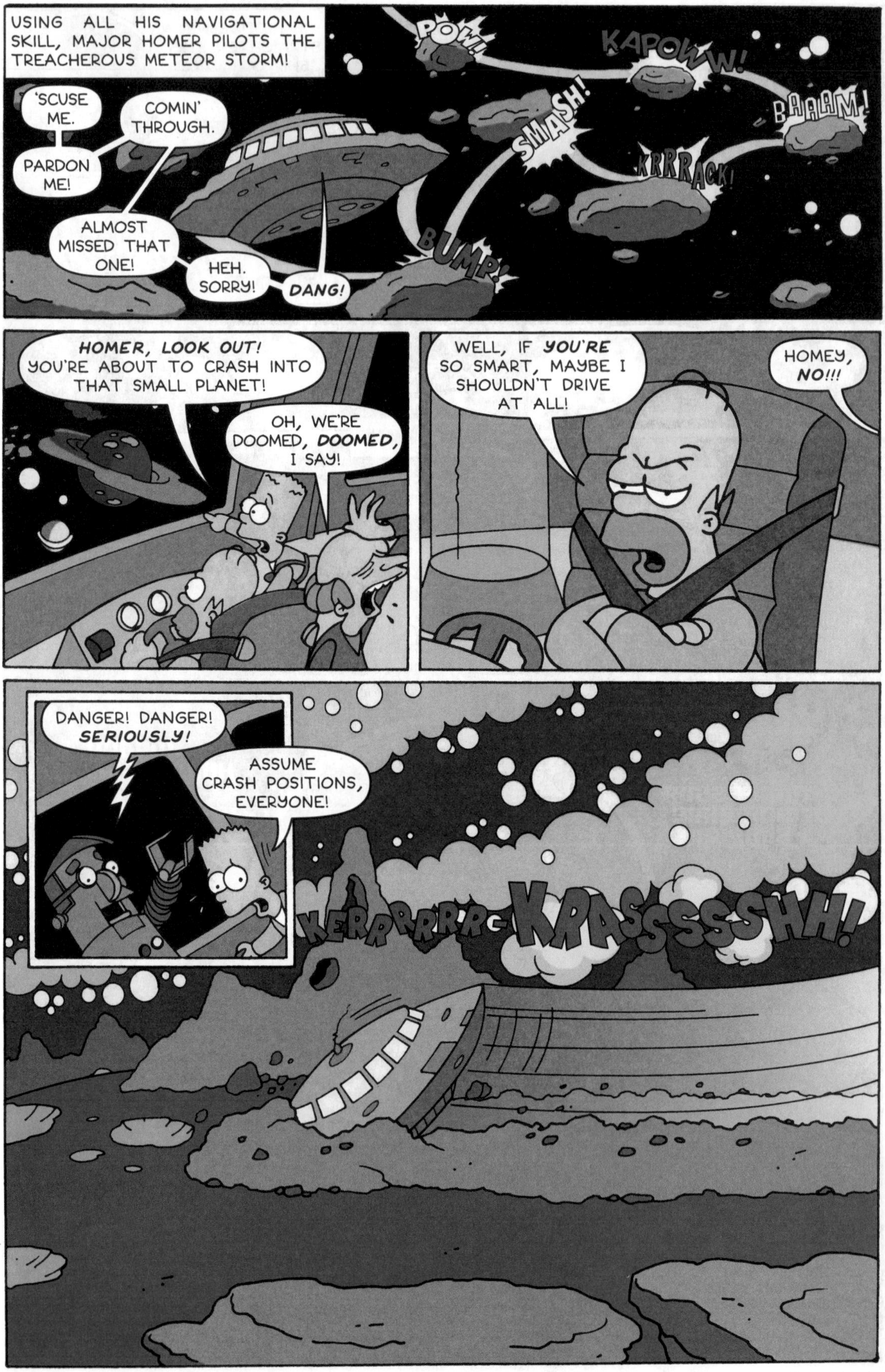
USING ALL HIS NAVIGATIONAL SKILL, MAJOR HOMER PILOTS THE TREACHEROUS METEOR STORM!
POW!
KAPOWWW!
SMASH!
BAAAM!
KRRRACK!
BUMP!
'SCUSE ME.
PARDON ME!
COMIN' THROUGH.
ALMOST MISSED THAT ONE!
HEH. SORRY!
DANG!
HOMER, LOOK OUT! YOU'RE ABOUT TO CRASH INTO THAT SMALL PLANET!
OH, WE'RE DOOMED, DOOMED, I SAY!
WELL, IF YOU'RE SO SMART, MAYBE I SHOULDN'T DRIVE AT ALL!
HOMEY, NO!!!
DANGER! DANGER! SERIOUSLY!
ASSUME CRASH POSITIONS, EVERYONE!
KERRRRRRR-KRASSSSSHH!

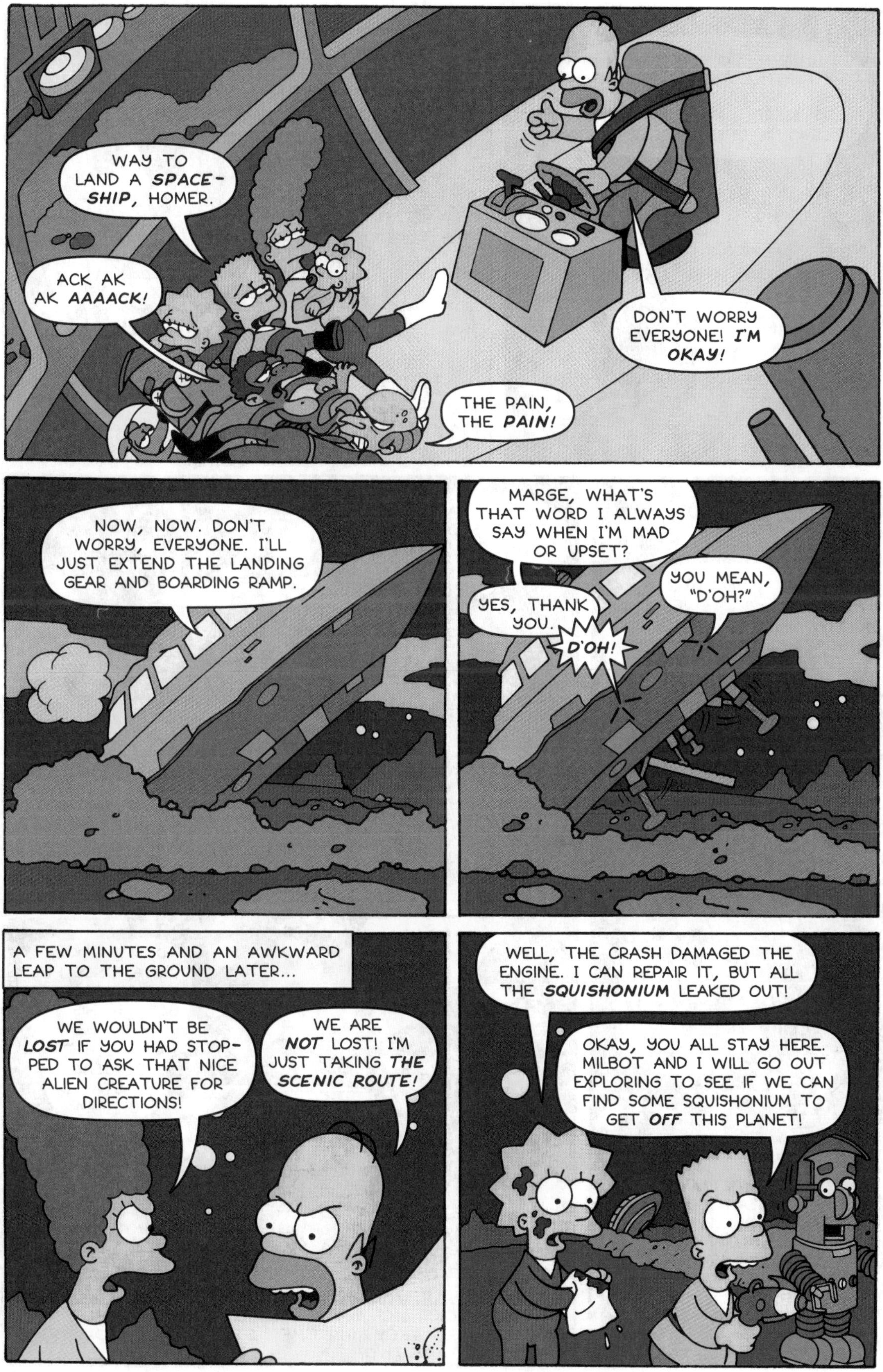
WAY TO LAND A SPACE-SHIP, HOMER.
ACK AK AK AAAACK!
DON'T WORRY EVERYONE! I'M OKAY!
THE PAIN, THE PAIN!
NOW, NOW. DON'T WORRY, EVERYONE. I'LL JUST EXTEND THE LANDING GEAR AND BOARDING RAMP.
MARGE, WHAT'S THAT WORD I ALWAYS SAY WHEN I'M MAD OR UPSET?
YOU MEAN, "D'OH?"
YES, THANK YOU.
D'OH!
A FEW MINUTES AND AN AWKWARD LEAP TO THE GROUND LATER...
WE WOULDN'T BE LOST IF YOU HAD STOP-PED TO ASK THAT NICE ALIEN CREATURE FOR DIRECTIONS!
WE ARE NOT LOST! I'M JUST TAKING THE SCENIC ROUTE!
WELL, THE CRASH DAMAGED THE ENGINE. I CAN REPAIR IT, BUT ALL THE SQUISHONIUM LEAKED OUT!
OKAY, YOU ALL STAY HERE. MILBOT AND I WILL GO OUT EXPLORING TO SEE IF WE CAN FIND SOME SQUISHONIUM TO GET OFF THIS PLANET!

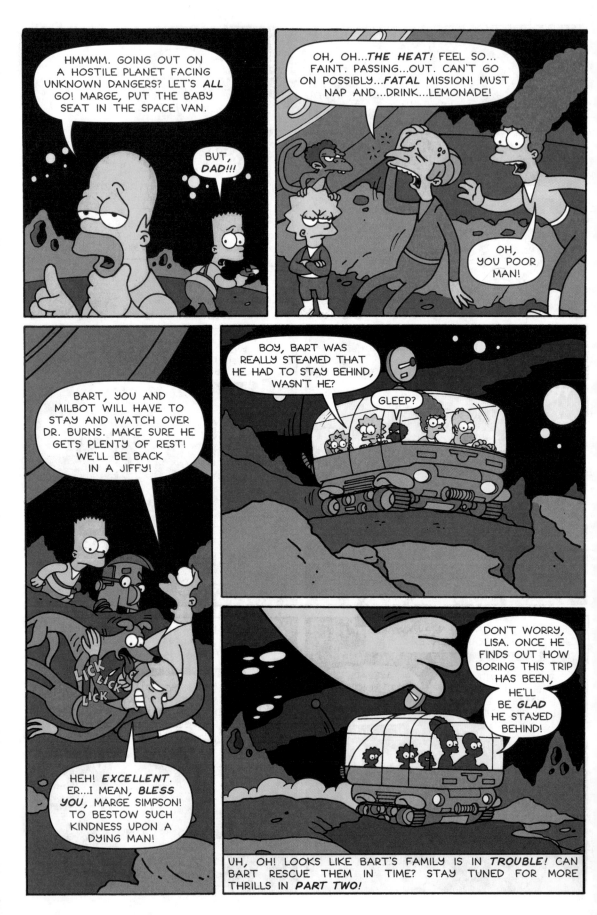

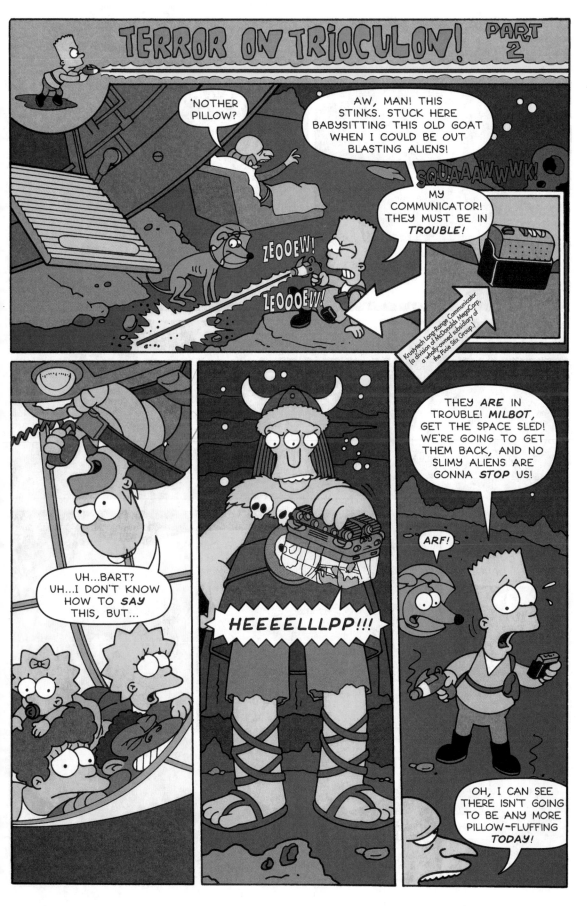

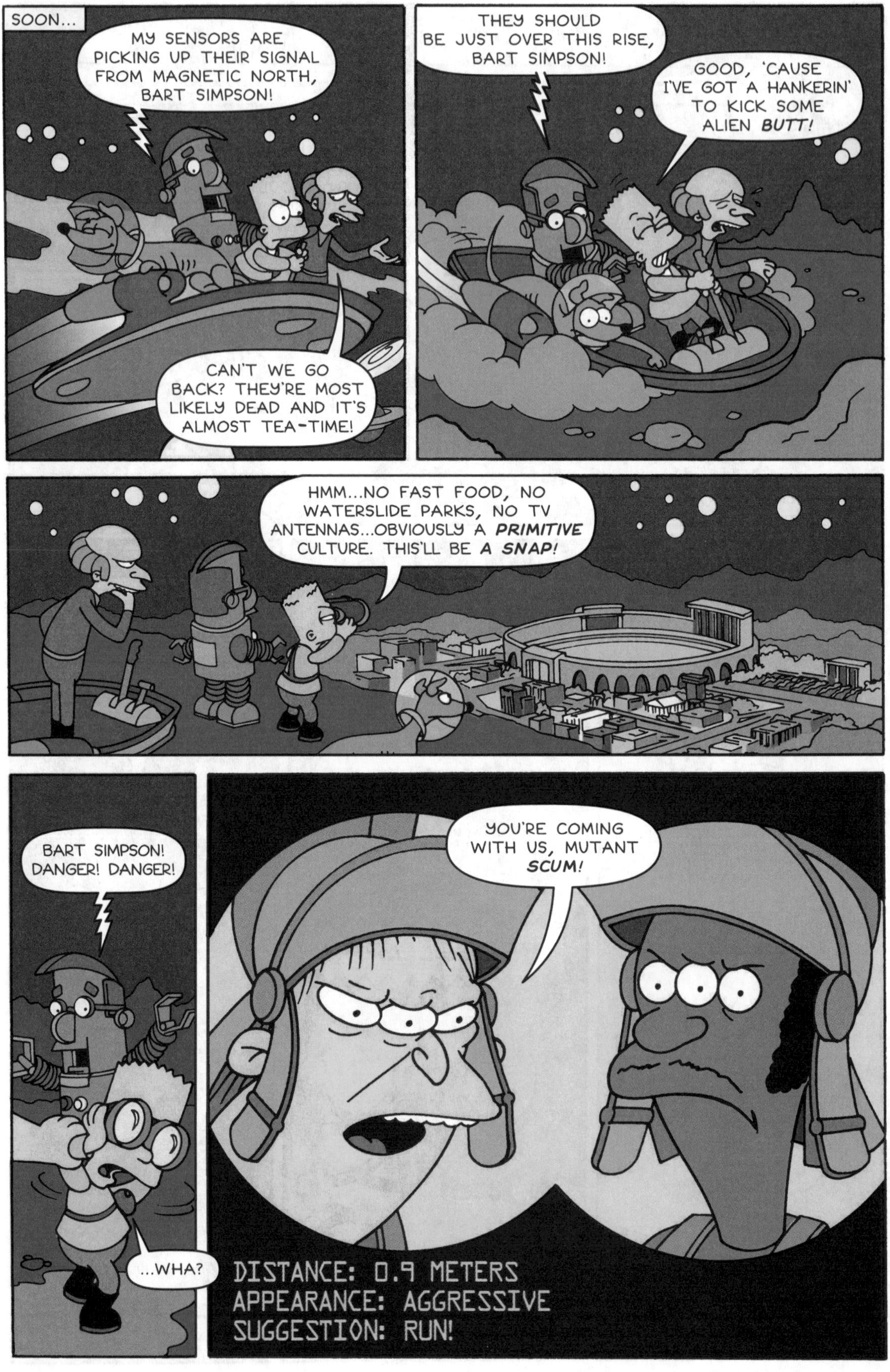
SOON...
MY SENSORS ARE PICKING UP THEIR SIGNAL FROM MAGNETIC NORTH, BART SIMPSON!
CAN'T WE GO BACK? THEY'RE MOST LIKELY DEAD AND IT'S ALMOST TEA-TIME!
THEY SHOULD BE JUST OVER THIS RISE, BART SIMPSON!
GOOD, 'CAUSE I'VE GOT A HANKERIN' TO KICK SOME ALIEN ***BUTT!***
HMM...NO FAST FOOD, NO WATERSLIDE PARKS, NO TV ANTENNAS...OBVIOUSLY A ***PRIMITIVE*** CULTURE. THIS'LL BE ***A SNAP!***
BART SIMPSON! DANGER! DANGER!
...WHA?
YOU'RE COMING WITH US, MUTANT ***SCUM!***
DISTANCE: 0.9 METERS
APPEARANCE: AGGRESSIVE
SUGGESTION: RUN!

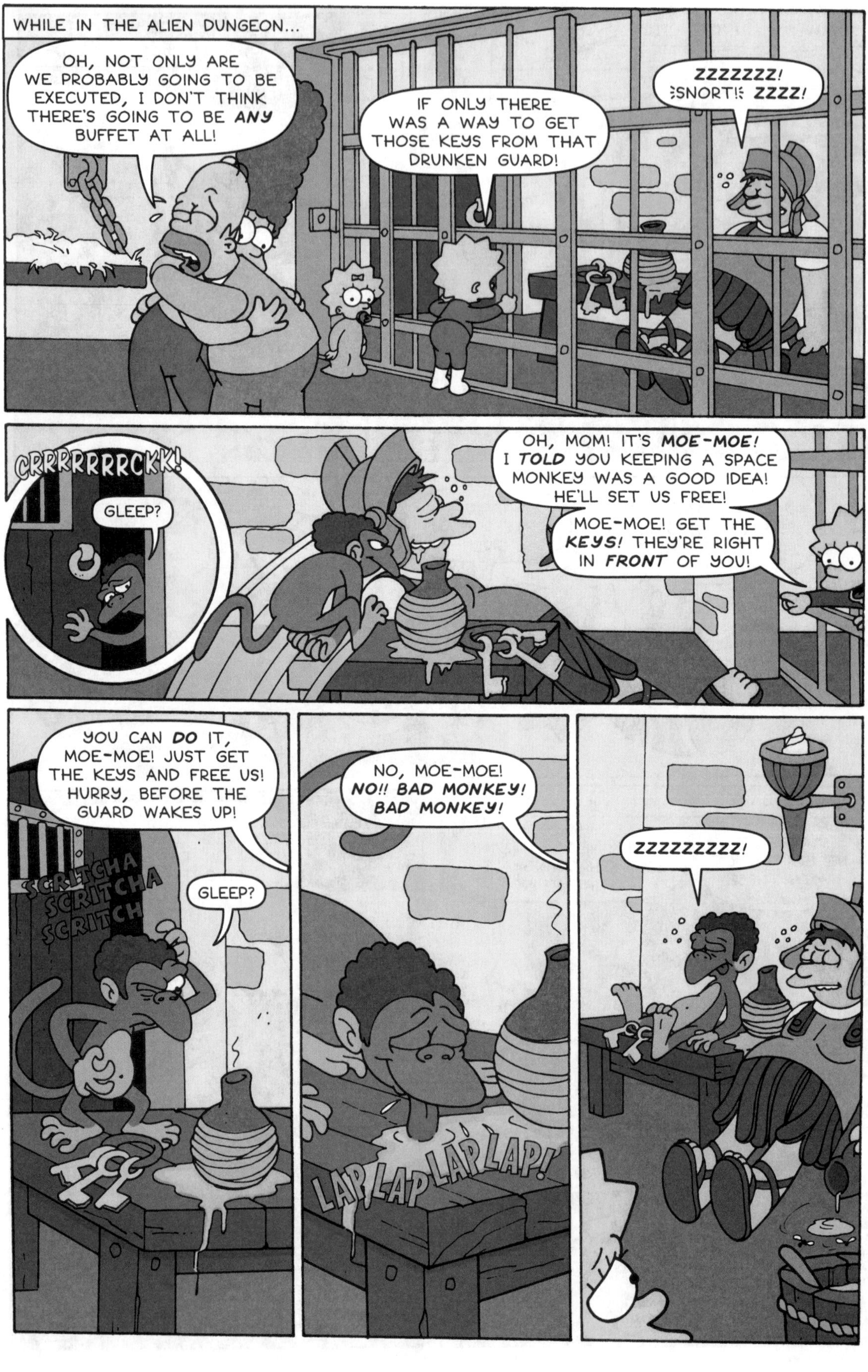
WHILE IN THE ALIEN DUNGEON...
OH, NOT ONLY ARE WE PROBABLY GOING TO BE EXECUTED, I DON'T THINK THERE'S GOING TO BE ANY BUFFET AT ALL!
IF ONLY THERE WAS A WAY TO GET THOSE KEYS FROM THAT DRUNKEN GUARD!
ZZZZZZZ! SNORT! ZZZZ!
CRRRRRRRCKK!
GLEEP?
OH, MOM! IT'S MOE-MOE! I TOLD YOU KEEPING A SPACE MONKEY WAS A GOOD IDEA! HE'LL SET US FREE!
MOE-MOE! GET THE KEYS! THEY'RE RIGHT IN FRONT OF YOU!
YOU CAN DO IT, MOE-MOE! JUST GET THE KEYS AND FREE US! HURRY, BEFORE THE GUARD WAKES UP!
SCRITCHA SCRITCHA SCRITCH
GLEEP?
NO, MOE-MOE! NO!! BAD MONKEY! BAD MONKEY!
LAP LAP LAP LAP!
ZZZZZZZZZ!

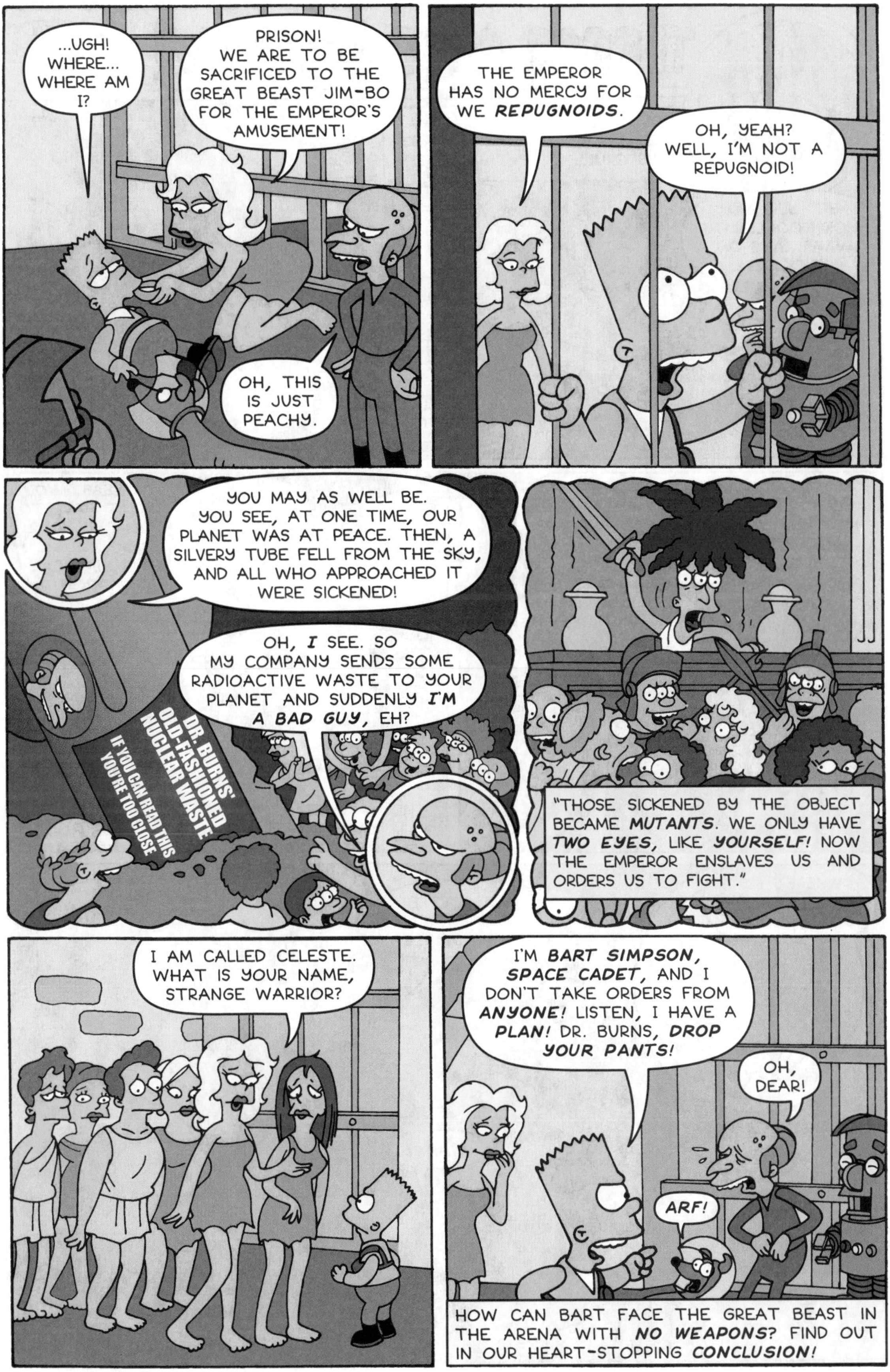
...UGH! WHERE... WHERE AM I?
PRISON! WE ARE TO BE SACRIFICED TO THE GREAT BEAST JIM-BO FOR THE EMPEROR'S AMUSEMENT!
OH, THIS IS JUST PEACHY.
THE EMPEROR HAS NO MERCY FOR WE REPUGNOIDS.
OH, YEAH? WELL, I'M NOT A REPUGNOID!
YOU MAY AS WELL BE. YOU SEE, AT ONE TIME, OUR PLANET WAS AT PEACE. THEN, A SILVERY TUBE FELL FROM THE SKY, AND ALL WHO APPROACHED IT WERE SICKENED!
DR. BURNS' OLD-FASHIONED NUCLEAR WASTE
IF YOU CAN READ THIS YOU'RE TOO CLOSE
OH, I SEE. SO MY COMPANY SENDS SOME RADIOACTIVE WASTE TO YOUR PLANET AND SUDDENLY I'M A BAD GUY, EH?
"THOSE SICKENED BY THE OBJECT BECAME MUTANTS. WE ONLY HAVE TWO EYES, LIKE YOURSELF! NOW THE EMPEROR ENSLAVES US AND ORDERS US TO FIGHT."
I AM CALLED CELESTE. WHAT IS YOUR NAME, STRANGE WARRIOR?
I'M BART SIMPSON, SPACE CADET, AND I DON'T TAKE ORDERS FROM ANYONE! LISTEN, I HAVE A PLAN! DR. BURNS, DROP YOUR PANTS!
OH, DEAR!
ARF!
HOW CAN BART FACE THE GREAT BEAST IN THE ARENA WITH NO WEAPONS? FIND OUT IN OUR HEART-STOPPING CONCLUSION!

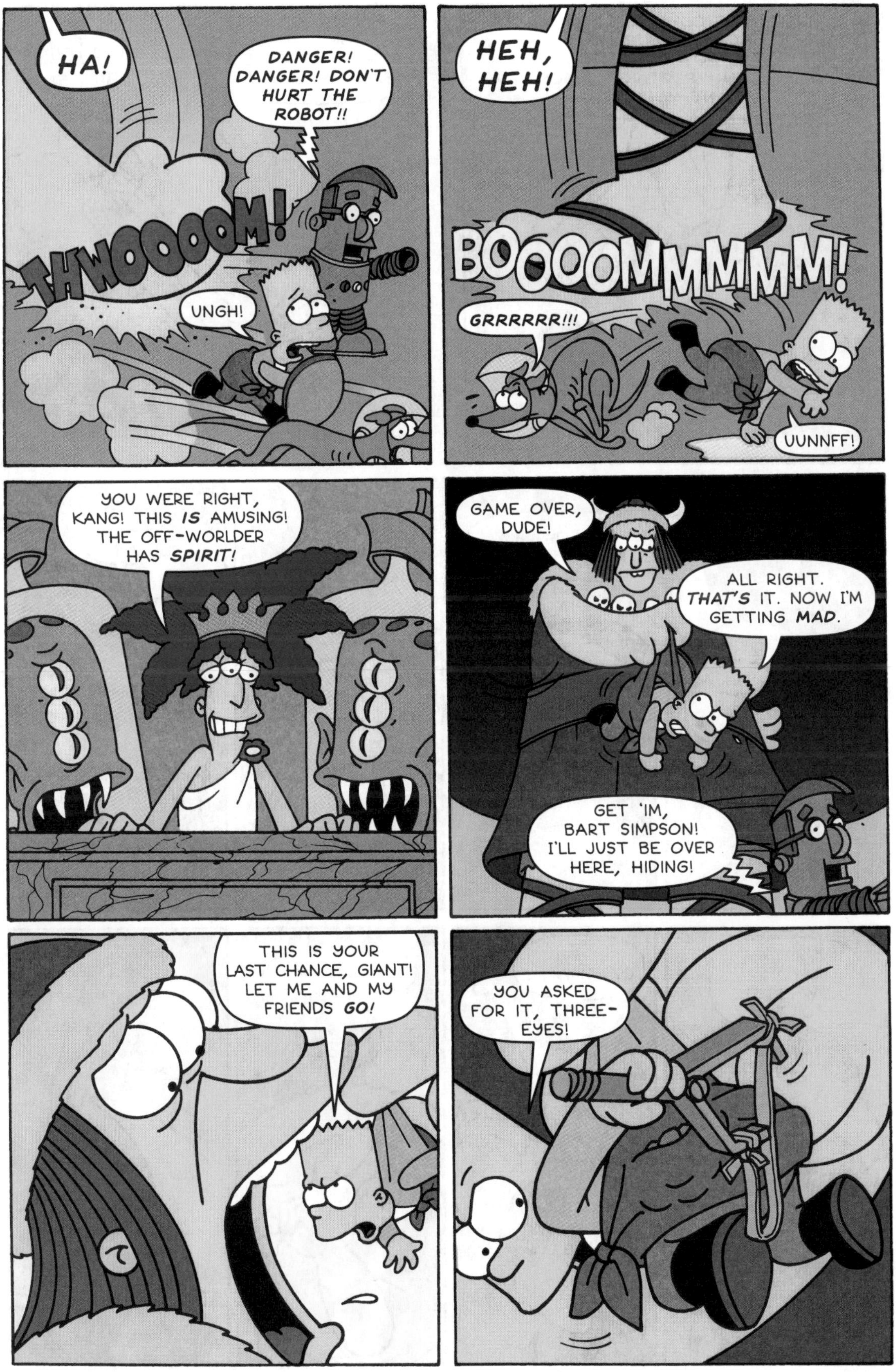
HA!
DANGER! DANGER! DON'T HURT THE ROBOT!!
THWOOOOOM!
UNGH!
HEH, HEH!
BOOOOMMMMMM!
GRRRRRR!!!
UUNNFF!
YOU WERE RIGHT, KANG! THIS *IS* AMUSING! THE OFF-WORLDER HAS *SPIRIT*!
GAME OVER, DUDE!
ALL RIGHT. *THAT'S* IT. NOW I'M GETTING *MAD*.
GET 'IM, BART SIMPSON! I'LL JUST BE OVER HERE, HIDING!
THIS IS YOUR LAST CHANCE, GIANT! LET ME AND MY FRIENDS *GO*!
YOU ASKED FOR IT, THREE-EYES!

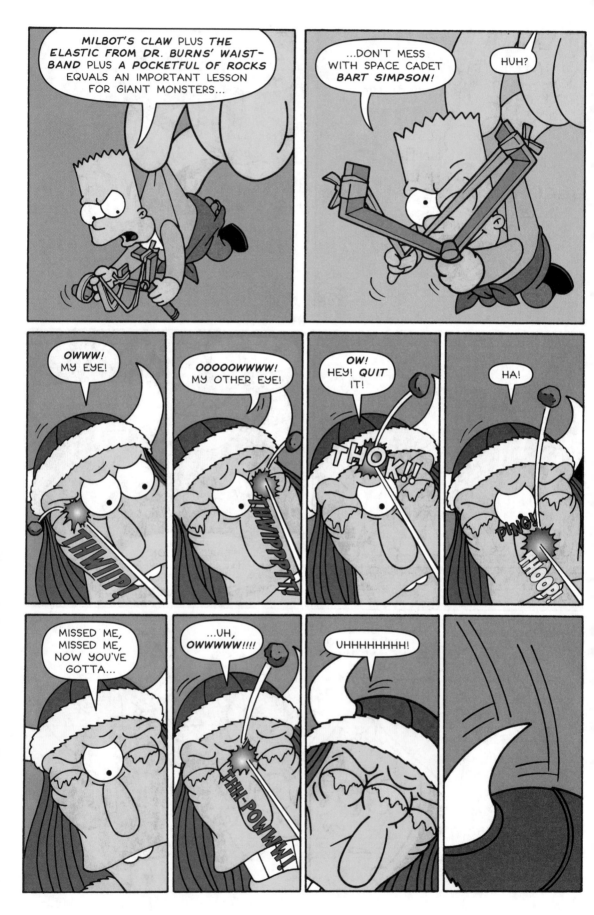

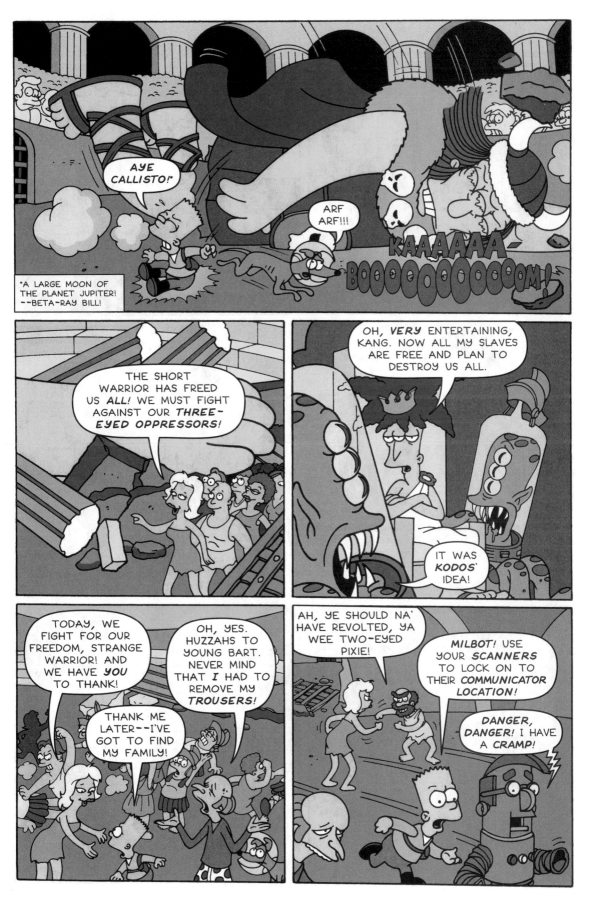

AYE CALLISTO!*

ARF ARF!!!

KAAAAAAA BOOOOOOOOOOOOM!

*A LARGE MOON OF THE PLANET JUPITER! --BETA-RAY BILL!

THE SHORT WARRIOR HAS FREED US **ALL**! WE MUST FIGHT AGAINST OUR **THREE-EYED OPPRESSORS**!

OH, **VERY** ENTERTAINING, KANG. NOW ALL MY SLAVES ARE FREE AND PLAN TO DESTROY US ALL.

IT WAS **KODOS'** IDEA!

TODAY, WE FIGHT FOR OUR FREEDOM, STRANGE WARRIOR! AND WE HAVE **YOU** TO THANK!

OH, YES. HUZZAHS TO YOUNG BART. NEVER MIND THAT **I** HAD TO REMOVE MY **TROUSERS**!

THANK ME LATER--I'VE GOT TO FIND MY FAMILY!

AH, YE SHOULD NA' HAVE REVOLTED, YA WEE TWO-EYED PIXIE!

MILBOT! USE YOUR **SCANNERS** TO LOCK ON TO THEIR **COMMUNICATOR** LOCATION!

DANGER, DANGER! I HAVE A **CRAMP**!

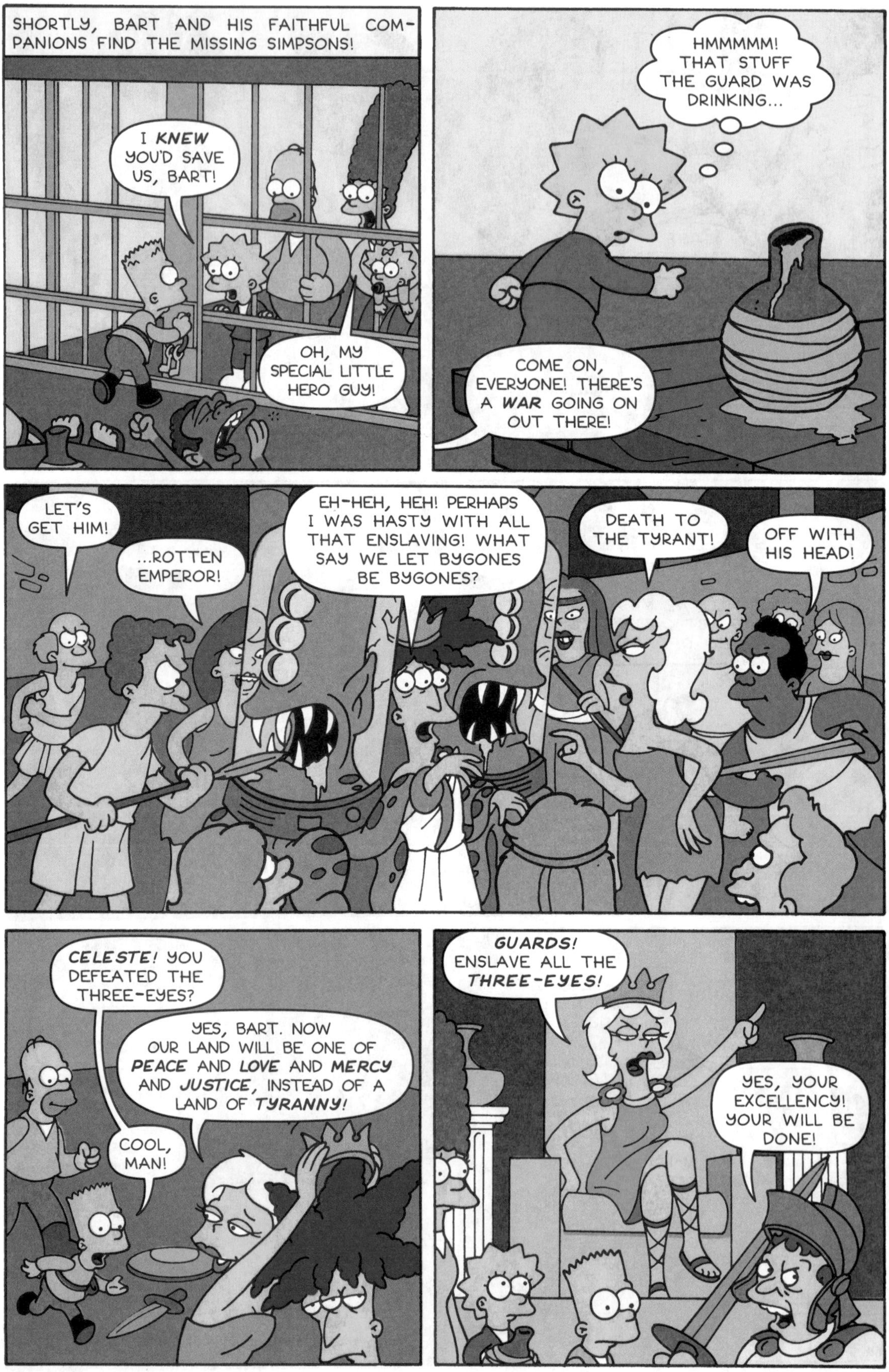
SHORTLY, BART AND HIS FAITHFUL COMPANIONS FIND THE MISSING SIMPSONS!
I KNEW YOU'D SAVE US, BART!
OH, MY SPECIAL LITTLE HERO GUY!
HMMMMM! THAT STUFF THE GUARD WAS DRINKING...
COME ON, EVERYONE! THERE'S A WAR GOING ON OUT THERE!
LET'S GET HIM!
...ROTTEN EMPEROR!
EH-HEH, HEH! PERHAPS I WAS HASTY WITH ALL THAT ENSLAVING! WHAT SAY WE LET BYGONES BE BYGONES?
DEATH TO THE TYRANT!
OFF WITH HIS HEAD!
CELESTE! YOU DEFEATED THE THREE-EYES?
YES, BART. NOW OUR LAND WILL BE ONE OF PEACE AND LOVE AND MERCY AND JUSTICE, INSTEAD OF A LAND OF TYRANNY!
COOL, MAN!
GUARDS! ENSLAVE ALL THE THREE-EYES!
YES, YOUR EXCELLENCY! YOUR WILL BE DONE!

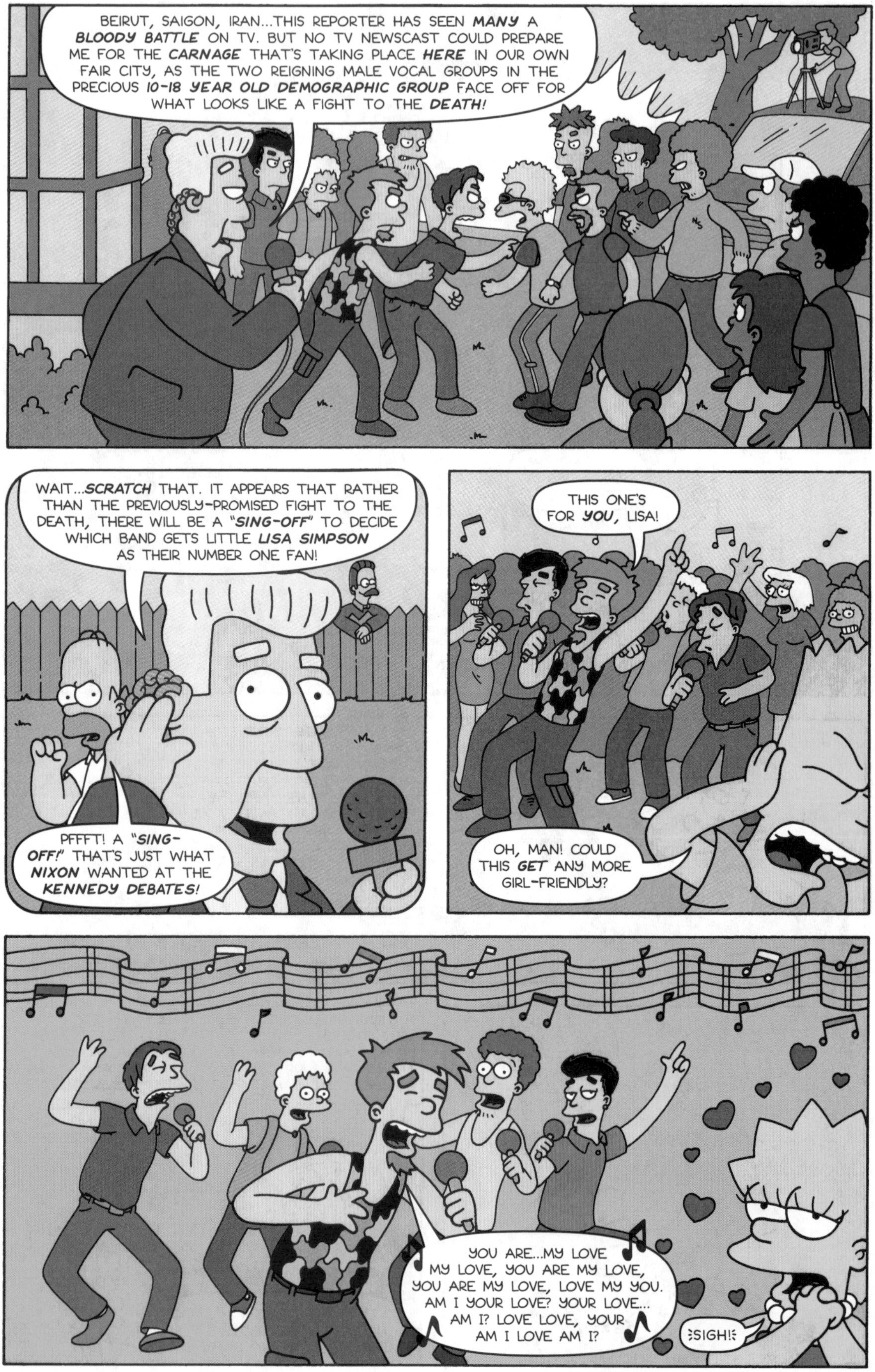
BEIRUT, SAIGON, IRAN...THIS REPORTER HAS SEEN **MANY** A **BLOODY BATTLE** ON TV. BUT NO TV NEWSCAST COULD PREPARE ME FOR THE **CARNAGE** THAT'S TAKING PLACE **HERE** IN OUR OWN FAIR CITY, AS THE TWO REIGNING MALE VOCAL GROUPS IN THE PRECIOUS **10-18 YEAR OLD DEMOGRAPHIC GROUP** FACE OFF FOR WHAT LOOKS LIKE A FIGHT TO THE **DEATH**!
WAIT...**SCRATCH** THAT. IT APPEARS THAT RATHER THAN THE PREVIOUSLY-PROMISED FIGHT TO THE DEATH, THERE WILL BE A "**SING-OFF**" TO DECIDE WHICH BAND GETS LITTLE **LISA SIMPSON** AS THEIR NUMBER ONE FAN!
PFFFT! A "**SING-OFF!**" THAT'S JUST WHAT **NIXON** WANTED AT THE **KENNEDY DEBATES**!
THIS ONE'S FOR **YOU**, LISA!
OH, MAN! COULD THIS **GET** ANY MORE GIRL-FRIENDLY?
YOU ARE...MY LOVE MY LOVE, YOU ARE MY LOVE, YOU ARE MY LOVE, LOVE MY YOU. AM I YOUR LOVE? YOUR LOVE... AM I? LOVE LOVE, YOUR AM I LOVE AM I?
SIGH!

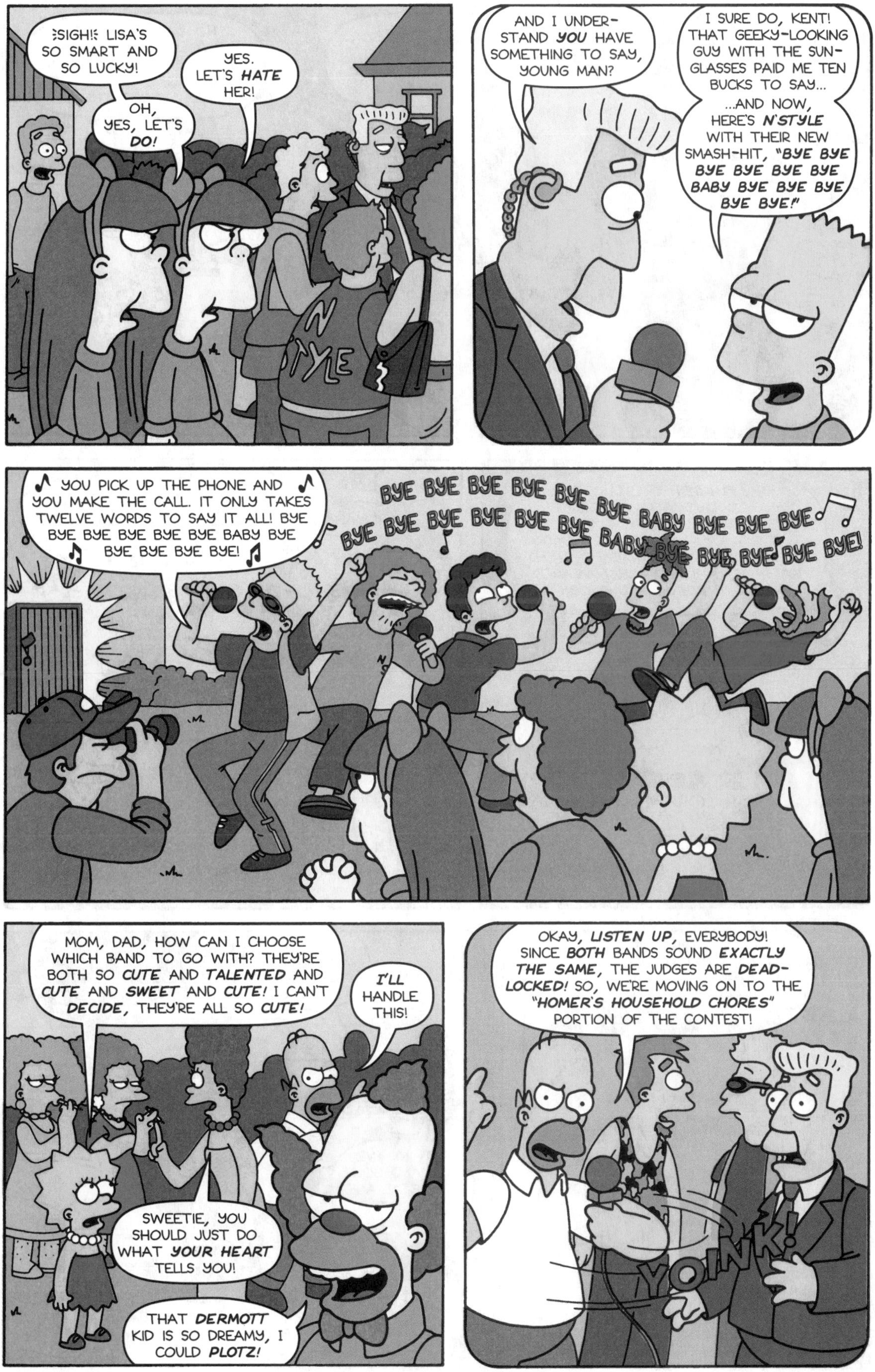

SIGH! LISA'S SO SMART AND SO LUCKY!
YES. LET'S HATE HER!
OH, YES, LET'S DO!
N STYLE
AND I UNDER-STAND YOU HAVE SOMETHING TO SAY, YOUNG MAN?
I SURE DO, KENT! THAT GEEKY-LOOKING GUY WITH THE SUN-GLASSES PAID ME TEN BUCKS TO SAY...
...AND NOW, HERE'S N'STYLE WITH THEIR NEW SMASH-HIT, "BYE BYE BYE BYE BYE BYE BABY BYE BYE BYE BYE BYE!"
♪ YOU PICK UP THE PHONE AND YOU MAKE THE CALL. IT ONLY TAKES TWELVE WORDS TO SAY IT ALL! BYE BYE BYE BYE BYE BYE BABY BYE BYE BYE BYE BYE! ♪
BYE BYE BYE BYE BYE BYE BABY BYE BYE BYE
BYE BYE BYE BYE BYE BYE BABY BYE BYE BYE BYE BYE!
MOM, DAD, HOW CAN I CHOOSE WHICH BAND TO GO WITH? THEY'RE BOTH SO CUTE AND TALENTED AND CUTE AND SWEET AND CUTE! I CAN'T DECIDE, THEY'RE ALL SO CUTE!
I'LL HANDLE THIS!
SWEETIE, YOU SHOULD JUST DO WHAT YOUR HEART TELLS YOU!
THAT DERMOTT KID IS SO DREAMY, I COULD PLOTZ!
OKAY, LISTEN UP, EVERYBODY! SINCE BOTH BANDS SOUND EXACTLY THE SAME, THE JUDGES ARE DEAD-LOCKED! SO, WE'RE MOVING ON TO THE "HOMER'S HOUSEHOLD CHORES" PORTION OF THE CONTEST!
YOINK!

GAIL SIMONE
RECIPE

DAN DECARLO
LUSCIOUS LAYOUTS

MIKE ROTE
ALL-PURPOSE ART

KAREN BATES
CREAMY COLORS/LUMPY LETTERS

BILL MORRISON
HEAD CHEF

MATT GROENING
TOP NUT

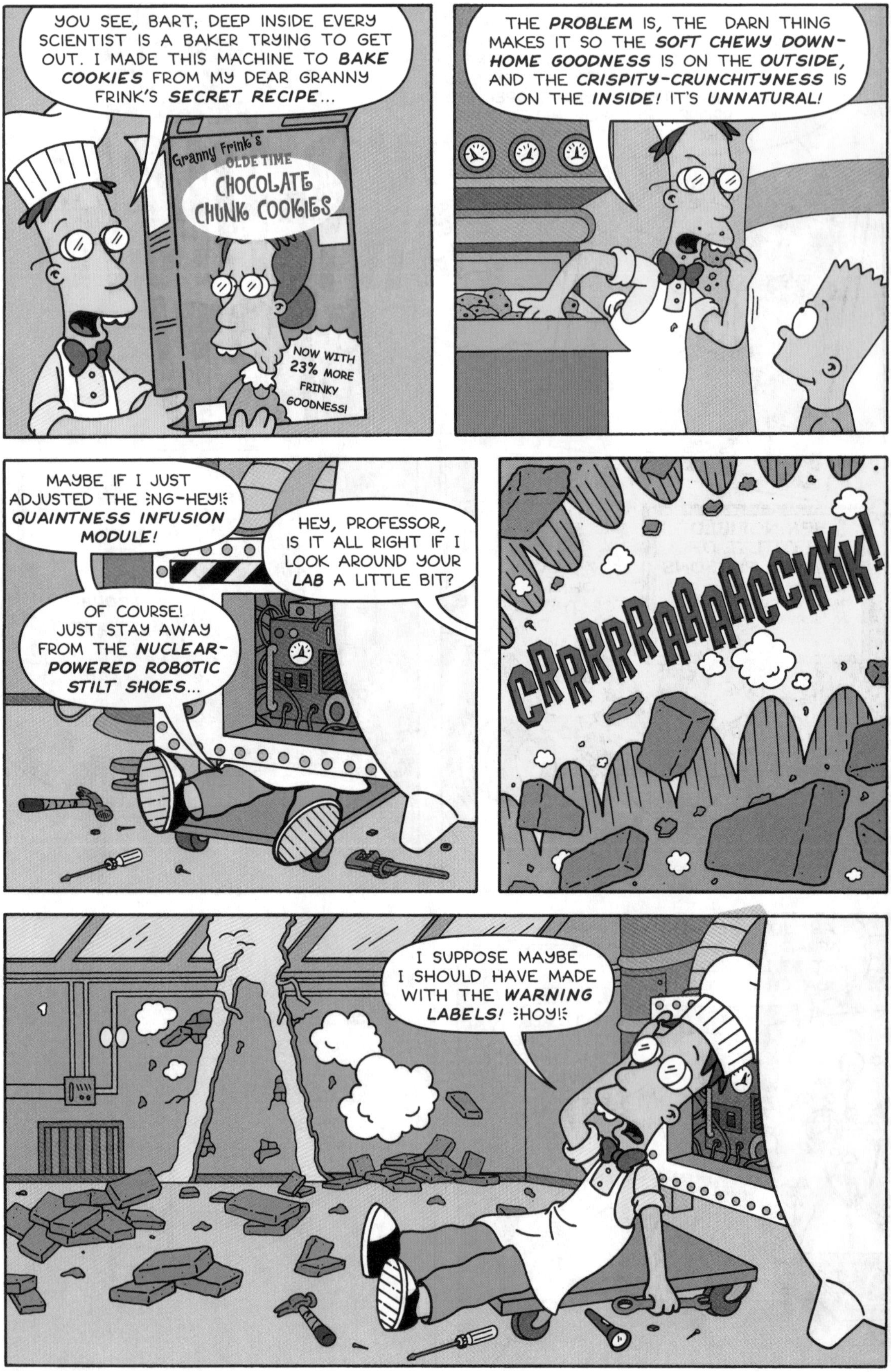
YOU SEE, BART; DEEP INSIDE EVERY SCIENTIST IS A BAKER TRYING TO GET OUT. I MADE THIS MACHINE TO BAKE COOKIES FROM MY DEAR GRANNY FRINK'S SECRET RECIPE...
Granny Frink's OLDE TIME CHOCOLATE CHUNK COOKIES
NOW WITH 23% MORE FRINKY GOODNESS!
THE PROBLEM IS, THE DARN THING MAKES IT SO THE SOFT CHEWY DOWN-HOME GOODNESS IS ON THE OUTSIDE, AND THE CRISPITY-CRUNCHITYNESS IS ON THE INSIDE! IT'S UNNATURAL!
MAYBE IF I JUST ADJUSTED THE NG-HEY! QUAINTNESS INFUSION MODULE!
HEY, PROFESSOR, IS IT ALL RIGHT IF I LOOK AROUND YOUR LAB A LITTLE BIT?
OF COURSE! JUST STAY AWAY FROM THE NUCLEAR-POWERED ROBOTIC STILT SHOES...
CRRRRRAAAACCKKK!
I SUPPOSE MAYBE I SHOULD HAVE MADE WITH THE WARNING LABELS! HOY!

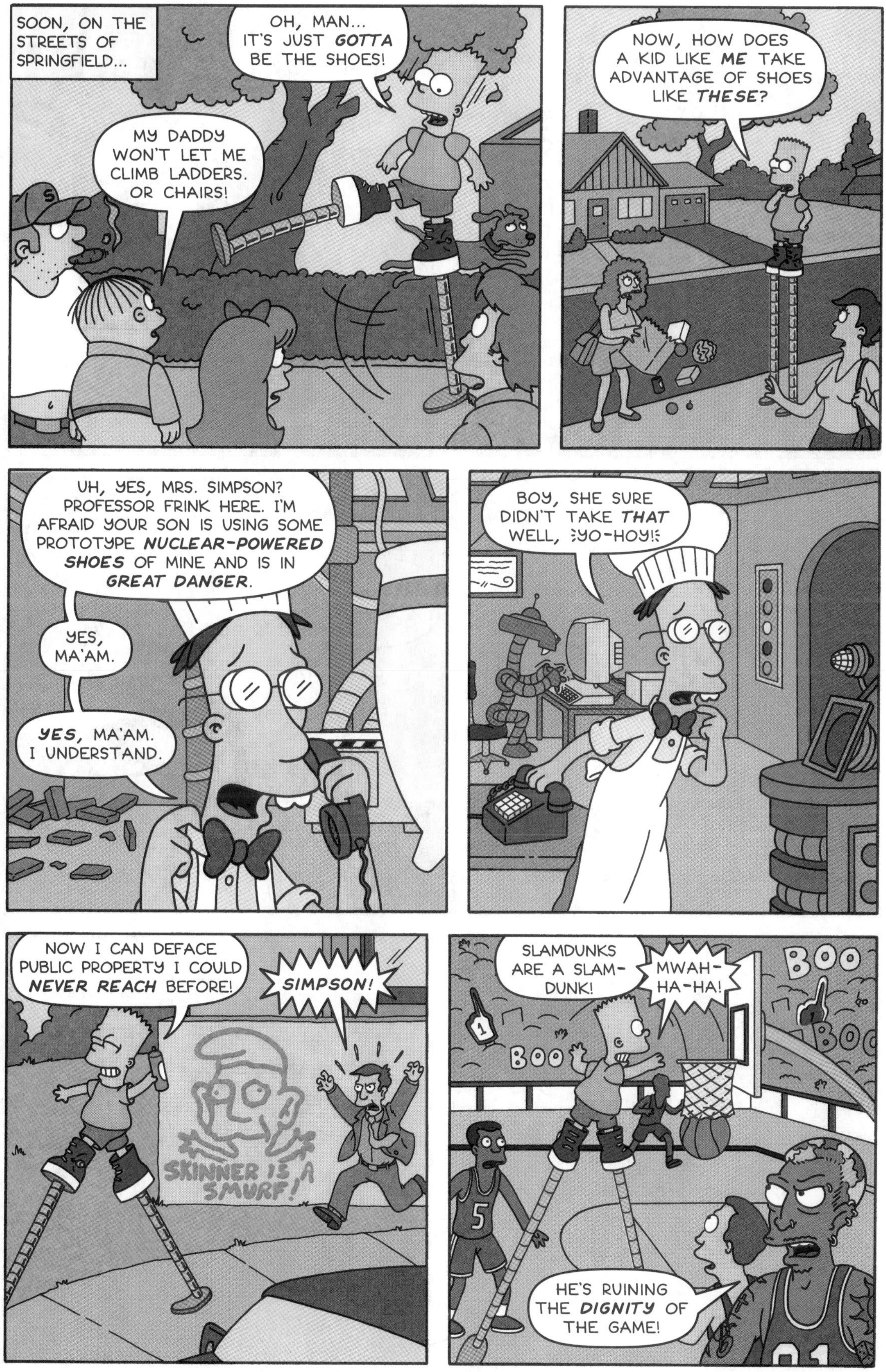
SOON, ON THE STREETS OF SPRINGFIELD...
OH, MAN... IT'S JUST GOTTA BE THE SHOES!
MY DADDY WON'T LET ME CLIMB LADDERS. OR CHAIRS!
NOW, HOW DOES A KID LIKE ME TAKE ADVANTAGE OF SHOES LIKE THESE?
UH, YES, MRS. SIMPSON? PROFESSOR FRINK HERE. I'M AFRAID YOUR SON IS USING SOME PROTOTYPE NUCLEAR-POWERED SHOES OF MINE AND IS IN GREAT DANGER.
YES, MA'AM.
YES, MA'AM. I UNDERSTAND.
BOY, SHE SURE DIDN'T TAKE THAT WELL, YO-HOY!
NOW I CAN DEFACE PUBLIC PROPERTY I COULD NEVER REACH BEFORE!
SIMPSON!
SKINNER IS A SMURF!
SLAMDUNKS ARE A SLAM-DUNK!
MWAH-HA-HA!
BOO
BOO
BOO
HE'S RUINING THE DIGNITY OF THE GAME!

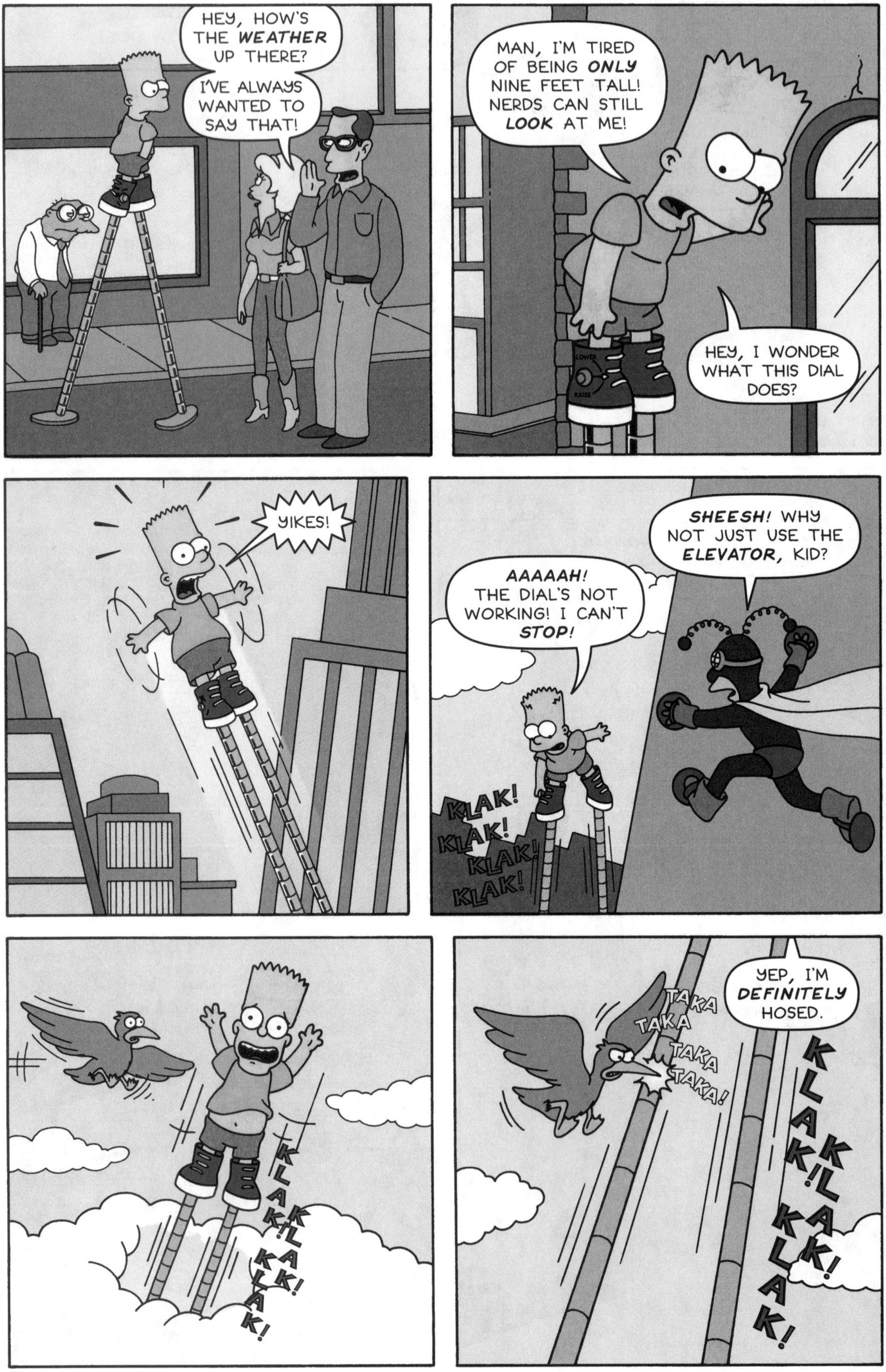

HEY, HOW'S THE **WEATHER** UP THERE?
I'VE ALWAYS WANTED TO SAY THAT!
MAN, I'M TIRED OF BEING **ONLY** NINE FEET TALL! NERDS CAN STILL **LOOK** AT ME!
LOWER
RAISE
HEY, I WONDER WHAT THIS DIAL DOES?
YIKES!
AAAAAH! THE DIAL'S NOT WORKING! I CAN'T **STOP!**
SHEESH! WHY NOT JUST USE THE **ELEVATOR,** KID?
KLAK! KLAK! KLAK! KLAK!
KLAK! KLAK! KLAK! KLAK!
TAKA TAKA TAKA TAKA!
YEP, I'M **DEFINITELY** HOSED.
KLAK! KLAK! KLAK! KLAK!

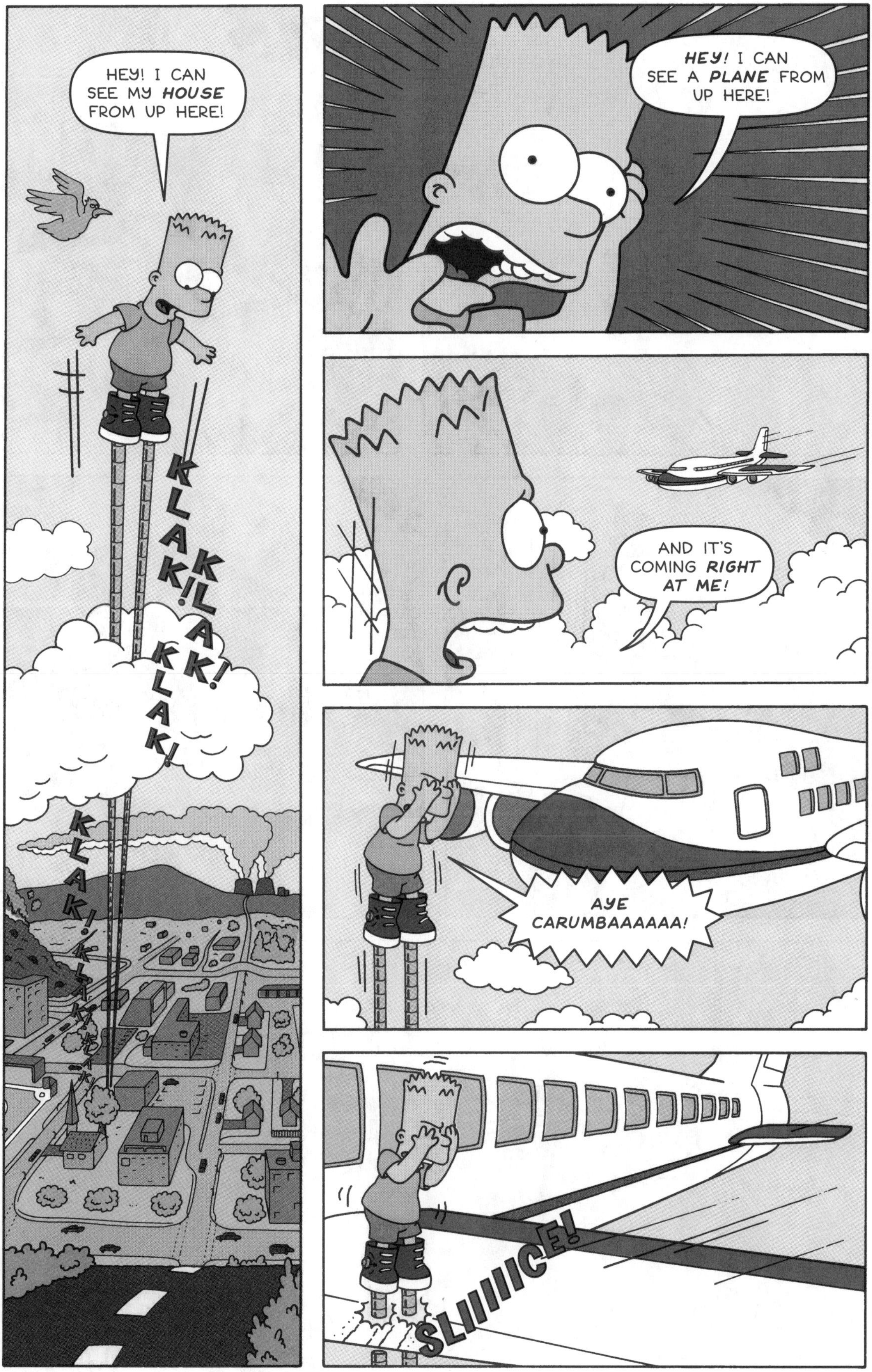
HEY! I CAN SEE MY HOUSE FROM UP HERE!
KLAK! KLAK! KLAK! KLAK! KLAK!
HEY! I CAN SEE A PLANE FROM UP HERE!
AND IT'S COMING RIGHT AT ME!
AYE CARUMBAAAAAAA!
SLIIIIICE!

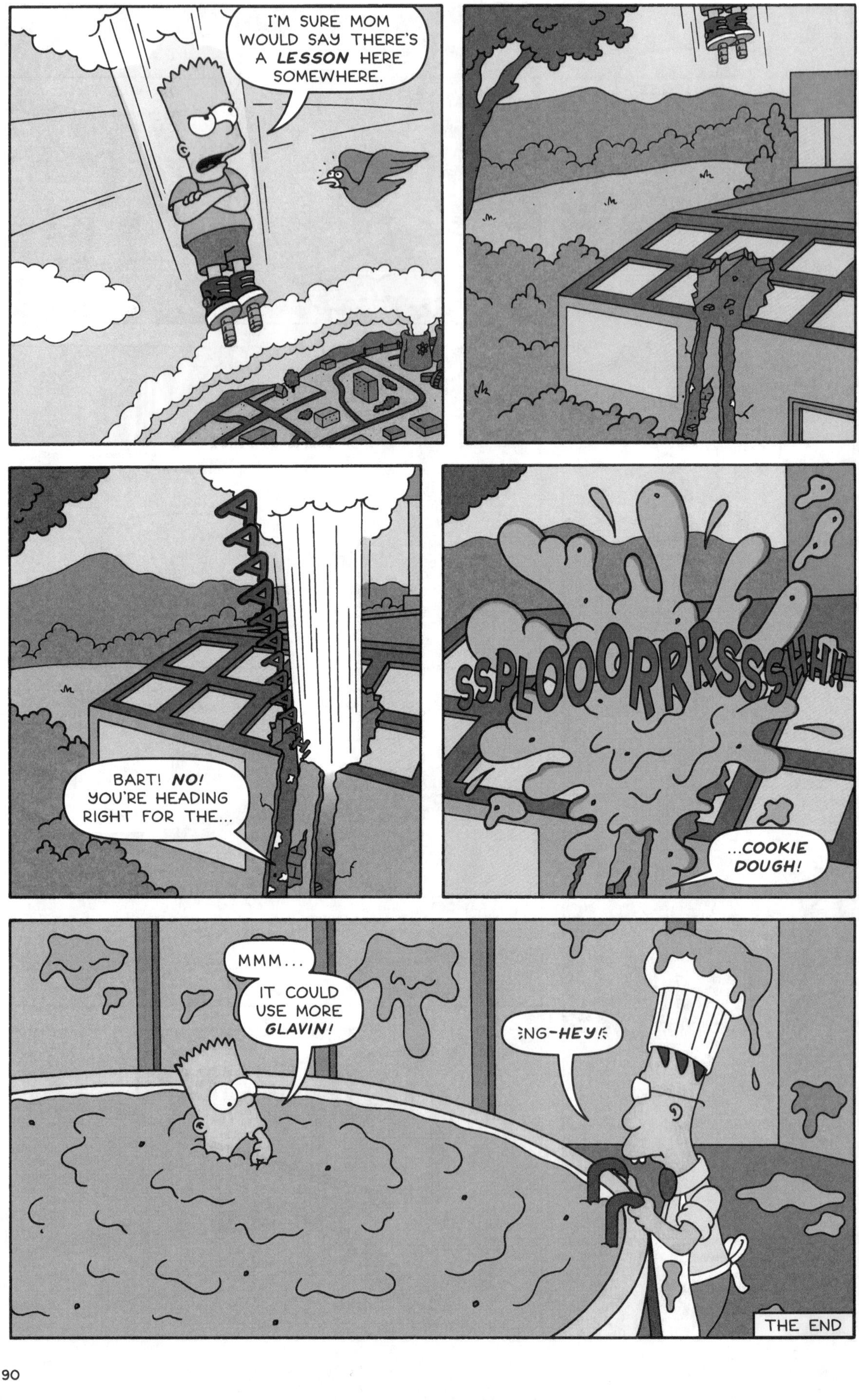

I'M SURE MOM WOULD SAY THERE'S A ***LESSON*** HERE SOMEWHERE.
AAAAAAAAAAAH!
BART! ***NO!*** YOU'RE HEADING RIGHT FOR THE...
SSPLOOORRRSSSHH!!
...***COOKIE DOUGH!***
MMM...
IT COULD USE MORE ***GLAVIN!***
NG-***HEY***
THE END

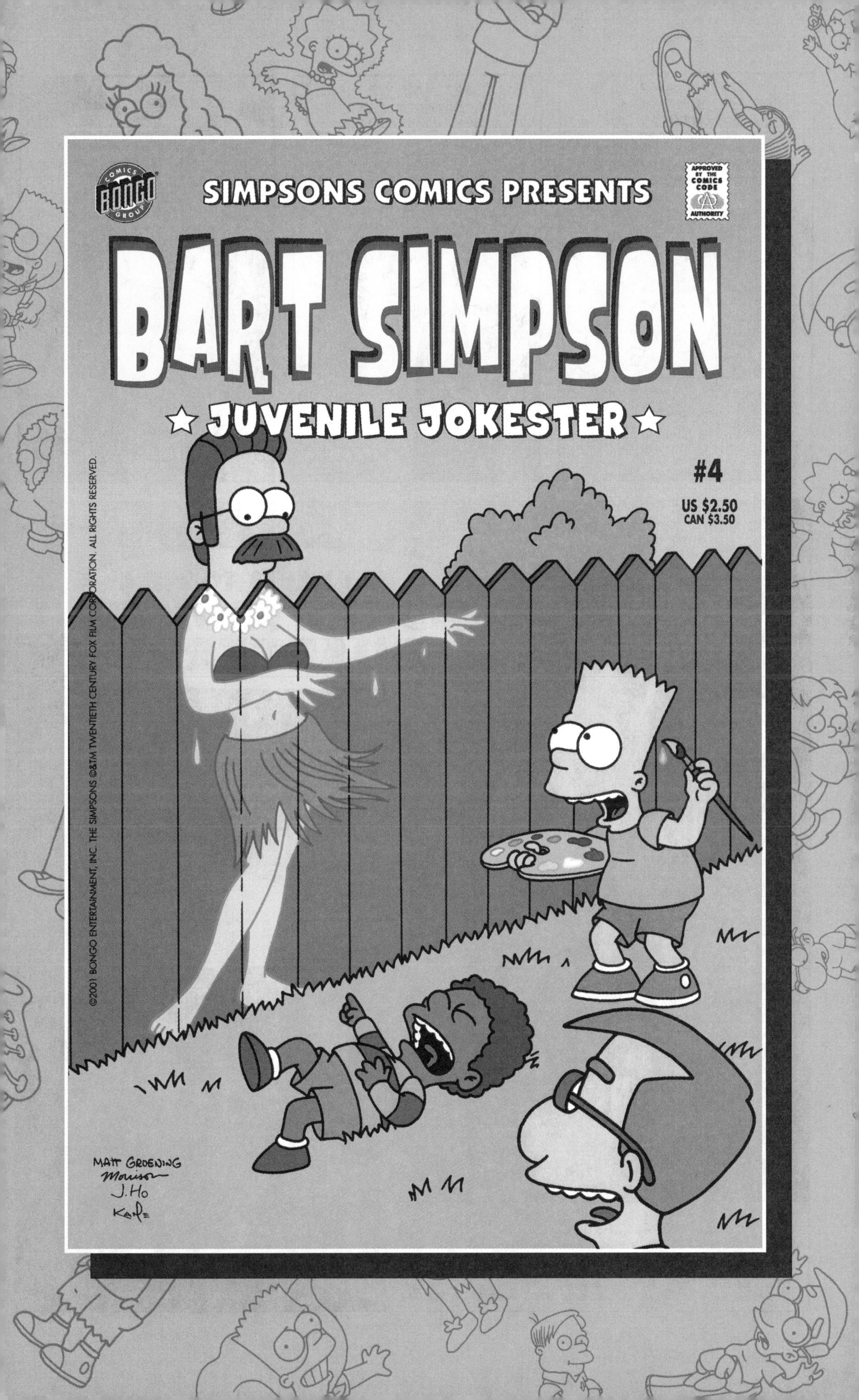

COMICS BONGO GROUP
SIMPSONS COMICS PRESENTS
APPROVED BY THE COMICS CODE AUTHORITY
BART SIMPSON
JUVENILE JOKESTER
#4
US $2.50
CAN $3.50
©2001 BONGO ENTERTAINMENT, INC. THE SIMPSONS ©&TM TWENTIETH CENTURY FOX FILM CORPORATION. ALL RIGHTS RESERVED.
MATT GROENING
J. Ho

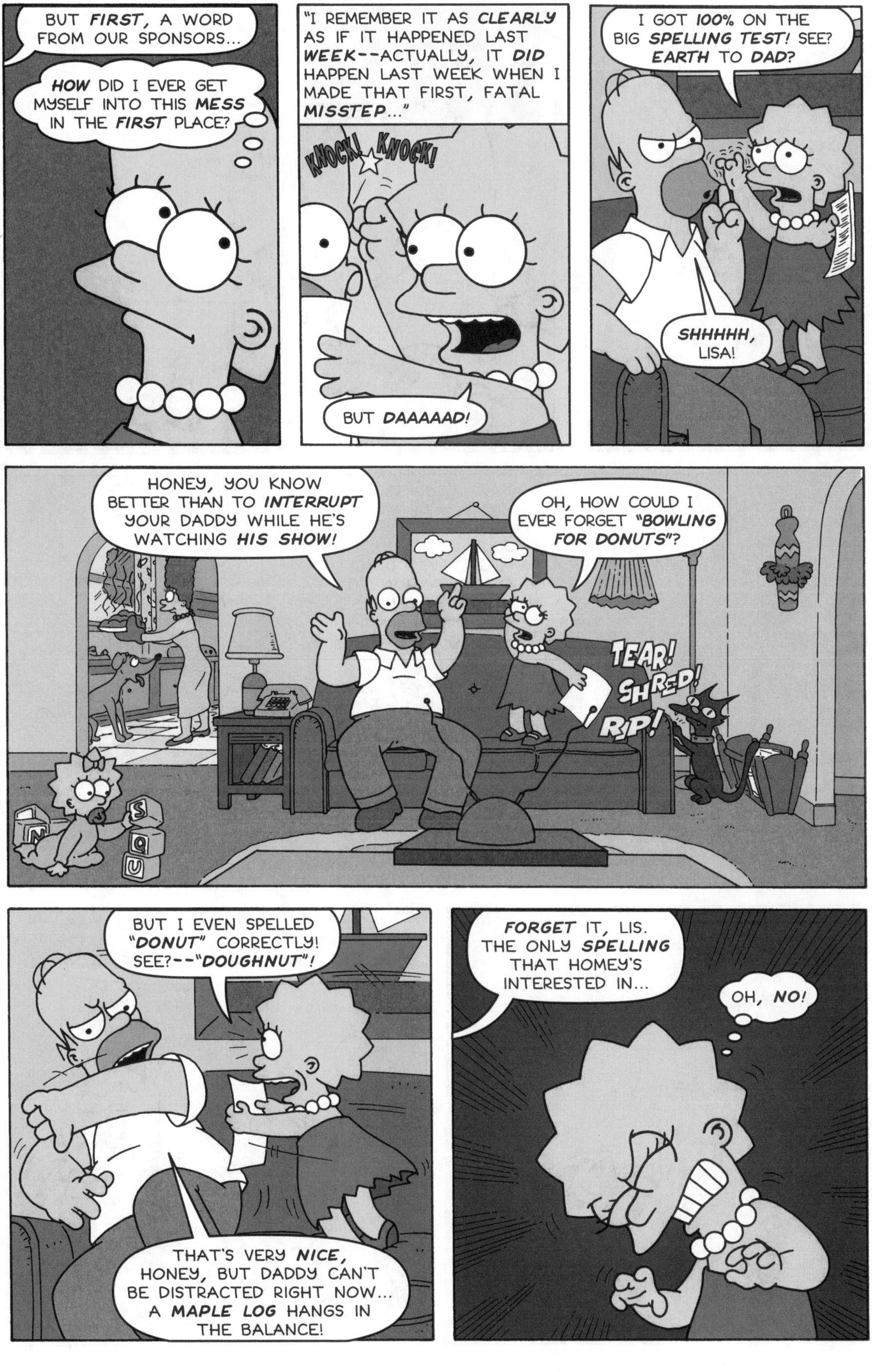
BUT FIRST, A WORD FROM OUR SPONSORS...
HOW DID I EVER GET MYSELF INTO THIS MESS IN THE FIRST PLACE?
"I REMEMBER IT AS CLEARLY AS IF IT HAPPENED LAST WEEK--ACTUALLY, IT DID HAPPEN LAST WEEK WHEN I MADE THAT FIRST, FATAL MISSTEP..."
KNOCK! KNOCK!
BUT DAAAAAD!
I GOT 100% ON THE BIG SPELLING TEST! SEE? EARTH TO DAD?
SHHHHH, LISA!
HONEY, YOU KNOW BETTER THAN TO INTERRUPT YOUR DADDY WHILE HE'S WATCHING HIS SHOW!
OH, HOW COULD I EVER FORGET "BOWLING FOR DONUTS"?
TEAR! SHRED! RIP!
BUT I EVEN SPELLED "DONUT" CORRECTLY! SEE?--"DOUGHNUT"!
THAT'S VERY NICE, HONEY, BUT DADDY CAN'T BE DISTRACTED RIGHT NOW... A MAPLE LOG HANGS IN THE BALANCE!
FORGET IT, LIS. THE ONLY SPELLING THAT HOMEY'S INTERESTED IN...
OH, NO!

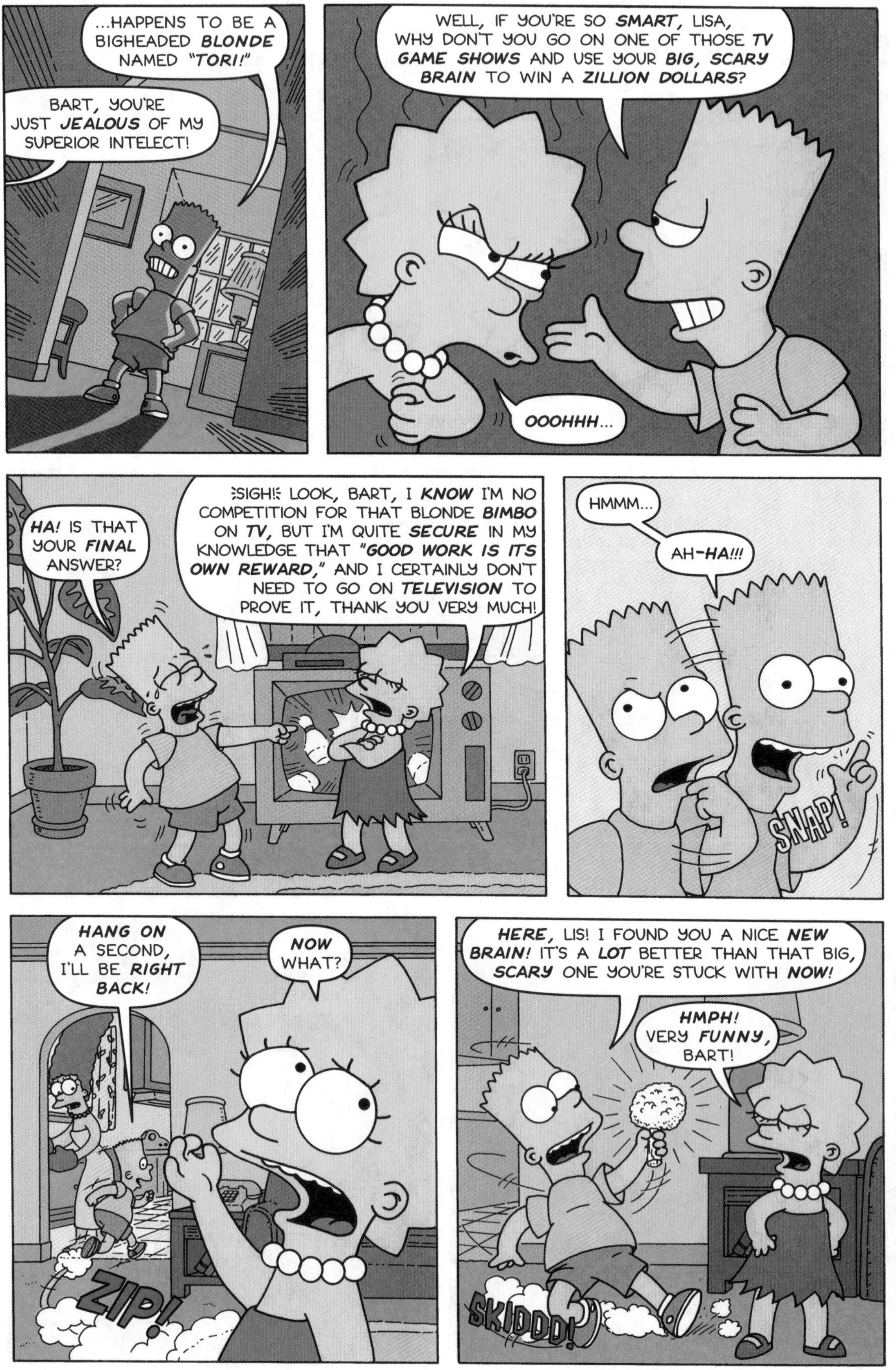

BART, YOU'RE JUST JEALOUS OF MY SUPERIOR INTELECT!
...HAPPENS TO BE A BIGHEADED BLONDE NAMED "TORI!"
WELL, IF YOU'RE SO SMART, LISA, WHY DON'T YOU GO ON ONE OF THOSE TV GAME SHOWS AND USE YOUR BIG, SCARY BRAIN TO WIN A ZILLION DOLLARS?
OOOHHH...
HA! IS THAT YOUR FINAL ANSWER?
:SIGH!: LOOK, BART, I KNOW I'M NO COMPETITION FOR THAT BLONDE BIMBO ON TV, BUT I'M QUITE SECURE IN MY KNOWLEDGE THAT "GOOD WORK IS ITS OWN REWARD," AND I CERTAINLY DON'T NEED TO GO ON TELEVISION TO PROVE IT, THANK YOU VERY MUCH!
HMMM...
AH-HA!!!
SNAP!
HANG ON A SECOND, I'LL BE RIGHT BACK!
NOW WHAT?
ZIP!
HERE, LIS! I FOUND YOU A NICE NEW BRAIN! IT'S A LOT BETTER THAN THAT BIG, SCARY ONE YOU'RE STUCK WITH NOW!
HMPH! VERY FUNNY, BART!
SKIDDD!

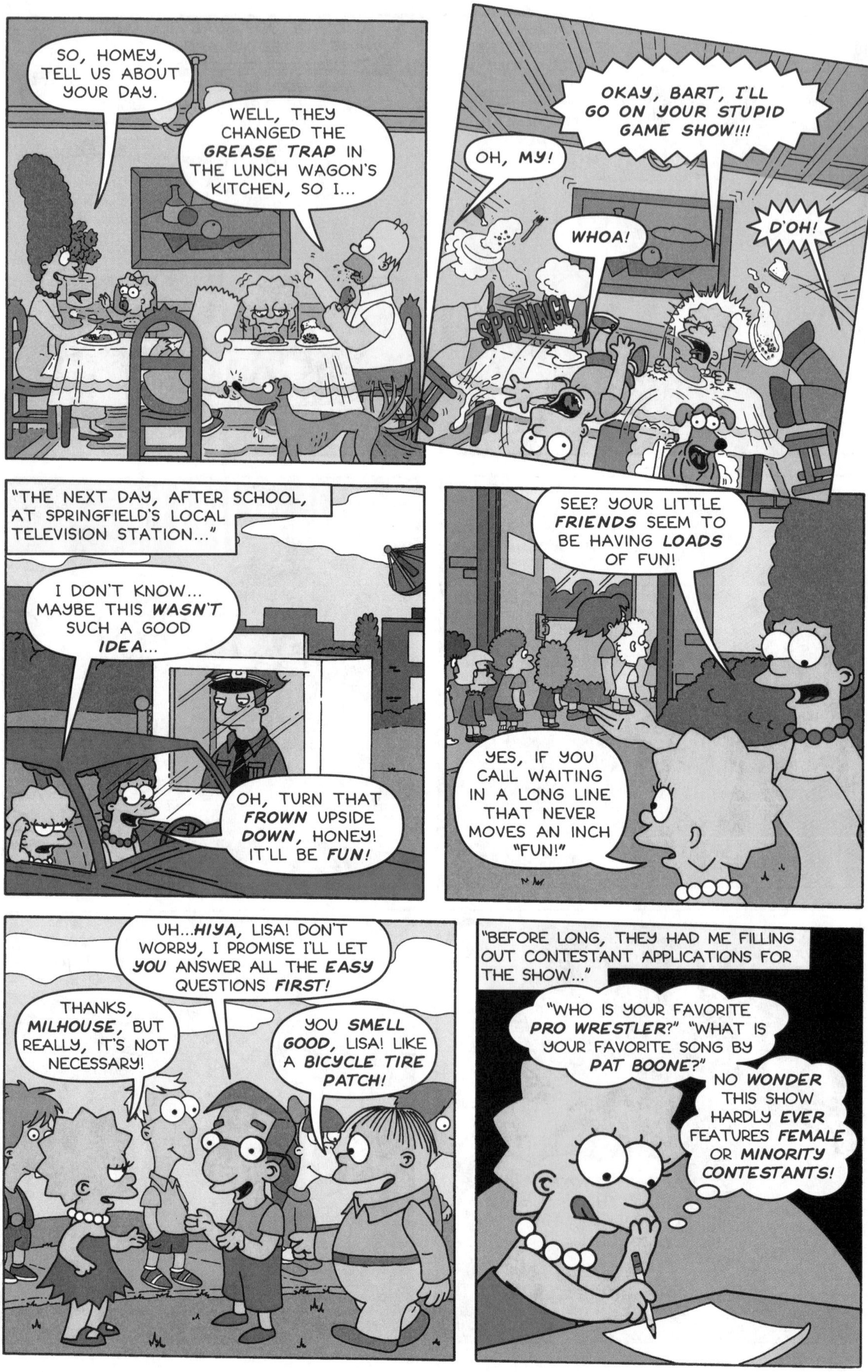

SO, HOMEY, TELL US ABOUT YOUR DAY.
WELL, THEY CHANGED THE **GREASE TRAP** IN THE LUNCH WAGON'S KITCHEN, SO I...
OKAY, BART, I'LL GO ON YOUR STUPID GAME SHOW!!!
OH, **MY**!
WHOA!
D'OH!
SPROING!
"THE NEXT DAY, AFTER SCHOOL, AT SPRINGFIELD'S LOCAL TELEVISION STATION..."
I DON'T KNOW... MAYBE THIS **WASN'T** SUCH A GOOD **IDEA**...
OH, TURN THAT **FROWN** UPSIDE **DOWN**, HONEY! IT'LL BE **FUN**!
SEE? YOUR LITTLE **FRIENDS** SEEM TO BE HAVING **LOADS** OF FUN!
YES, IF YOU CALL WAITING IN A LONG LINE THAT NEVER MOVES AN INCH "FUN!"
UH...**HIYA**, LISA! DON'T WORRY, I PROMISE I'LL LET **YOU** ANSWER ALL THE **EASY** QUESTIONS **FIRST**!
THANKS, **MILHOUSE**, BUT REALLY, IT'S NOT NECESSARY!
YOU **SMELL GOOD**, LISA! LIKE A **BICYCLE TIRE PATCH**!
"BEFORE LONG, THEY HAD ME FILLING OUT CONTESTANT APPLICATIONS FOR THE SHOW..."
"WHO IS YOUR FAVORITE **PRO WRESTLER**?" "WHAT IS YOUR FAVORITE SONG BY **PAT BOONE**?"
NO **WONDER** THIS SHOW HARDLY **EVER** FEATURES **FEMALE** OR **MINORITY CONTESTANTS**!

99

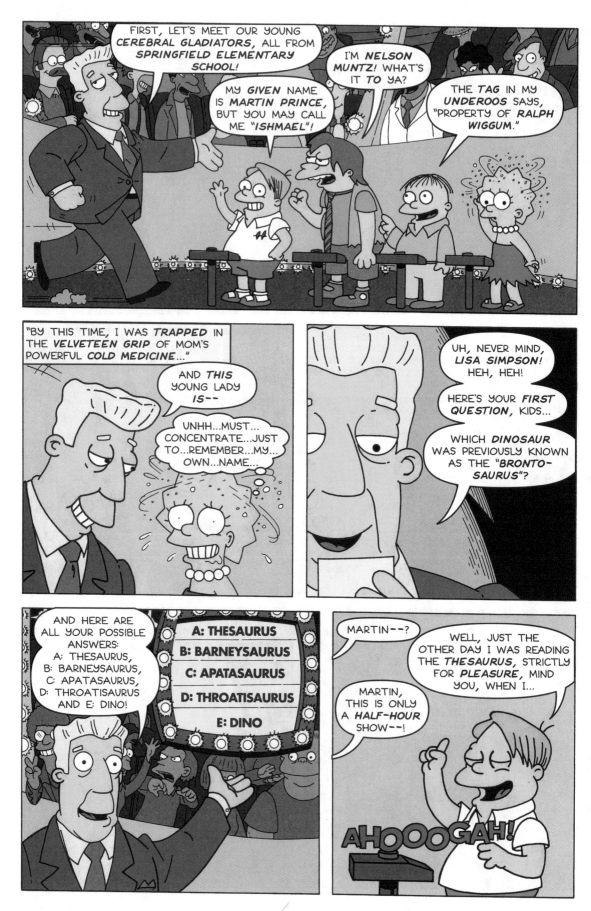

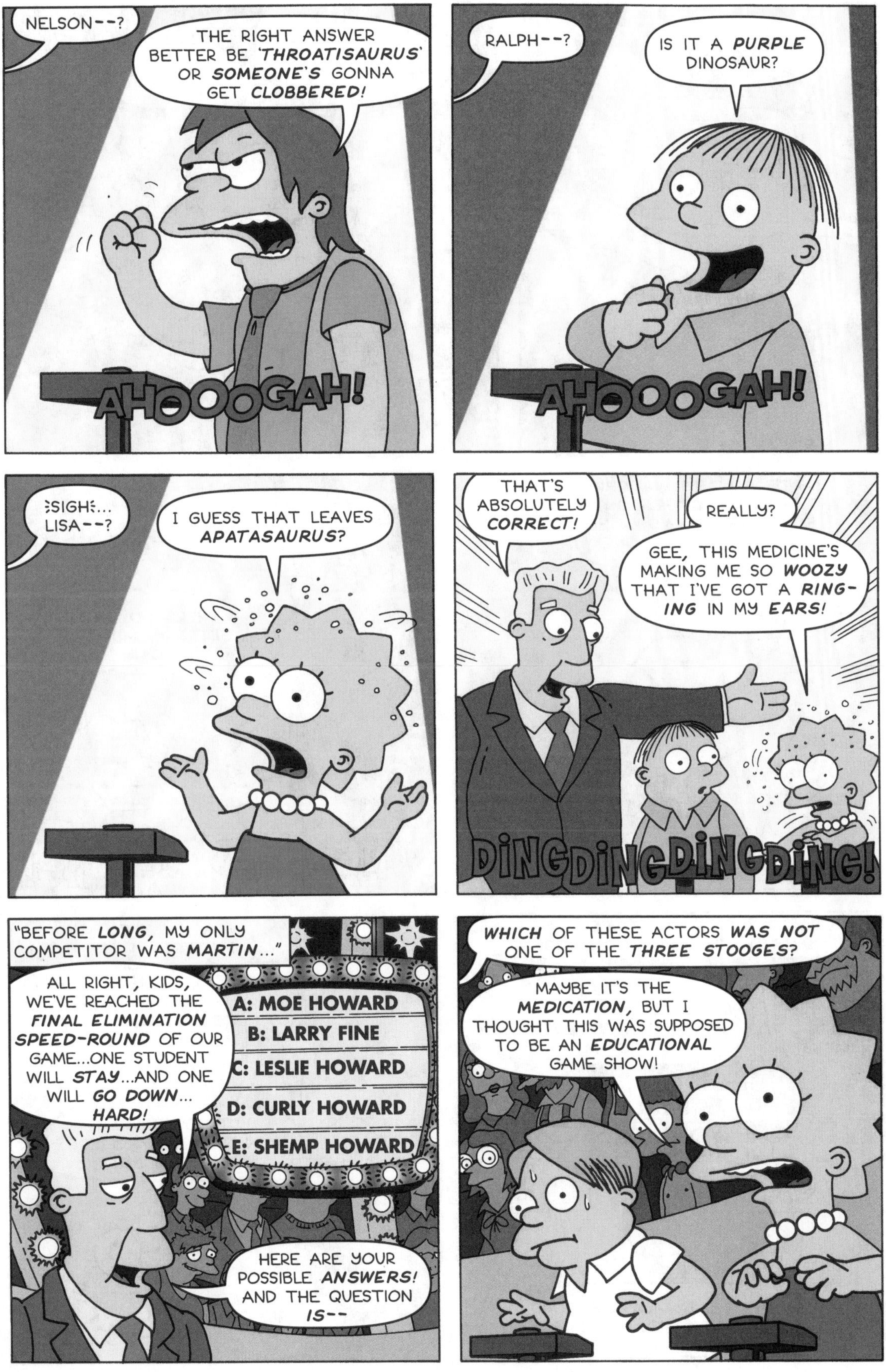
NELSON--?
THE RIGHT ANSWER BETTER BE 'THROATISAURUS' OR SOMEONE'S GONNA GET CLOBBERED!
AHOOOOGAH!
RALPH--?
IS IT A PURPLE DINOSAUR?
AHOOOOGAH!
:SIGH:... LISA--?
I GUESS THAT LEAVES APATASAURUS?
THAT'S ABSOLUTELY CORRECT!
REALLY?
GEE, THIS MEDICINE'S MAKING ME SO WOOZY THAT I'VE GOT A RING-ING IN MY EARS!
DINGDINGDINGDING!
"BEFORE LONG, MY ONLY COMPETITOR WAS MARTIN..."
ALL RIGHT, KIDS, WE'VE REACHED THE FINAL ELIMINATION SPEED-ROUND OF OUR GAME...ONE STUDENT WILL STAY...AND ONE WILL GO DOWN... HARD!
A: MOE HOWARD
B: LARRY FINE
C: LESLIE HOWARD
D: CURLY HOWARD
E: SHEMP HOWARD
HERE ARE YOUR POSSIBLE ANSWERS! AND THE QUESTION IS--
WHICH OF THESE ACTORS WAS NOT ONE OF THE THREE STOOGES?
MAYBE IT'S THE MEDICATION, BUT I THOUGHT THIS WAS SUPPOSED TO BE AN EDUCATIONAL GAME SHOW!

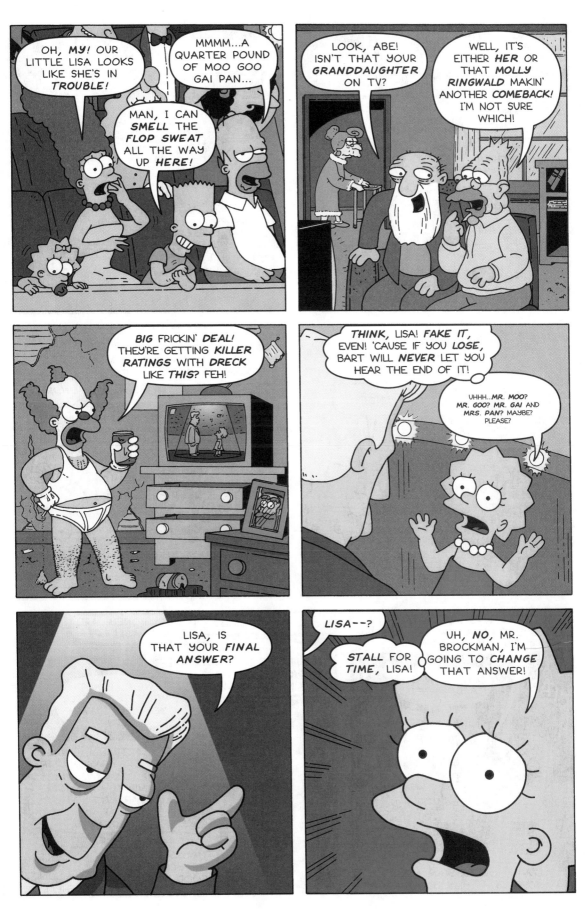

GAIL SIMONE
SODA JERK SCRIPT

DAN DECARLO
LO-CAL LAYOUTS

JASON HO
SIX-PACK PENCILS & FIZZY INKS

CHRIS UNGAR
CARBONATED COLORS

KAREN BATES
LEMON-LIME LETTERS

BILL MORRISON
ALL-NATURAL EDITS

MATT GROENING
BEST BURPS

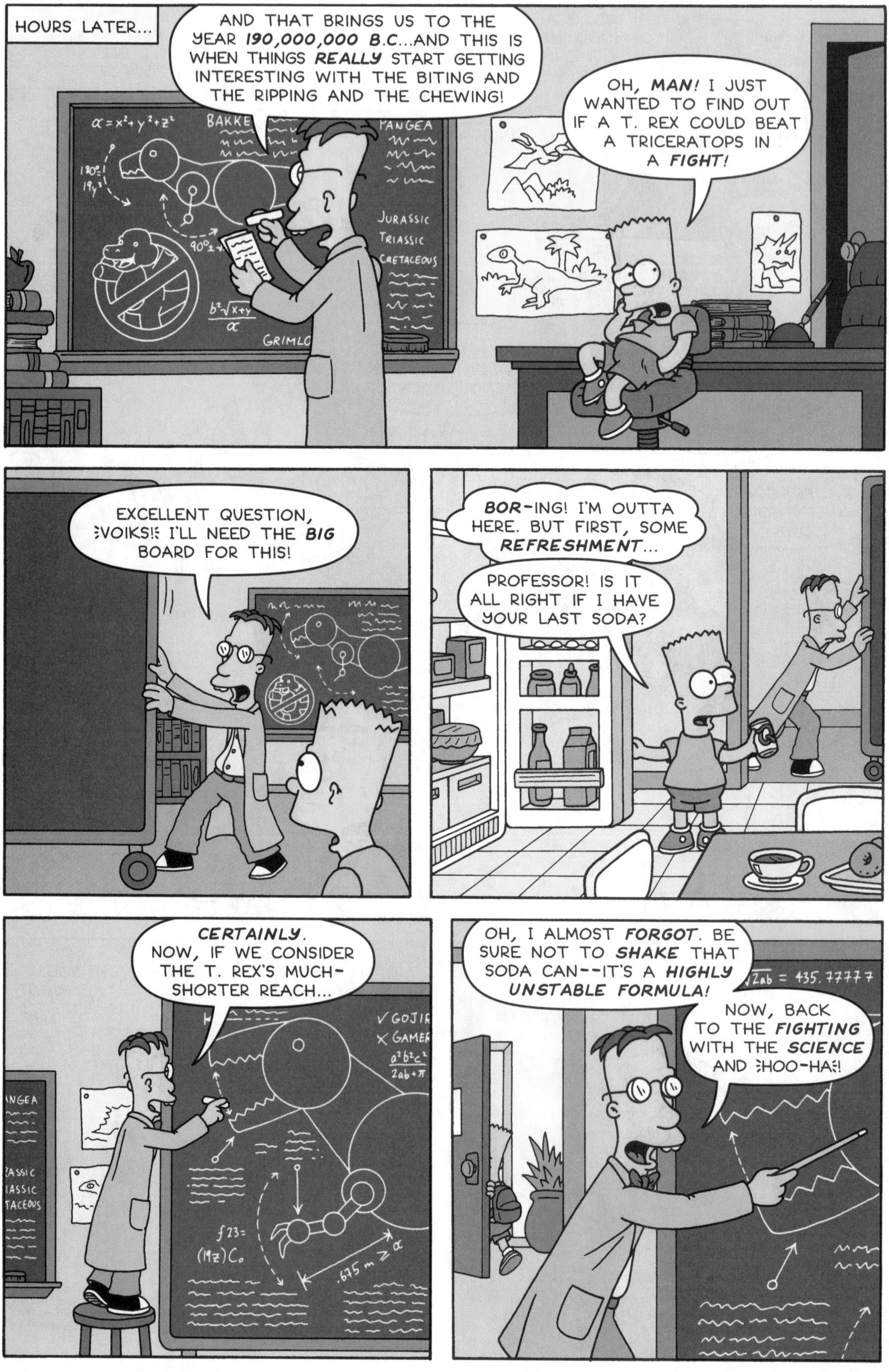
HOURS LATER...
AND THAT BRINGS US TO THE YEAR 190,000,000 B.C...AND THIS IS WHEN THINGS REALLY START GETTING INTERESTING WITH THE BITING AND THE RIPPING AND THE CHEWING!
OH, MAN! I JUST WANTED TO FIND OUT IF A T. REX COULD BEAT A TRICERATOPS IN A FIGHT!
EXCELLENT QUESTION, ⁝VOIKS!⁝ I'LL NEED THE BIG BOARD FOR THIS!
BOR-ING! I'M OUTTA HERE. BUT FIRST, SOME REFRESHMENT...
PROFESSOR! IS IT ALL RIGHT IF I HAVE YOUR LAST SODA?
CERTAINLY. NOW, IF WE CONSIDER THE T. REX'S MUCH-SHORTER REACH...
OH, I ALMOST FORGOT. BE SURE NOT TO SHAKE THAT SODA CAN--IT'S A HIGHLY UNSTABLE FORMULA!
NOW, BACK TO THE FIGHTING WITH THE SCIENCE AND ⁝HOO-HA⁝!

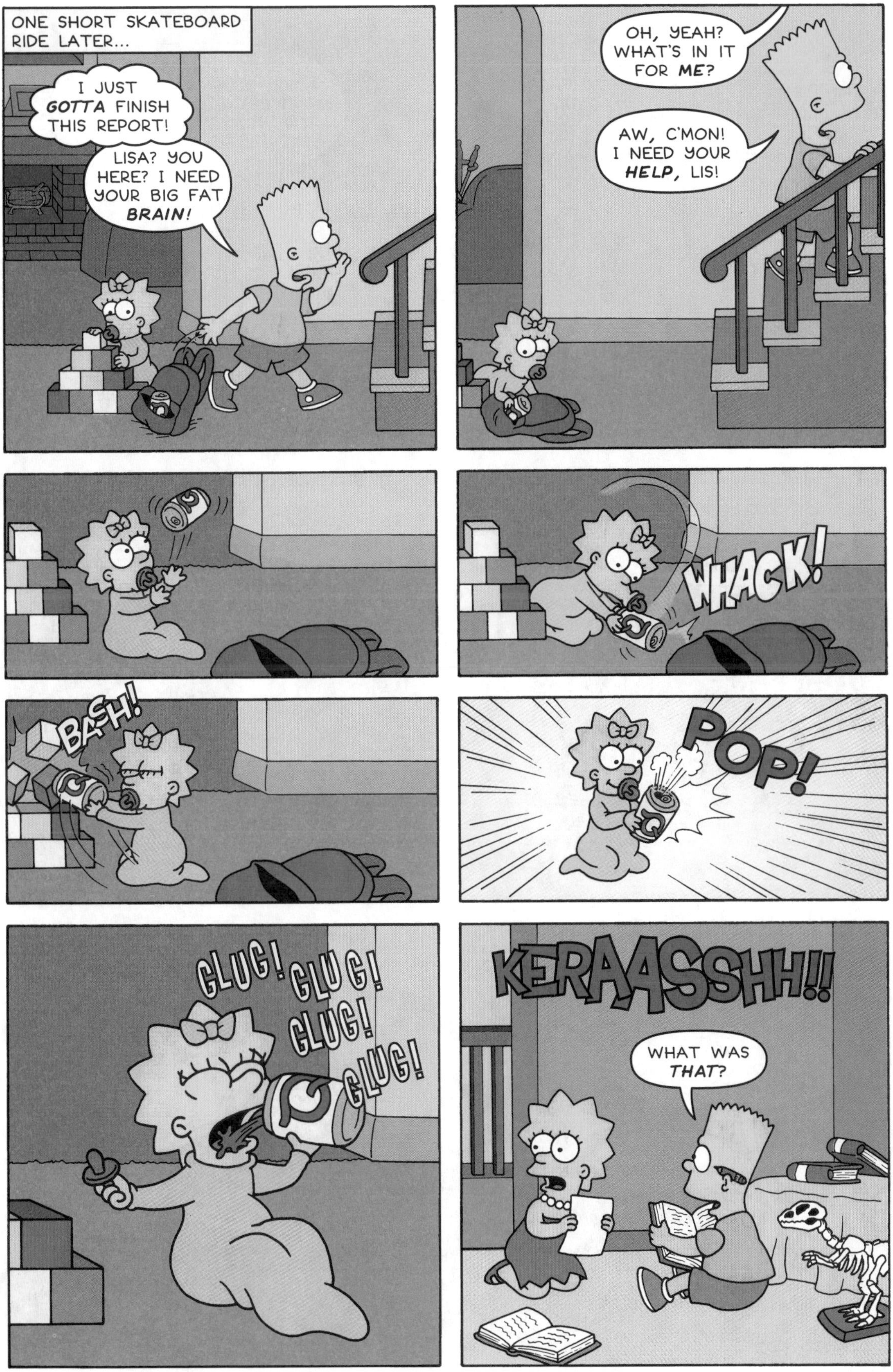

ONE SHORT SKATEBOARD RIDE LATER...
I JUST **GOTTA** FINISH THIS REPORT!
LISA? YOU HERE? I NEED YOUR BIG FAT **BRAIN!**
OH, YEAH? WHAT'S IN IT FOR **ME**?
AW, C'MON! I NEED YOUR **HELP,** LIS!
WHACK!
BASH!
POP!
GLUG! GLUG! GLUG! GLUG!
KERAASSHH!!
WHAT WAS *THAT*?

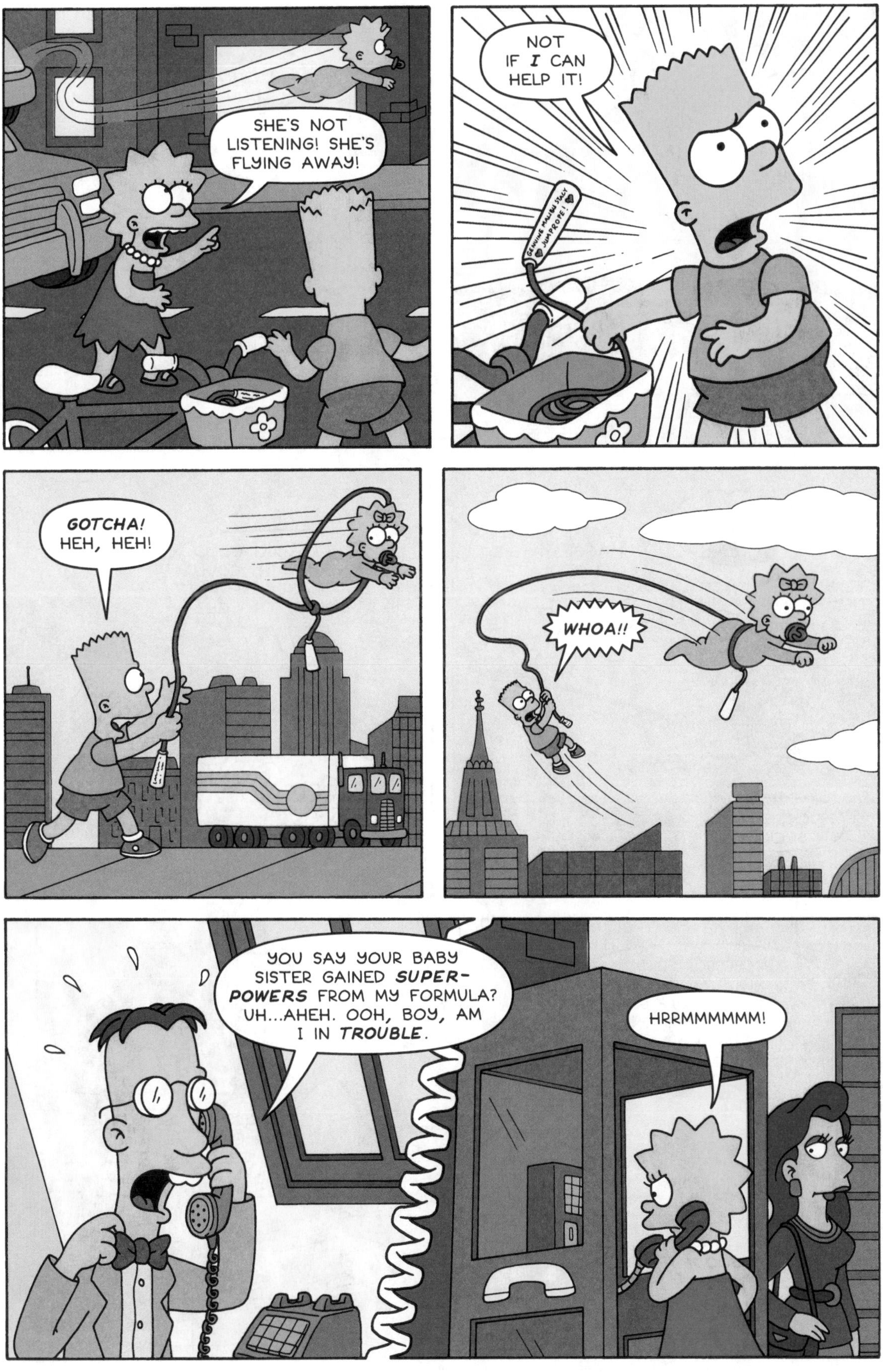
SHE'S NOT LISTENING! SHE'S FLYING AWAY!
NOT IF I CAN HELP IT!
GENUINE MALIBU STACY JUMPROPE!
GOTCHA! HEH, HEH!
WHOA!!
YOU SAY YOUR BABY SISTER GAINED SUPER-POWERS FROM MY FORMULA? UH...AHEH. OOH, BOY, AM I IN TROUBLE.
HRRMMMMMMM!

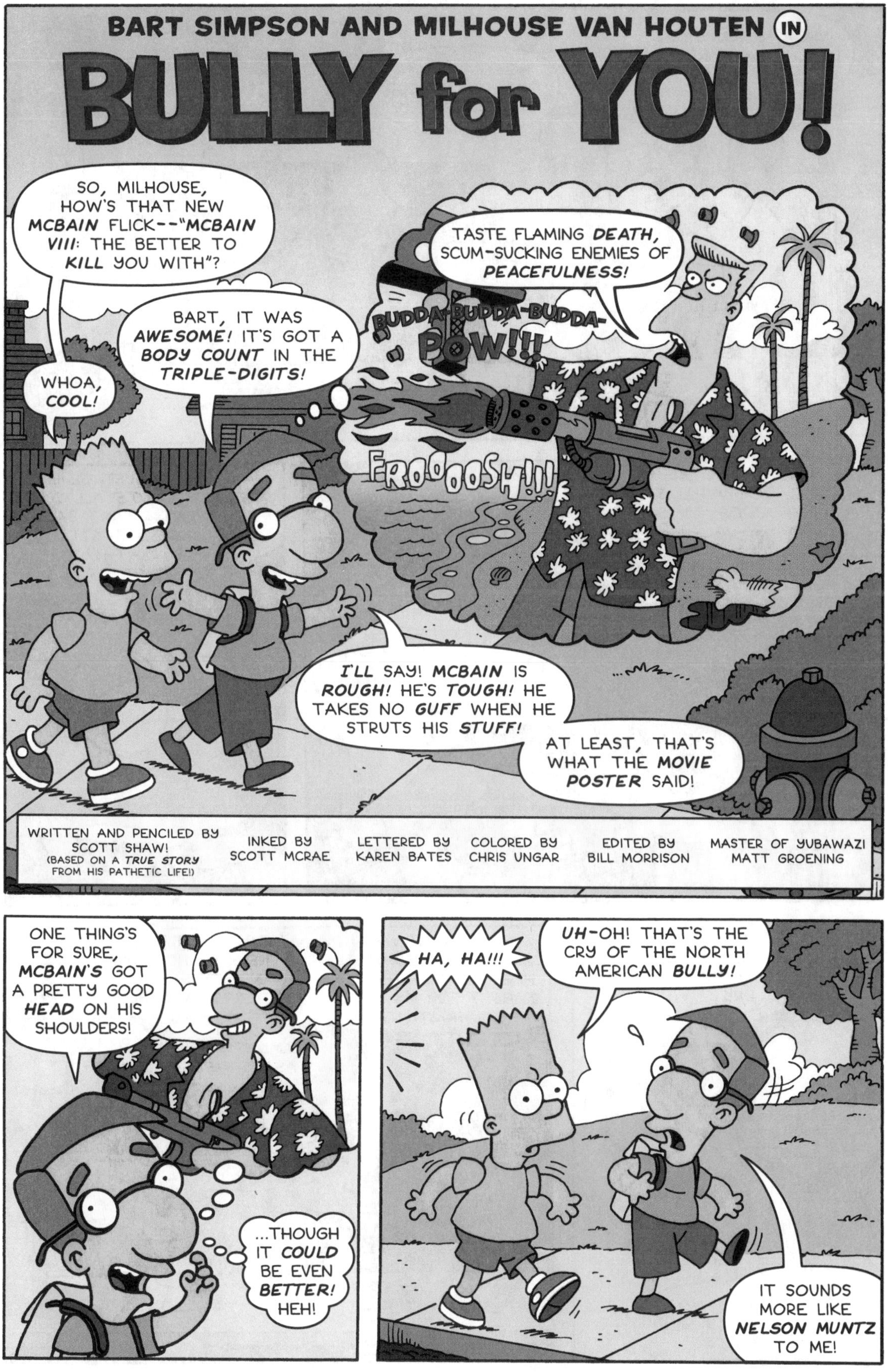
BART SIMPSON AND MILHOUSE VAN HOUTEN IN
BULLY for YOU!
SO, MILHOUSE, HOW'S THAT NEW MCBAIN FLICK--"MCBAIN VIII: THE BETTER TO KILL YOU WITH"?
BART, IT WAS AWESOME! IT'S GOT A BODY COUNT IN THE TRIPLE-DIGITS!
WHOA, COOL!
TASTE FLAMING DEATH, SCUM-SUCKING ENEMIES OF PEACEFULNESS!
BUDDA-BUDDA-BUDDA-POW!!!
FROOOOOSH!!!
I'LL SAY! MCBAIN IS ROUGH! HE'S TOUGH! HE TAKES NO GUFF WHEN HE STRUTS HIS STUFF!
AT LEAST, THAT'S WHAT THE MOVIE POSTER SAID!
WRITTEN AND PENCILED BY SCOTT SHAW! (BASED ON A TRUE STORY FROM HIS PATHETIC LIFE!)
INKED BY SCOTT MCRAE
LETTERED BY KAREN BATES
COLORED BY CHRIS UNGAR
EDITED BY BILL MORRISON
MASTER OF YUBAWAZI MATT GROENING
ONE THING'S FOR SURE, MCBAIN'S GOT A PRETTY GOOD HEAD ON HIS SHOULDERS!
...THOUGH IT COULD BE EVEN BETTER! HEH!
HA, HA!!!
UH-OH! THAT'S THE CRY OF THE NORTH AMERICAN BULLY!
IT SOUNDS MORE LIKE NELSON MUNTZ TO ME!